DR. SORAN SMILED THINLY . . .

as he pulled himself up onto the next highest peak, and stepped quickly onto the narrow metal scaffolding that bridged two plateaus. Soon he would be with his dead wife again, and if that meant destroying millions of lives in a fiery inferno, that was a price he was willing to pay.

Halfway across, he glanced up. Into a stranger's face. A stranger's, but somehow vaguely familiar. A human, hair chestnut shot with silver, wearing a Starfleet uniform Soran had not seen in almost a century . . .

"Just who the hell are you?" Soran whispered, but he knew the answer even before a voice replied behind him.

"He's James T. Kirk. Don't you read history?"

Look for STAR TREK Fiction from Pocket Books

Star Trek: The Original Series

The Ashes of Eden
Federation
Sarek
Best Destiny
Shadows on the Sun
Probe
Prime Directive
The Lost Years
Star Trek VI: The Undiscovered Country
Star Trek V: The Final Frontier
Star Trek IV: The Voyage Home
Spock's World
Enterprise
Strangers from the Sky
Final Frontier

#1   Star Trek: The Motion Picture
#2   The Entropy Effect
#3   The Klingon Gambit
#4   The Covenant of the Crown
#5   The Prometheus Design
#6   The Abode of Life
#7   Star Trek II: The Wrath of Khan
#8   Black Fire
#9   Triangle
#10 Web of the Romulans
#11 Yesterday's Son
#12 Mutiny on the Enterprise
#13 The Wounded Sky
#14 The Trellisane Confrontation
#15 Corona
#16 The Final Reflection
#17 Star Trek III: The Search for Spock
#18 My Enemy, My Ally
#19 The Tears of the Singers
#20 The Vulcan Academy Murders
#21 Uhura's Song
#22 Shadow Lord
#23 Ishmael
#24 Killing Time
#25 Dwellers in the Crucible
#26 Pawns and Symbols
#27 Mindshadow
#28 Crisis on Centaurus
#29 Dreadnought!
#30 Demons

#31 Battlestations!
#32 Chain of Attack
#33 Deep Domain
#34 Dreams of the Raven
#35 The Romulan Way
#36 How Much for Just the Planet?
#37 Bloodthirst
#38 The IDIC Epidemic
#39 Time for Yesterday
#40 Timetrap
#41 The Three-Minute Universe
#42 Memory Prime
#43 The Final Nexus
#44 Vulcan's Glory
#45 Double, Double
#46 The Cry of the Onlies
#47 The Kobayashi Maru
#48 Rules of Engagement
#49 The Pandora Principle
#50 Doctor's Orders
#51 Enemy Unseen
#52 Home Is the Hunter
#53 Ghost Walker
#54 A Flag Full of Stars
#55 Renegade
#56 Legacy
#57 The Rift
#58 Face of Fire
#59 The Disinherited
#60 Ice Trap
#61 Sanctuary
#62 Death Count
#63 Shell Game
#64 The Starship Trap
#65 Windows on a Lost World
#66 From the Depths
#67 The Great Starship Race
#68 Firestorm
#69 The Patrian Transgression
#70 Traitor Winds
#71 Crossroad
#72 The Better Man
#73 Recovery
#74 The Fearful Summons
#75 First Frontier
#76 The Captain's Daughter

Star Trek: The Next Generation

Star Trek Generations
All Good Things
Q-Squared
Dark Mirror
Descent
The Devil's Heart
Imzadi
Relics
Reunion
Unification
Metamorphosis
Vendetta
Encounter at Farpoint

#1 *Ghost Ship*
#2 *The Peacekeepers*
#3 *The Children of Hamlin*
#4 *Survivors*
#5 *Strike Zone*
#6 *Power Hungry*
#7 *Masks*
#8 *The Captains' Honor*
#9 *A Call to Darkness*
#10 *A Rock and a Hard Place*
#11 *Gulliver's Fugitives*
#12 *Doomsday World*

#13 *The Eyes of the Beholders*
#14 *Exiles*
#15 *Fortune's Light*
#16 *Contamination*
#17 *Boogeymen*
#18 *Q-in-Law*
#19 *Perchance to Dream*
#20 *Spartacus*
#21 *Chains of Command*
#22 *Imbalance*
#23 *War Drums*
#24 *Nightshade*
#25 *Grounded*
#26 *The Romulan Prize*
#27 *Guises of the Mind*
#28 *Here There Be Dragons*
#29 *Sins of Commission*
#30 *Debtors' Planet*
#31 *Foreign Foes*
#32 *Requiem*
#33 *Balance of Power*
#34 *Blaze of Glory*
#35 *Romulan Stratagem*
#36 *Into the Nebula*
#37 *The Last Stand*

Star Trek: Deep Space Nine

The Way of the Warrior
Warped
The Search

#1 *Emissary*
#2 *The Siege*
#3 *Bloodletter*
#4 *The Big Game*
#5 *Fallen Heroes*

#6 *Betrayal*
#7 *Warchild*
#8 *Antimatter*
#9 *Proud Helios*
#10 *Valhalla*
#11 *Devil in the Sky*
#12 *The Laertian Gamble*
#13 *Station Rage*

Star Trek: Voyager

#1 *Caretaker*
#2 *The Escape*
#3 *Ragnarok*
#4 *Violations*
#5 *Incident at Arbuk*

STAR TREK®
GENERATIONS™

A NOVEL BY J.M. DILLARD

Based on STAR TREK GENERATIONS
Story by Rick Berman & Ronald D. Moore & Brannon Braga
Screenplay by Ronald D. Moore & Brannon Braga

POCKET BOOKS

New York   London   Toronto   Sydney   Tokyo   Singapore

POCKET BOOKS, a division of Simon & Schuster Inc.
1230 Avenue of the Americas, New York, NY 10020

This book is published by Pocket Books, a division of Simon & Schuster Inc., under exclusive license from Paramount Pictures.

ISBN: 0-671-53753-9

First Pocket Books paperback printing December 1995

10 9 8 7 6 5 4 3 2 1

POCKET and colophon are registered trademarks of Simon & Schuster Inc.

Printed in the U.S.A.

For my amazing mother

ACKNOWLEDGMENTS

Special thanks are due to the following people, all of whom contributed in some way (whether they know it or not) to make this project not only possible, but downright pleasant:

Mike and Denise Okuda
John Ordover
Amanda Conti
Renee Martinez
Suza Francina

And of course, my beloved consort, George.

Part One

☆

SPACEDOCK, EARTH

2293 Old Earth Date

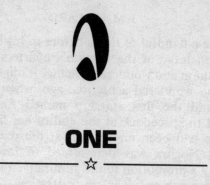

ONE

☆

In the captain's quarters aboard the *Enterprise*-A the nautical clock chimed, breaking the silence to softly mark the passage of time. James Kirk paused over the suitcase open on his bunk, neatly folded civilian tunic in hand, and straightened to listen. As he did, a second clock—an antique mantelpiece, cased in polished dark cherry and wound for the first time in years, specially for this occasion—began to strike the hour.

Nineteen hundred hours. Spock and McCoy would be arriving soon to accompany him on the long gauntlet of traditional firewatch parties—the crew's celebration of the last night aboard a vessel at the end of a long mission.

Nineteen hundred hours, the sound of time moving inexorably onward. The night had already begun and would move all too swiftly to its inevitable conclusion.

Kirk dropped the tunic inside the suitcase and moved over to the bulkhead to press a control, key in a code. A panel slid up, and he retrieved a handful of small cases, each of which hid a medal. He did not stop to examine them, but placed them carefully in the suitcase, just as he

3

J. M. DILLARD

had done a handful of times before in his life, when he
had taken leave of the captain's quarters in the very
same fashion and wondered whether it might be his last.

He had wondered a lifetime ago, when he was still
young and the first starship named *Enterprise* had
returned to spacedock at the end of her five-year mission. He had been angry then at the realization that
Admiral Nogura was determined to force him into
accepting a promotion to the admiralty, and a desk job.
Now there was no anger, no frustration—only sadness
and an overwhelming sense of loss. And a faint stirring
of pride at the memory of when, all those years ago, he
had fought to get his ship back—had taken on
Heihachiro Nogura, the head of Starfleet himself, and
won.

This time, Kirk did not wonder whether this would be
the last night he would stand aboard the *Enterprise* as
her captain. There could be no doubt that it was. He and
the ship were both to be decommissioned, along with the
senior bridge crew: Spock, McCoy, Uhura—even Scotty, who had chosen to take retirement rather than
remain in Starfleet without the opportunity to serve with
this particular crew.

There could be no more gambits, no more ploys to get
his ship back, to stave off the inevitable. He had exhausted them all; and now he himself was exhausted
after fighting so many years to keep his command. He
absently massaged an aching muscle in his back, recently
injured while working in the mines on the Klingon penal
colony of Rura Penthe. He had not been able to bring
himself to trouble McCoy about it; it would have been
an admission of the truth—that he was getting too old to
withstand the rigors of the captaincy.

He looked about for something else to pack, reached for a holo on the dresser, and gazed into the smiling countenance of his and Carol's son, David. David, too, had fallen prey to time some years before, when he died at Klingon hands. Kirk gently set the picture back down, beside the mantel clock and antique paper book set aside for the occasion. David's holo was always the first thing he set in a cabin to make it his own, the last thing he packed before leaving. It would stay on his dresser until morning, when he packed it along with his captain's uniform.

The intercom whistled; he winced at the twinge of pain in his back as he wheeled abruptly to punch the toggle and respond. "Kirk here."

A familiar feminine voice filtered through the grid. "Uhura, Captain. I—"

He interrupted, "I thought you were supposed to be on your way to a firewatch party, Commander."

"I am, sir." He could hear her smile. "But I had a few minutes left, and I wanted to spend them on duty."

"Understood," Kirk said softly.

"Sir, the subspace interference has eased. I was finally able to clear a channel to Starbase Twenty-three. I can even get you that visual now—but I'm warning you, the reception isn't that great."

"Uhura, you're a marvel."

"I know, sir."

"Patch it through to my quarters." Aware of the sudden rapidity of his heartbeat, he strode over to the viewer and watched a burst of visual static on the screen. It resolved itself into the greenish and slightly fritzed image of Carol Marcus, against a setting Jim recognized as her hospital bed on the starbase. He had visited her there once, before he was called away to what the media were already calling the Khitomer mission—his and the *Enterprise*-A's final mission. Carol had been almost fatally wounded in an apparent Klingon attack; she had been unconscious his entire stay, and he had left fearful that he would never see her again.

He had promised himself that, if and when he had another chance to speak to her, it would be to say that he was coming home to her, never again to leave. The pain of losing the *Enterprise* was eased by knowing that Carol was all right, that she would be waiting for him.

"Carol?" The words came out in a rush. "Carol, thank God, you have no idea how good it is to see you awake. When I left you, I was so afraid—"

She spoke at the same time. "Jim. Oh, God, Jim, they said the Klingons charged you with Gorkon's murder and shipped you off to that terrible prison. I was so afraid—"

They both broke off at the same instant and laughed gently, delightedly. "It looks like you survived," Carol said at last. It was hard to tell with the bad reception, but she seemed the same shade of pastel green as her normally golden hair, as the pillows propped behind her—which gave him the impression that she was terribly pale. Yet she seemed herself, and in her lap lay a padd; she had been sitting up working.

He grinned. "Always. How about you?"

"Doctor tells me I can be out of here in a day, at most two. So you're really all right?"

"I'm all right. Just out of a job, starting tomorrow. I'm sitting in spacedock, Carol. They're decommissioning us." He tried to sound cavalier, but the heaviness came through despite his efforts.

Her smile faded; she was silent a beat, then said, "I'm truly sorry, Jim."

"It's not like I didn't see it coming." He shrugged and managed a lighter tone. "So . . . what are you going to be doing in a day or two?"

She brightened and straightened in her seat; he fancied he detected a gleam of intensity in her eyes, the one she always got when speaking about work that was important to her. "I'm going to rebuild the Themis research station, Jim. Now that things with the Klingons are settling down—"

He cut her off. "Carol, you almost *died.* It's time to take things easy, not to rush into a massive undertaking."

Her lip quirked with fond exasperation. "You're one to talk. How many times have *you* almost been killed? And still I couldn't hold you back from that damned ship of yours with a tractor beam—"

"Well, you've got the opportunity now." He tried to keep the irony he felt from his tone. "I've got time on my hands now. And I want to spend it with you."

"Well, of course. You know I'm always glad to see you, Jim. But it won't be much of a vacation on Themis. There's nothing to see except a scorched research station. . . ."

"Dammit," he said lightly, "could you help me out a little here? I'm not talking about a weekend on Themis while you work. I'm talking about a honeymoon."

She released a startled little laugh, and despite the fuzzy reception, seemed to color a bit. "Jim," she admonished, smiling, and with that one word managed to convey, *You're joking, right?*

"I'm serious," he said. "Don't tell me you haven't

been expecting this." He had thought it had been clear to her; he tried now vainly to recall the conversation, the precise words they had used to state that they would marry once he retired, but the specific memory eluded him.

"I haven't been expecting this." Her smile vanished, replaced by an expression of concern. "Jim, you know the time we spend together is special to me, but . . . we never said anything about legalities."

"I'm saying it now. I love you, Carol. I always thought we'd be together once I retired. That we'd settle down. You even said Marcuslabs could use someone like me—"

"As for Marcuslabs, I'll hire you in a heartbeat, if you want. You're someone with connections who could go all over the galaxy facilitating the creation of new research stations. Plenty of travel, a chance to practice your diplomacy. But I wouldn't be able to travel with you." She let go a long breath. "Jim, I love you, but you couldn't settle down if you wanted to. You'll be on the move, restless, looking for excitement until the day you die. If you're suggesting we buy a little condo somewhere and take up housekeeping—it'd be death for both of us."

"I see," he said quietly.

"Jim, don't be hurt."

"No . . . no, you're right," he admitted weakly; what was worse, he meant it. Somewhere, in the deepest recesses of his mind, he had seen this very scene played out before, had known it was coming—yet he still felt as though the deck had been pulled from under his feet. "I'm not hurt, just . . . tired. Looking for someplace to rest. It's been a tough last mission."

"Then come see me. We should talk."

Behind him, the door chimed. He glanced toward it, then back at Carol. "I have to go. Firewatch parties."

"I love you, Jim."

He touched the screen as if to take her hand, to hold on to her—on to the present, but he could sense her and time slipping away from him, like the ship on which he stood.

The screen darkened; Kirk turned toward the door and said, "Come."

Spock entered, carrying two packages—a smaller stacked atop a larger, both precisely wrapped in colored paper. He hesitated, looking reserved and somewhat awkward, just inside the door.

"What's this?" Kirk gestured with feigned surprise at the packages.

"A gift, sir." Spock handed him the larger box. "Perhaps it is not the custom; but it seemed . . . somehow appropriate to mark the end of our years of service together."

Kirk smiled faintly, touched, and sat on his bunk to open it. He removed the paper carefully; inside the box, swathed in tissue, was a gleaming brass-and-polished-wood sextant—a centuries-old tool sailors once used to navigate by the stars.

"To help me find my way?" Kirk asked lightly, running his fingers over it in admiration. "Spock—thank you. It's beautiful. . . ."

As he spoke, the door chimed once more. "Come," Jim said, and McCoy entered.

There was a wide grin on the doctor's face and two dust-covered flagons in his arms; but to Jim, the smile seemed forced. Purple shadows had gathered beneath

McCoy's ice blue eyes; he looked as haggard as Kirk felt after the hardships endured on Rura Penthe.

My God, Jim thought. *He's* old . . . *and so am I.*

"Well," McCoy said cheerfully, holding up the flasks. "I see the Vulcan beat me to it. I, too, came bearing gifts."

"Two bottles? I hope they're both for me." Kirk squinted at them, wishing he had his spectacles.

"Not in the least." The doctor lifted one and blew on the label; Kirk raised his hands to protect himself from the approaching cloud of dust. "This one's oldest, so it's yours."

Kirk took the bottle and smiled at the date on the label.

"For auld lang syne," said McCoy, with the slightest quaver in his voice; or was it Jim's imagination? "And this one—"

He blew on the second bottle's label and handed it to Spock.

"Why, Dr. McCoy," the Vulcan said with mild surprise. "This is alcohol."

"Good old-fashioned Saurian brandy, to be precise," the doctor said with gusto. "Drink it and remember me—and the importance of loosening up once in a while."

"I shall," Spock replied. "If you will attempt to recall the importance of logic when you gaze upon this." He proffered McCoy the smaller package.

McCoy unwrapped it and lifted out a palm-sized circle of burnished metal, on which was etched an intricate maze of geometric design. He frowned at it. "It's lovely, Spock. . . . But . . . what *is* it?"

"A Vulcan mandala. One contemplates it to quiet the

mind and emotions, in preparation for the reception of logic."

"Oh. Thank you." McCoy slipped it into his jacket pocket. "I'll be sure to look at it every time I need a little logic. Now that you won't be around to provide it for me . . ."

"Gentlemen." Kirk rose and went over to the dresser. "I'm no good at wrapping things, but . . . these are for you." He handed the small paper book to Spock.

Spock looked down at the book and allowed the merest ghost of a smile to pass over his features. *"Horatio Hornblower.* Thank you, Captain."

"To remember me by," Jim said.

McCoy lifted a brow. "Don't you think *Don Juan* would have been a little more appropriate?"

"Watch your tongue, Doctor, or I'll keep your present," Kirk retorted, gesturing toward the mantel clock. "I was tempted to keep it anyway." He opened the crystal face and set the minute hand back to the hour; the clock began again to chime, a rich, melodic sound that echoed faintly off the bulkheads.

Lips parted with delight, McCoy listened, clearly enchanted.

"To remember the good times." Kirk smiled.

"Jim . . . it's beautiful. I think that's the finest present anyone's ever given me—with the exception of my grandkids, of course." The doctor's expression grew suddenly somber as he gazed up at his friends. "I can't imagine what life will be like without you two. It isn't really ending, is it? After all these years, it can't be over. . . ."

"Don't get maudlin on me, Doctor." Jim's tone grew firm. They had a long night ahead of them—one in which he'd be asked a hundred times what he was going to do with himself now that he didn't have the *Enterprise;* and a hundred times, he would have to reply graciously. He didn't need to start out the evening depressed. "And stop talking like we'll never see each other again."

"Well—when *will* we see each other?"

"How about tomorrow? I was thinking of heading to Yosemite, and thought you two might enjoy going there with me again—"

"Can't do it," McCoy said glumly. "I'm going to stay with Joanna and her family, and we're talking about heading off to do some research out in the B'renga sector. And Spock's headed home—"

"Home?" Jim glanced swiftly at his first officer for verification.

Spock gave a single nod. "I am . . . discussing the possibility of doing some diplomatic work with Ambassador Sarek. I shall be returning to Vulcan tomorrow. I am afraid I cannot accompany you to Yosemite."

"I see," Jim said softly. And for the first time, he realized that he was not simply parting for a few months' shore leave, but saying good-bye to his two best friends.

A sudden indescribable loneliness overtook him, melancholy coupled with premonition. He flashed on an image of himself, years before, seated in front of a crackling campfire in Yosemite Park, grinning up at his two friends' faces, orange with reflected firelight.

That's right; he had scaled El Capitan, the most rugged peak in the park, and had fallen. And Spock had caught him. And Bones, outraged as usual by his captain's risk-taking, had asked him whether he had been trying to kill himself.

It was funny, Kirk had answered then, *but even as I was falling, I knew I wouldn't die . . . because the two of you were with me. I've always known I'll die alone.*

Spock would no longer be there to catch him, nor McCoy to sputter in outrage. The thought that he was losing all that was dearest to him—Carol, Spock, Bones, the *Enterprise*—finally struck home. He was alone now; unfettered, moorless.

A shudder passed through him. *Someone walking on my grave . . .*

But the thought seemed too self-pitying. He dismissed it resolutely, forced himself to smile. "Well . . . we *will* be getting together again at some point." He rose. "Gentlemen. Thank you for the gifts. I think it's time we were off to the festivities."

"The last firewatch." McCoy drew a breath that caught in his throat as he studied his two friends. "Are we really ready for this?"

"Not at all," Jim answered honestly. "Let's go."

TWO

☆ ─────────────

One year later, Pavel Chekov, Commander, Starfleet, stood in the midst of a vast and undulating ocean of wheat and gazed up at the cloudless sky. He had been standing patient watch for some time—long enough to be heated and dazzled by the bright sun; long enough, certainly, to grow reflective about the object of his search.

The parallel seas of blue and gold, one above, one below, seemed infinite, and evoked the same dizzying sensation of freedom, of disconnectedness, he had felt over the past year since leaving the *Enterprise* and the service. Transitions were never easy, but as a Starfleet officer, Chekov had learned to take them in stride; only this one had proved the most challenging of all. A year or two before, he had thought to avoid that sensation by re-forming old connections. He had contacted Irina Galliulin, his love from his Academy days, the one woman he wanted to spend the rest of his life with—only to learn that she was soon to marry.

And so he had acquired a small dacha outside Moscow and spent his off-time there alone, except for those opportunities to gather with old friends. When the invitation came from Starfleet to attend the christening of the *Enterprise*-B, he jumped at the chance.

He stood beside Montgomery Scott now, who also frowned up at the sky. He enjoyed Scott's company—in part, because Scott was clearly enjoying himself, enjoying retirement. He had settled in his native Scotland with his sister's family, playing the role of doting uncle with gusto, producing a rapid spate of engineering articles for technical journals. And, he had relayed to Chekov with obvious pride, Starfleet had hired him as a part-time consultant in the design of new vessels. Yet his family ties and his labor of love for Starfleet still left him with enough freedom to reunite with old friends. He was looking as healthy as Chekov had ever seen him; his face was well tanned, with a faint ruddy glow that spoke of contentment rather than Scotch, and though his form was still stout, he seemed to Chekov slightly leaner as of late.

Chekov envied him. Perhaps, with time, he, Chekov, would find his own niche, as Scott had. But for the time he identified more with the captain—with Jim, he corrected himself silently. It was difficult, almost impossible, for him to dispense with the notion of rank after all these years; as strange as hearing Scott address him as *Pavel*. Kirk clearly was consumed with the same restlessness, the same dissatisfaction Chekov experienced daily; he had seen it in the captain's—Jim's—eyes.

Chekov's reverie ceased abruptly as he spotted a tiny black speck in the midst of all that blue. He raised an arm and pointed to it as he turned excitedly to Scott. "There he is—there, to the south!"

Scott lifted a hand to his weathered forehead, displacing a silver fringe of hair as he shielded his eyes from the glare. After a moment's scrutiny, he clicked his tongue. "What are ye, blind? That's a bird."

Chekov squinted, ready to protest until he made out the wings. He sagged slightly as anticipation left him.

"Rappelling the Crystalline Trench," Scott said suddenly, in the same indignant tone. "Rafting down lava flows . . . orbital skydiving . . . It's like the man is running a bloody decathlon across the galaxy."

Chekov frowned at the note of disapproval in Scott's voice. Certainly there was nothing wrong with orbital skydiving; in fact, Chekov had hoped to try it himself—after he saw how Jim Kirk fared with it. He opened his mouth to say something in the captain's defense. Perhaps Scott, with his comfortable family life, did not understand what it was to feel restless, unanchored, eager for excitement.

But Chekov never got the chance to explain things to Scott; a sonic boom, followed almost instantly by another, distracted him. "That should be him now," he said. "I think he's just crossed the sound barrier."

The two shaded their eyes from the sun and stared up at the sky. For a few seconds, Chekov thought he might have been mistaken again; but then, slightly to the west of where he anticipated, a dark speck appeared in the midst of the cerulean blue. It loomed suddenly larger, and larger, and this time, it most definitely was *not* a bird, but the form of a man hanging from a parachute.

He sailed down rapidly and landed unceremoniously flat on his back several meters away in the wheat. Chekov and Scott hurried over to him.

Kirk sat up and pulled off his helmet, revealing the

broad grin of a delighted child. "Right on target! I jump out over the Arabian Peninsula . . . and I end up here, right on the dime." He got to his feet, brushing away his two friends' attempts at assistance, cheerfully oblivious to the wisps of smoke still emanating from his charred, scorched suit.

"Actually, Captain," Chekov offered, "your precise target area was thirty-five meters"—he gestured to the west—"that way."

Kirk's lip quirked wryly, in the same manner Chekov had seen so many times on the bridge, when Spock had offered concise but unwanted details; perhaps, Chekov thought, he had offered the information precisely because Spock could not be there with them. "Thanks for pointing that out," the captain said. He began pulling off his suit, but drew up and winced suddenly in obvious pain.

Scott was shaking his head with fresh disapproval. "I've warned ye about that back of yours. You should have a doctor take a look at it."

Kirk made a sound of skepticism and started to remove his harness. "Tomorrow," he told Chekov excitedly, knowing that the younger man shared his enthusiasm for daredevil feats to a much greater extent than did his former engineer, "I want to make a tri-elliptical jump. That's where you jump out over northern China, and make three complete orbits before you start reentry. . . ."

Chekov was sincerely interested in hearing about tri-elliptical jumps—and perhaps even trying one himself—but Kirk had apparently suffered a memory lapse. The very notion that the captain might have become forgetful embarrassed Chekov; gently, he said, "Captain. Perhaps you have forgotten that tomorrow is the christening ceremony. . . ."

Kirk clearly had not. A flash of irritation crossed his features, then faded to stubborn resolve as he said curtly, "I'm not going." He paused, then fumbled at the straps on his body harness. "Scotty, help me with this chute."

Scott stepped forward and reached for the straps, his expression again stern and reproachful. "What do ye mean, you're not going? We promised."

"When I retired, I swore I'd never set foot on a starship again, and I meant it."

"Captain . . ." Chekov chided mildly, meaning: *We know you don't really mean it, sir.* He was not quite sure what prompted Kirk's sudden outburst of mulishness, except possibly the recent disappointing news that Spock and McCoy would not be joining them for the christening ceremony. Nor would Uhura, who was vacationing in a far-off region of the galaxy before returning to teach at the Academy, or Sulu, who was off commanding the *Excelsior.*

"I don't want to hear any more about it," Kirk told them both. "I'm not going and that's *final."*

Yes, *sir,* Chekov almost said, but he and Scott shared a knowing glance; he had heard the uncertainty in the captain's tone, and would not be at all surprised if Kirk had another change of heart before morning.

In the instant before the turbolift doors slid open, Jim Kirk drew a deep breath and steeled himself. A year before, in his final moments as captain on the bridge of his ship, he had sworn that he would never set foot on another starship again . . . for the simple, painful reason that he would never again be in the command chair. Yet despite his protestations to Scott and Chekov the day before, he had yielded to duty, responsibility—and no small amount of curiosity—and accompanied his friends to the christening of the *Enterprise*-B.

But from the moment he arrived on spacedock, he was unable to shake the feeling that it had been a mistake to come, that something indescribable was *wrong*. Perhaps it was just the weight of the past and his current pointless existence settling over him, or perhaps the simple disappointment that the friends who should have stood beside him now—Spock and Bones—could not be here. Spock was involved with a diplomatic mission on behalf of Vulcan and could not free himself, though he had sent a terse, elegant message honoring the former crew of the *Enterprise*-A and congratulating the new crew of the *Enterprise*-B. As for McCoy, he and his family were attending his granddaughter's graduation from the Vulcan Science Academy; he, too, had sent a polite message of congratulations to Starfleet—and a private message to Jim, saying: *Miss you, old friend. I'll be with you in spirit. . . .*

Jim's unease had begun with a restless night of troubling dreams; and in the fleeting second as he stared at the seam in the lift doors, he was haunted by dimly colored images from the night before, from dreams that had been strands of memory braided with imagination:

Yosemite. El Capitan. Climbing, gripping cool rock with his fingers, his hands, breathing in sweet Terran air, gazing out at hawks flying past. Spock appearing out of the literal blue, distracting him, and then:

The fall, just as it had happened those years ago, so swiftly that it shoved the air from his lungs, made him dizzy as he flailed, clawing vainly at smooth rock . . .

Abruptly, the superimposed flash of himself seated at the campfire beside Spock and Bones, explaining why he had not been afraid.

. . . even as I was falling, I knew I wouldn't die, because the two of you were with me . . .

Captain, Spock said, as the setting shifted again, and they were on the *Enterprise*-A in Jim's quarters, on his last night as captain. *I shall be returning to Vulcan.*

And then he was falling again—falling into infinity, past El Capitan, over the Arabian Peninsula with the air roaring in his ears, waiting for Spock to catch him.

But Spock was gone—on Vulcan—and Bones was nowhere to be found, either. Jim was alone—for the first time really alone, terrified and in free fall. Even so, he heard the doctor's voice whisper in his ear:

Miss you, old friend . . .

And then, the question Bones had asked Spock so long ago, on the Klingon Bird-of-Prey soon after the Vulcan had returned to the living: *What did it feel like, being dead?*

Ridiculous, to be so unsettled by dreams. Kirk gave his head a slight shake and detached himself from the memory. Self-pity was useless; it might seem wrong that Spock and McCoy were not here beside him—but he was grateful for Scotty and Chekov, the two friends who flanked him now. He glanced at them and saw that Chekov's apprehension matched his own, while Scott's expression was one of wistfulness, mixed with an overwhelming curiosity about the turbolift's new design.

Yet despite his resolve to forget last night's dreams, he felt his unease grow. The only thing that felt comfortable about the whole affair was the chance to wear his uniform again.

The lift doors opened onto blinding light and applause. Dazzled, Kirk blinked until his vision cleared to reveal a holocam with spotlight, a bevy of journalists with padds, and the applauding bridge crew. He forced a gracious smile, and felt Scott and Chekov tense self-consciously beside him.

"Captain Kirk," one of the reporters called, "how does it feel to be back on the *Enterprise* bridge?"

The question was the only one he could make out clearly amid the sudden barrage: *Captain, could I have a min—*

Captain Scott, do you have any comment on the—

Commander Chekov, after seeing the new Enterprise, *do you regret—*

Blessedly, a uniformed figure pushed forward through the crowd and stepped in front of the light. Kirk knew even without looking at the insignia who it would be; authority conferred a certain confident grace, a determined manner of walking that marked a captain on his own bridge.

And a tension that permeated the air around him. *Like a coiled spring,* Jim thought. *Was I ever that intense?*

"Excuse me," the man told the reporters as he strode past them. "Excuse me, there will be plenty of time for questions later."

The journalists at once fell silent, and receded like a tide—all except the cameraman, who angled himself for a better picture, throwing the light directly into Kirk's eyes. Kirk tried not to squint, not to let his annoyance show in his frozen smile, directed now at the lean young officer who stood before him.

"I'm Captain John Harriman." The current commander of the *Enterprise* directed a polite nod at each of the retired officers. "I'd like to welcome you all aboard."

"It's our pleasure." Despite his discomfort, Kirk's smile warmed genuinely. Harriman seemed to him painfully young, painfully eager, painfully earnest about his first command—no doubt exactly the way a certain James T. Kirk had been when he had first taken command of a ship called *Enterprise*. And while Harriman was doing a fair job of hiding his nervousness, he did not quite succeed in masking his awe of the men who stood before him.

"I just want you to know how excited we all are to have a group of living legends with us on our maiden voyage," Harriman said. "I remember reading about your missions when I was in grade school."

Scott and Chekov stiffened; Harriman's expression grew embarrassed as he realized his gaffe. His panic was so sincere that Kirk's lips quirked in amusement.

"Well," he said easily, "may we have a look around?"

"Please." Harriman gestured at the gleaming bridge, plainly relieved at the rescue. "Please . . ."

"Demora!" Chekov's face brightened with sudden pleasure as he caught a familiar face among the sea of uniforms in the background. He headed off as the other three ceremoniously made their way toward the conn.

"This is the new command chair," Harriman explained unnecessarily to his two politely attentive guests. He laid a proud hand on the armrest. "If you take a look at the comm panel, you'll see a number of small but significant improvements over the *Enterprise*-A. . . ."

He droned on for a moment; Scott seemed raptly attentive, but Kirk did not hear. Harriman and Scott quickly moved on to the helm, but Kirk lingered a moment to rest his hand enviously upon the back of the new captain's chair.

It seemed wrong that another man should sit here; wrong that Bones and Spock should not be here, standing in their customary places beside him. He felt an abrupt, odd sense of discomfort, and flashed again on the memory of his last night as captain of the *Enterprise*, and the sudden chill he had felt when Spock and McCoy confessed they were going their separate ways.

. . . even as I was falling, I knew I wouldn't die . . . because the two of you were with me . . .

Stop, he told himself firmly. He was being maudlin, self-pitying again—yet he could not quite shake the eerie sense of premonition prompted by dreams.

"So, Captain . . ." someone said.

He jerked his head up to see a reporter with a padd.

In the same breezy tone, she continued, "This is the first *Starship Enterprise* in thirty years without James T. Kirk in command. How do you feel about that?"

How the hell do you expect me to feel? he wanted to say, angered by her casualness. *This ship was my life— was everything. And now . . .*

Instead, he drew a breath and summoned back the frozen smile. "Just fine. I'm glad to be here to send her on her way."

He tried to step past her, to join Harriman and Scott, but she angled into his path, blocking escape.

"And what have you been doing since you retired?"

"I've been . . . keeping busy." Trapped, he paused and tried to catch Harriman's eye, but the young captain and Scott were enthusiastically discussing the redesigned helm.

"Excuse me, Captain," Chekov called, with sufficient command authority that the journalist backed off.

Kirk shot him a look of gratitude.

Chekov gave a knowing smile, then gestured with obvious pride at the officer beside him—a young Terran woman whose oddly familiar golden face and dark eyes were framed by a shoulder-length sweep of ebony hair. "I'd like you to meet the helmsman of the *Enterprise*-B."

Don't I know you? Kirk was on the verge of asking, but Chekov continued:

"Ensign Demora Sulu—Captain James Kirk."

Kirk's lips parted in astonishment; for a moment, he just stared as the ensign offered her hand and said, with unmistakably Sulu-ish confidence and good humor, "It's a pleasure to meet you, sir. My father's told me some . . ." Her eyes took on a faint glimmer of merriment. ". . . interesting stories about you."

Jim found his voice at last. "Your father . . . Hikaru Sulu is your *father?*" He had known that Sulu had a child—a little *girl,* certainly not a daughter old enough to enter the Academy, much less handle the helm of a starship. Chekov had served as honorary uncle and godparent, which would certainly explain his doting demeanor now, but . . .

Demora straightened proudly. "Yes, sir."

Chekov leaned forward and prompted, sotto voce, "You met her once before, but she was . . ." Hand held palm down and waist high, he indicated her former height.

Kirk shook his head in disbelief. It made sense, of course: the round cheeks beneath shining dark eyes, the gracious good nature. He could never have mistaken her for anyone else's daughter. "Yes, yes, I remember. Even then you were talking about being a helmsman, like your father. But that wasn't so long ago. It couldn't have been more than—"

"Twelve years, sir," Chekov said.

"Yes . . . well . . ." Kirk hesitated. To her credit, Demora showed not a hint of amusement or annoyance, but waited, respectful and poised, while the captain did some quick mental calculations, then sighed in acquiescence. "Congratulations, Ensign," he said at last, and smiled genuinely. "It wouldn't be the *Enterprise* without a Sulu at the helm."

"Thank you, sir," Demora replied, with voice and gaze that revealed she had inherited her father's forthright sincerity and warmth. "If you'll excuse me . . ." She turned to Chekov. "Let me show you the new inertial system. . . ."

Kirk imagined he could hear the words she barely managed not to say: *Uncle Pavel. . . .*

The two wandered off. Kirk watched them go, and a sudden overwhelming sadness overtook him as he thought of his own child, David, of Carol, of lost chances. Rather than easing with time, his sense of loss over David's death had deepened, as if his own approaching end made him see more clearly the opportunities missed in life. If he had known from the beginning that he had a son, his life might now be very different.

Perhaps—just perhaps—he could have done things differently, and David would still be alive. . . .

Perhaps he would be with the two of them now, instead of trying to outrun his loneliness while Carol buried her grief with work. He had seen her only twice in the past year, and each time she had been consumed by the details of rebuilding the station on Themis. He was beginning to think that her sorrow, too, had increased; that maybe the sight of him reminded Carol too much of her late son—much the way that the sight of Demora at the helm reminded him strongly of Sulu now.

He glanced up as Scotty approached, beaming broadly.

"Damn fine ship if you ask me," Scott said with gusto. "What I wouldn't give for a tour of engineering. . . ."

Kirk made a noncommittal sound, then gazed back at Demora, who was taking her position at the helm. "You know, Scotty, it amazes me."

Scott's good cheer remained undampened. "And what would that be, sir?"

"Sulu. When did he find the time for a family?"

Scotty followed Kirk's gaze to Demora and released a silent *ah.* "Sulu's given the world another fine officer, hasn't he?"

"She seems like a fine young woman."

"That she is." Scott faced him again. "It's like you always said. If something's important enough, you make the time."

Kirk gave an absent nod. For a moment, neither spoke—until Scott said, in a voice low but keen with revelation, "So . . . *that's* why you've been running around the galaxy like an eighteen-year-old. Finding retirement a little lonely, are we?"

Kirk glanced at him sharply. "With that kind of tact, I'm glad you're an engineer and not a psychiatrist."

Still all eagerness and intensity, Harriman approached and interrupted with an exaggerated formality that spoke of the camera focused on them. "Excuse me, gentlemen. If you'll take your seats . . ."

"Oh . . . of course." Kirk straightened and reactivated the public-relations smile; so did Scott, and the two of them settled into two of the three seats set on the bridge for the occasion.

As Harriman took the conn and the crew members their stations, Chekov joined them and sank into the third one, casting a final proud-uncle glance at Demora and whispering to Kirk, "I was never that young."

Kirk cast him a fond glance. "No. You were younger."

"Prepare to leave spacedock," Harriman ordered, with something less than ease. Kirk felt a stirring of sympathy for the young captain. It had been difficult enough to take command of the first *Enterprise* all those years ago—and young Jim Kirk hadn't had to face three "living legends" and a horde of journalists at the time.

"Aft thrusters ahead one quarter, port and starboard at station keeping," Harriman continued, then swiveled in his chair to face his guests of honor. "Captain Kirk, I'd be honored if you would give the order to get under way."

"No," Kirk replied instantly. He did not intend to be rude; Harriman was simply trying to be polite, to show respect, but to Kirk the offer seemed patronizing. He had no desire to serve as figurehead, to give a symbolic order which, to his mind, only served to underscore the fact that the *Enterprise* was no longer his. He did not care to pretend that it was, even for a moment. "No. Thank you."

Harriman seemed to take his refusal as modesty. "Please. I insist."

The bridge fell silent; Kirk became uncomfortably aware that the gaze of every person—including the bank of journalists on the other side of the bridge—was fixed upon him. He glanced helplessly at Scotty, Chekov, the smiling, expectant Harriman, and rose to his feet. The anticipation seemed deafening, his pronouncement anticlimactic.

"Take us out," he said flatly.

The crew again broke into wild applause. Kirk sat, trying not to squint at the glaring lights, hoping the camera could not record his embarrassment and annoyance.

"Very good, sir," Chekov whispered wryly.

"Brought a tear to my eye," Scott deadpanned.

On impulse power, the ship sailed smoothly out of spacedock and into the solar system. Kirk might have actually relaxed and enjoyed the ride, but he, Scotty, and Chekov were trapped in their seats by the camera and journalists like doomed prisoners in front of a firing squad. He smiled into the dazzling light until his jaw ached, until his head hurt, giving ridiculous answers to ridiculous questions such as: *Here you are, back on the bridge of the* Starship Enterprise. . . . *How does it* feel?

The three of them had paused reluctantly at that; he had cast a look at Chekov, then Scott, realizing that none wanted to answer and each was hoping the others would.

Jim had silently sighed, then summoned the PR smile and said, *Just fine* . . . at the exact moment Chekov and Scott had each surrendered and chorused, *Fine.*

And so it went, until Harriman rescued them by saying, "Well, ladies and gentlemen, we've just cleared the asteroid belt. Our course will take us out beyond Pluto and then back to spacedock. . . . Just a quick run around the block."

The journalists turned all in a row, as if suddenly realizing that here was a fresh victim. One of them immediately asked, "Captain, will there be time to conduct a test of the warp—"

He broke off at the shrill beep emanating from the communications console. The comm officer called, in a voice that reflected the surprise felt by all, "We're picking up a distress call, Captain."

Harriman's eyes went wide for an instant, but he recovered himself enough to order, "On speakers."

Kirk winced at the loud burst of static that followed. A male voice, desperate, distorted, barely comprehensible, filtered through the speakers:

"This is the transport ship *Lakul.* We're caught in some kind of energy distortion. We can't break free . . ." Here the words became garbled, but Kirk was able to make out: ". . . need immediate help . . . it's tearing us . . ."

Another painful burst of static filled the air; the comm officer played a rapid fugue on his panel, then shook his head at Harriman. Simultaneously, the science officer checked her console and reported, "The *Lakul* is one of two ships transporting El Aurian refugees to Earth."

Harriman blinked once, twice, at this information, then cleared his throat. Seconds were passing—critical seconds, which could save or doom lives, Kirk knew, and he held his breath as he prayed the young captain would overcome his surprise in time to act. Somehow, he

29

managed not to move, not even to clench his fists as he waited for Harriman to speak.

Harriman turned toward the helm. "Can you locate them?"

Almost before the question was out of Harriman's mouth, Demora responded calmly, "The ships are bearing at three one zero mark two one five. Distance: three light-years."

"Signal the nearest starship," Harriman ordered. "We're in no condition to mount a rescue. We don't even have a full crew aboard."

The navigator checked his console and half turned toward his captain. "We're the only one in range, sir."

Harriman let go a small, perplexed sigh just as the camera light was turned on him. Another second passed, leaving Kirk fidgeting on the edge of his seat, drumming his fingers on his thighs, ready to rise and commandeer the vessel if the younger captain did not take swift action. At last, Harriman drew in a breath and straightened his tunic.

"Well, then . . . I guess it's up to us." He swiveled toward Demora. "Helm, lay in an intercept course and engage at maximum warp."

Kirk released a silent sigh, then tensed, startled as Scott leaned in toward him and said softly, with a glint of amusement in his eye, "Something wrong with your chair, Captain?"

Kirk shot him a sour look as the *Enterprise* leapt into warp.

Within a minute, Demora glanced up from her console. "We're within visual range of the energy distortion, Captain."

"On screen," Harriman said.

All eyes focused on the main viewscreen, which revealed a bizarre sight: stars and space dissected by a writhing, crackling lash of pure energy, hot white shot with streaks of violet, blue, gold. To Kirk, it seemed alive, angry.

"What the hell is that?" Chekov whispered.

"I've found the transport ships," Demora reported. The view shifted slightly to reveal two buffeted transport vessels, trapped like struggling insects in a violent, pulsing spiderweb. "Their hulls are starting to buckle under the stress. They won't survive much longer."

She hung on to her console as the *Enterprise*-B suddenly lurched, throwing Kirk against Chekov.

"We're encountering severe gravimetric distortions from the energy ribbon," the navigator said.

Clutching the arms of his chair, Harriman ordered, "We'll have to keep our distance. We don't want to get pulled in, too." He frowned at the screen, clearly pondering his next move.

To Kirk, the solution seemed obvious; he gave Harriman another two seconds, then blurted out, "Tractor beam . . ."

Scott immediately directed a well-aimed elbow at his former captain's rib. Kirk fell silent at once; he knew that this was Harriman's ship, not his. Yet the situation was quickly growing desperate. . . .

Harriman glanced over his shoulder with a glum expression that was free from annoyance. Either he was too gracious to register the insult, or was genuinely grateful for any help. "We don't have a tractor beam."

Kirk made no effort to hide his indignant reaction. "You left spacedock without a tractor beam?"

"It won't be installed until Tuesday," Harriman replied matter-of-factly. He turned back toward the helm. "Ensign Sulu—try generating a subspace field around the ships. That might break them free."

"Aye, sir." Demora bent over her console.

No, Kirk wanted to say, but before he had a chance for another outburst, Demora shook her head and glanced up. "There's too much quantum interference, Captain."

Once again, Harriman squinted at the lashing streaks of energy on the viewscreen and frowned. Kirk had nothing but sympathy for the young captain, whose first day in command was turning into something of a nightmare on a ship that was undermanned and ill prepared. But if Harriman failed to come up with another plan, sympathy or not—

"What about venting plasma from the warp nacelles?" Harriman asked no one in particular. "That might disrupt the ribbon's hold on the ships."

"Aye, sir," the navigator replied. "Releasing drive plasma . . ."

Harriman visibly held his breath for a moment, then glanced back at Kirk, who gave him a pained, encouraging smile.

"It's not having any effect, sir," the navigator said. "I think—"

"Sir!" Demora cried. "The starboard vessel's hull is collapsing!"

On the screen, one of the ships, now engulfed by one of the fiery tendrils, exploded into a brilliant starburst. All on the *Enterprise* bridge fell silent as the starburst dimmed and dissolved into hurtling shards of debris.

"How many people were on that ship?" Chekov asked, aghast; it was not his place to speak out, to put such a pointed question, which should have belonged to the ship's captain. But in the horror of the moment, no one seemed to care or notice—certainly not Harriman, who stared, eyes wide and lips parted, at the screen.

"Two hundred sixty-five," Demora said softly.

Two pairs of shoulders sagged ever so faintly under the weight of that answer—one pair belonging to Harriman, the other to Kirk.

The devil with politeness, Kirk told himself. *Two hundred sixty-five . . . I know the hell he's going through, but I can't sit by and watch it happen again. If he doesn't ask, by God, I'll tell him. . . .*

Demora spoke again, her tone more urgent. "The *Lakul's* hull integrity is down to twelve percent, sir."

Harriman swiveled slowly and met Kirk's anxious gaze. Uncertainty flickered over the younger captain's face. Kirk understood; Harriman did not wish to seem incapable in front of his crew—and the now very silent reporters. But here was experienced help, and there were another two hundred–odd lives at stake. . . .

"Captain Kirk," Harriman said, with admirable dignity and humility, "I would appreciate any suggestions you might have."

The words triggered an amazing reaction within Kirk. It was the same sensation he had had in the dream the night before: free fall, the way he had felt in Yosemite, falling from El Capitan, the way he had felt orbital skydiving only the day before. Yet this time he experienced the intense exhilaration he had sought in those adventures, and never found—because this time, he was making a difference.

He shot out of his chair like a cork from a champagne

bottle, and was beside Harriman in less than a second, with a look that he hoped conveyed his gratitude and respect.

"First," he said, in a voice so low only the younger captain could hear, "move us within transporter range and beam those people to the *Enterprise*."

Harriman gazed up at him with unmasked surprise. "But what about the gravimetric distortions? They'll tear us apart."

Kirk put a hand on his shoulder and said, very softly and without reproach, "Risk is part of the game if you want to sit in that chair."

Harriman wavered—only for an instant—then squared his shoulders and turned grimly toward the image on the screen. "Helm," he ordered, "close to within transporter range."

Kirk squinted at the sudden glare, and glanced up to see the cameraman moving in on the command chair for a close-up. "And second," he snapped, making sure his voice carried over the entire bridge, "turn that damned thing off."

The cameraman hesitated—only for an instant; the scowls on the two captains' faces apparently convinced him. He turned the camera off and joined the other silent reporters.

The *Enterprise* eased forward; on the viewscreen, the streak of deadly energy loomed closer, closer . . . until, unexpectedly, it lashed out at the *Enterprise*, barely missing it. Kirk let out a mental sigh and directed silent thanks to Sulu for passing on his skill at the helm.

"We're within range, sir," Demora said.

Harriman kept his pale eyes focused on the screen. "Beam them directly to sickbay."

Directly? Kirk almost said—intraship beaming was risky business, at best—but before he could utter a sound, Harriman glanced up at him, apparently reading his thoughts; had the situation not been so critical, he might have smiled.

"It's all right, Captain. As I said, the new ship's got some amazing new capabilities."

Brow furrowed with concern, Chekov stepped forward and bent beside Harriman's chair. "Sir. How big is your medical staff?"

Harriman's momentary flicker of pride turned to embarrassment. "The medical staff doesn't arrive until Tuesday."

Chekov wasted no time in questioning it; he rose and pointed at two reporters watching nearby. "You and you. You've just become nurses. Let's go."

The three hurried to the turbolift as Demora said, "Main Engineering reports fluctuations in the warp plasma relays."

Scott was on his feet before she finished speaking. "Bypass the relays and go to auxiliary systems," he said, moving quickly toward the helm. Kirk gave him a swift, bemused glance that said, *Weren't you jabbing me in the ribs not two minutes ago . . . ?*

Scott wasted no time acknowledging it.

"Sir." A skinny young lieutenant fresh from the Academy turned from the aft console with an air of panic. "I'm having trouble locking on to them." He gazed back at his board and shook his head with an expression of pure puzzlement. "They appear to be in some sort of . . . temporal flux."

"Scotty?" Kirk called, but before he could turn to face his former engineer, Scott had left the helm and was

35

standing beside the young lieutenant, frowning down at the console.

He let go a hiss of amazement. "What the hell—?"

Kirk strode over to stand beside him; Scott angled his face toward his former captain without taking his gaze off the perplexing readout. "Their life signs are . . . *phasing* in and out of our space-time continuum."

"Phasing?" Kirk asked. "To where?" He stared down at the board, but the data made no more sense than Scott's words.

Scott did not answer, but moved in to work the controls as the lieutenant gratefully moved aside.

"Sir!" the navigator cried, in a tone as electrifying as the sight on the screen. "Their hull's collapsing!"

For the second time, the energy tendril engulfed the doomed ship, like a great dazzling python squeezing its prey. As Kirk watched, the *Lakul* erupted into a fiery hail of spinning debris. He turned at once to Scott, whose eyes held the haggard, defeated look Kirk had come to dread so long ago.

"I got forty-seven of them," Scott said softly, though in the sudden silence his words seemed to fill the entire bridge. His gaze dropped. "Out of one hundred fifty."

No time to react with sorrow; the floor beneath Kirk's feet heaved, hurling him against Harriman's chair. Somehow he managed to hold on, somehow reacted instinctively to the sound of shrieking metal by shielding his face with his forearm against the sudden rain of sparks and bulkhead fragments.

And then it was over just as quickly, and the ship righted itself with an abrupt hitch that almost made him lose his balance again. He lowered his arm and took in his surroundings; a scorched bulkhead, but no hull breach, as he'd feared. No serious injuries—except the navigator, who lay sprawled across the console with terrible limpness, his eyes open, his head bloodied, his neck at such an impossible angle that Kirk did not need to check to know that he was dead.

Beside him, dull grief in her eyes, Demora sat stiffly, holding on to her console with white-lipped intensity.

"Report!" Kirk shouted over the klaxon's howl, as Scott gently moved the dead man aside and took his place.

Demora drew in a visible, gathering breath. "We're caught in a gravimetric field emanating from the trailing edge of the ribbon."

This time, Harriman needed no prompting, no advice. "All engines, full reverse!"

THREE

☆ ————

Seconds earlier, aboard the *Lakul,* Tolian Soran sat cross-legged on the deck of the crowded passenger cabin and stared blankly up at the viewscreen, where the blazing ribbon thrashed through the night of space.

Unlike the others beside him, some silent with shock, others murmuring, weeping at the news that their sister ship had been destroyed, Soran did not fear the ribbon. Indeed, he welcomed it.

Since the first day he had been rescued by the *Lakul,* he had been gathering the strength to end his own life. He had been trying to do just that—steering the lifepod into the Borg's death beams when he realized that Sadorah City, his home, Leandra's home, was destroyed. His wife and children were dead, killed as he had watched, in safety and horror, from an off-planet observatory.

By pure chance, the fleeing *Lakul* had detected him, and beamed him aboard—quite against his will. He was dead inside already of grief; he wished merely for his body to join his mind and family. But he had not been permitted.

Soran gazed up at the fearsome sight on the viewscreen and smiled grimly. The ribbon looked like blazing doom, like the Borg death rays that had carved up his homeworld. They had come for him at last, to allow him to die as he was meant to, as Leandra and Emo and Mara had.

The shuddering ship reeled, stricken.

At last, Soran thought. Amid the screams, the chaotic ballet of tumbling bodies, he sat with arms folded tight about his knees, and let himself be tossed.

The bulkheads around him began to crumple; a shard of metal debris stung his forehead, sending blood trickling over his brow, into his eye. Yet Soran merely smiled.

And in the midst of the tumult, the light lashed forth, piercing the bulkhead to crackle in their very midst, lifting the hairs on Soran's head, arms, the back of his neck. He filled his lungs, embracing death, waiting for dissolution, his mind focused on a solitary thought:

Leandra . . .

Darkness. Stillness. Silence.

So this is it, he thought with amazement. *Death . . .* Yet he was still aware of his own consciousness, and that awareness brought with it disappointment. He had hoped to dissolve into nothingness, thoughtlessness, the void. But here he was, listening to his own breathing, his own heartbeat . . . aware of the movement of cool, moist air against his skin.

And the warm flesh of another against his.

He opened his eyes to darkness. Not total blackness, for beyond the open window, stars twinkled, sending down their gentle light. He stirred, and felt the soft, yielding velvet of bedclothes beneath his bare back, heard the gentle cascade of breaking ocean waves, smelled the subtle fragrance of brine mixed with the aroma of exotic flora.

Even in the dimness, he knew: This was Talaal, the resort where he had spent his wedding night.

He turned on his side and found her lying beside him, her face limned silver by starglow, her dark hair long and soft, scented like the flowers.

"Leandra," he whispered, and wept, the dam of pent-up emotion finally breaking. He slid his arms around her and held her to his heart, burying his face in her hair. Miracle of miracles, she was solid, warm—no dream, but *real,* truly here in his arms.

"Leandra, oh gods, dear gods, Leandra . . ."

The universe was once again sane, just.

"Tolian?" she murmured sleepily. "Darling, what is it?" His torment brought her back to consciousness. "What's wrong? Were you dreaming?"

"Yes, dreaming," he said bitterly, lips brushing her hair. "Promise me. Promise me you'll never leave. . . ."

"Of course I'll never leave you, Tolian. You know that. But what—"

Her image faded, paled like a vanishing ghost. He cried out, horrified to find that he no longer clasped her soft solid body, but empty air. Yet he could see her faintly before him, a ribbon of moonlight illuminating her lovely face, her troubled eyes. See her, and not touch her . . .

"Leandra!" he cried, but he could not hear the words that issued from her moving lips. At the same time, he became aware of another reality enveloping them, surrounding them: he was standing with the refugees from the *Lakul* aboard a different ship—a Federation ship.

"No!" Soran screamed with fury and grief, clawing at Leandra's outstretched hand; his own passed through empty air. "Noooo . . . !"

For a fleeting instant, Pavel Chekov paused in the open doorway and stared in awe—not at the state-of-the-art medical equipment, or the sleeker, more spacious sickbay design, but at the horrific tableau within.

Some fifty *Lakul* survivors—all graceful humanoids, the last remnants of the long-lived El Aurian race—lay draped unconscious over diagnostic beds, sat stunned on the carpets, or huddled moaning against bulkheads. It was not their physical injuries that made Chekov and the two reporters who flanked him briefly recoil. Most seemed relatively unscathed—in body, at least; but what horrified Chekov most was the look in the El Aurians' eyes, a look he knew he would never be able to forget.

He could not shake the notion that he had just walked into an eighteenth-century madhouse.

Those conscious stared at some distant, alluring sight, one so beautiful that some were stricken into silence. Others clawed at the air, grasping vainly at the invisible desired. Yet none shared the same vision; each was lost to his own inner world. Moans, whispers, soft weeping filled the air in an eerie discordant litany.

The colors are touching me
I'm caught in the glass
I can see the seconds
Help me. Help me . . .

Chekov had understood that morning why Captain Kirk had not wanted to come aboard the *Enterprise*-B. Chekov had not wanted to either; he had seen no good reason to sit aboard a starship feeling useless. Yet like the captain, he had not been able to stay away.

But the moment Kirk had taken command of the ship, Chekov felt an overwhelming sense of exhilaration. For the first time in a year, he felt a sense of purpose—a sense of rightness, of belonging—which he had not experienced since retirement, so he did not hesitate to take charge of sickbay. His emergency medical training as head of security aboard the *Reliant* would serve him now in good stead.

He hesitated in the doorway to sickbay for only an instant, then came to himself and quickly located diagnostic scanners. He handed one to each of the journalists —one male, one female, both Terran—with brief instructions.

Before he finished, the ship gave a sudden lurch, flinging them against a nearby bulkhead. "Good lord!" the man cried out, his scanner clattering to the floor as Chekov collided against him. "What was that?"

Chekov regained his footing quickly, scooped up the scanner, and handed it back to the man, who simply stared back in fear.

"Take it," he ordered. "We've got to get moving—"

The woman's eyes were wide. "But what *was* that? Do you think the energy ribbon—"

The ship shuddered again; she dropped her scanner and clung to the bulkhead.

"It doesn't matter what it is," Chekov said shortly. "We'll leave that to those on the bridge. These people need our help." And at the dull, frightened stares that replied, he thundered, exasperated, "Don't think. Just *move,*" with such force that the two finally retrieved their scanners and followed him into the moaning crowd.

Don't make me go; please, let me stay. . . .
I'm caught, let me go
Help me. Someone, help me. . . .

"It's all right," Chekov soothed. He crouched down beside a beautiful, ageless woman with long auburn hair who seemed unharmed. Her sorrowful pale eyes never focused on him, but remained fixed on some far distant point. "It's all right. Miss . . . ma'am . . . can you hear me?"

She did not reply, did not seem at all aware of his presence as he quickly ran the scanner over her. Nothing serious, just some bruised ribs. The same held true for the next survivor—the same near-catatonia, a few scrapes. By the third patient, Chekov looked over at the male journalist, who was tending a slightly wounded victim beside him.

"Only minor injuries so far," he said, and the man gave a nod to indicate he had found the same; two El Aurians down, the female reporter rose and nodded in agreement. Chekov continued, "But it looks like they're all suffering from some kind of neural shock."

"What would cause it?" the woman asked. "The stress of being attacked?"

As she spoke her male cohort made his way to another patient sitting on a biobed, a pale man with an even paler shock of silvery hair and eyes that made Chekov think of a candle blazing too fiercely. A thread of bright blood crossed the center of the man's forehead to the bridge of his nose, then curved beneath one eye and down his cheek.

"Probably not," Chekov answered. "At least, not a mass reaction like this. Perhaps the energy ribbon—"

"Why?" the pale man suddenly shrieked. Chekov turned to see the slender El Aurian grabbing the much larger journalist by his shoulders and pulling him close. "Why?"

At the insane desperation in the wounded man's eyes, Chekov quietly hurried over to a supply cabinet.

The reporter wisely remained calm and did not struggle in the El Aurian's grip. "It's all right," he said soothingly. "You're safe. You're on the *Enterprise*."

"No . . ." The word was a ragged sob, a plea; the bleeding man tightened his grip dangerously on the reporter. "I have to go—I have to get back! You don't understand! *Let me go!*"

Without warning, he released his hold, then lunged at the reporter's neck. Before he could squeeze the man's windpipe, Chekov stepped swiftly behind him and emptied a hypospray into his arm.

The El Aurian fell unconscious beside the wide-eyed journalist, who put a hand to his throat as he asked, "What was he talking about?"

Chekov never got the chance to answer; beside him, a woman stumbled. He caught her arm, stopping her in midfall. "Easy there . . ."

There seemed no physical reason for her weakness; a scan revealed no injury. She was a small woman, not beautiful but handsome, with the agelessness typical of El Aurians, and a cascade of tiny black braids that fell halfway to her waist from beneath a large purple cap. She gazed up at Chekov with dark face, dark eyes so deep and full of such radiant peace and, at the same time, such agonizing pain that he drew in his breath.

"It's going to be okay," he said, smiling warmly at her

in an effort to distract her from that pain. "Here, just lie down. . . ."

And he led her to a biobed.

In the years to come, when he remembered that day and thought of James Kirk, he would also think of that woman, and wonder what had become of her.

The *Enterprise* engines groaned, straining against the pull of the energy tendril, to no avail; the ship shuddered constantly, helpless, as the ribbon lashed against her.

"Inertial dampers failing," Demora reported on the shaking bridge, just before Scott called out:

"Engines not responding!"

Harriman gripped the arms of his trembling chair with enough force to turn his knuckles pale yellow; he glanced up at Kirk and said quietly, "I didn't expect to die my first day on the job."

With a small, grim smile, Kirk bent closer to the younger captain's ear, holding on to the edge of the chair to keep his balance. "The first thing you learn as captain is how to cheat death." He straightened, then called, "Scotty?"

Indignant at what he knew his captain would ask next, Scott shouted, "There's just no way to disrupt a gravimetric field of this magnitude!"

In the midst of her shuddering, the ship reeled hard again; Demora clutched her console and cried, "Hull integrity at eighty-two percent!"

Kirk said nothing, simply kept his eyes focused on Scott, who at last grudgingly allowed, "But, I do have a theory. . . ."

Kirk grinned. "I thought you might."

Scott nodded at the ominous sight on the screen. "An

antimatter discharge directly ahead . . . it might disrupt the field long enough for us to break away."

Kirk nodded slowly as he considered it. "A photon torpedo?"

"Aye."

The older captain turned toward Demora. "Load torpedo bays, prepare to fire on my command."

"Captain." Demora swiveled toward him, unmasked dismay in her eyes. "We don't have any torpedoes."

"Don't tell me. Tuesday." Kirk closed his eyes briefly, then opened them at Harriman, who gave a defeated nod.

"Captain," Scott said, "it may be possible to *simulate* a torpedo blast using a resonance burst from the main deflector dish."

Fighting to keep his balance on the unsteady deck, Kirk turned to him with a fresh surge of hope. "Where are the deflector relays?"

"Deck fifteen," Demora replied at once. "Section twenty-one alpha."

Harriman rose, his bearing unsteady because of the shaking floor beneath his feet. "I'll go. You have the bridge." And without pausing to hear the response, he headed for the turbolift.

"No," Kirk said sharply. As tempting as it was for him to slip into the empty captain's chair, this was Harriman's ship; and the younger man had just proven his worth. Only a true captain would swallow his pride and turn over command for his crew's sake.

Harriman straightened, and turned to stare at the older captain behind him. "No," Kirk said. "A captain's place is on the bridge of his ship." He paused. "I'll take care of it."

Harriman smiled with his eyes only; his jaw was set grimly as he gave Kirk a nod that acknowledged far more than the older captain's words.

Kirk turned to Scott as he headed for the turbolift. "Keep her together until I get back."

"I always do," Scott said.

Kirk gave him a smile just before the turbolift doors slid shut.

And when the lift doors opened onto level fifteen, he was again in exhilarating free fall, a combination of the sheerest terror and bliss. Terror, because he remembered the dreams of the night before and knew Spock would not be there to catch him; bliss, because he was once again doing what he had been born to do—make a difference. There was no time for thought, for reflection, only for pure mindless action.

Jim ran down the trembling corridor with a speed he had thought himself no longer capable of, following the signs to section twenty-one alpha until at last he made it to the deflector room, with its massive generators towering behind a stand of consoles.

His heart was pounding, his breath coming in gasps, but none of it mattered; it was the first time in over a year he had truly felt alive. He found the bulkhead panel and pried it off, then began to work at rerouting the deflector circuitry.

He hadn't been at it more than a minute when the wall intercom whistled and Scott's voice filtered through, barely audible over the ship's groaning. "Bridge to Captain Kirk."

"Kirk here," he shouted, not taking his gaze from his work. What needed to be done was simple; and if he didn't let Scott interrupt him, he would be done in seconds. . . .

"Captain," Scott cried, in the plaintive tone Kirk knew so well—well enough to know that this time, things were seriously critical. Even had Scott not contacted him, he would have known from the feel of the *Enterprise*'s shaking—even this *new Enterprise*'s shaking—that a major hull breach was imminent. "I don't know how much longer I can hold her together!"

In the background, he could hear Demora's voice: "Forty-five seconds to structural collapse!"

Kirk took the critical seconds needed to make the final adjustment, then slammed the wall panel closed with a sense of triumph. "That's it! *Go!*"

He heard Scott terminate the intercom link, and rose unsteadily to make his way out into the shuddering corridor. There was no sense in hurrying; they would either be safe now, or die. He had done all that he could do.

Before he had taken more than a dozen steps, the ship's shaking eased dramatically. He grinned gently; so, his strange premonition of death had proven to be false. He was glad, of course, for himself and all those aboard the ship—and yet he felt a faint, odd disappointment. It wouldn't have been such a terrible way to go. Would he ever again get another chance like this to make a difference?

He was in midstride when it came: an explosion so deafening, so teeth-chattering, that it seemed to have erupted from within his own head. He was lifted from the floor, slammed against bulkhead or deck—he could not discern which. In a dazzlingly brilliant millisecond, he saw everything around him dissolve into the violet white heat of the energy ribbon, felt his own body dissolving, merging with the pulse.

He was, as he had always known he would be, alone. There was no time for reflection or regret in the primal moment of dissolution, only a glimmer of gladness that McCoy and Spock were safe wherever they were, that they would continue without him.

And then there was silence, and the beginning of the ultimate, infinite free fall. . . .

FOUR

☆

Several seconds earlier, Montgomery Scott terminated the link to the deflector room and stared at the thrashing energy tendril on the main screen—like a great bolt of lightning gone berserk, it looked. The *Enterprise* was shuddering constantly now, pommeled to the sound of distant thunder like a storm-tossed sailing vessel in the midst of a violent sea. Scott held his breath as young Captain Harriman leaned forward to give an order to Sulu's daughter.

"Activate main deflector."

Along with the silent, prayerful crew, Scott watched as a brilliant beam of energy burst from the main deflector dish and erupted into a tiny nova off the starboard hull.

He was breathless, yes, but not as frightened as the young lieutenant beside him at the console. Scott had had a full life, and over the past year had found a measure of contentment in consultant work and family.

At least, he had thought himself content. But at the moment Captain Kirk had smiled at him from the turbolift—

Keep her together until I get back.

—Scott had felt a thrill he had almost forgotten, and seen a spark long extinguished blaze once more in his captain's eyes.

In his younger days, Scott would have been terrified— but too determined to survive to let his terror show, to let it interfere with what had to be done. Now all that was gone. Oh, there was still fear of dying, yes, but it was tempered by experience and the perspective of age. He had faced such impossible situations many times before and always walked away whole.

Even if this time he did not, he had far less to lose than the young ones surrounding him. He could sense their fear, and for some odd reason it calmed him, made him determined to be of help.

He set a hand on the shoulder of the young lieutenant beside him, who had been so distracted by the unfolding drama on the screen that he jumped nervously at the touch. Scott gave him a reassuring half smile; the young officer grimaced sheepishly, then returned his gaze to the screen.

Scott too turned toward their fate, and watched as the energy tendril reacted to the deflector blast by leaping backward, then roiling like angry storm clouds.

The shuddering lessened; Scott drew in a deep breath and let it go. "We're breaking free."

The young lieutenant's grimace turned to a smile; Harriman's shoulders and bottom lip dropped in concert. Scott began to straighten, with the intent of going over to congratulate the young captain—

The screen went blinding white as the ship lurched hard to port. Scott clawed at the console, lost purchase, and came down on his backside on the deck. The lieutenant was thrown sideways into Scott's chair and nearly fell on top of him, but regained his balance in time.

Scott stayed where he was, waiting for the next strike for one second, for two. For three, and as he sat, the shaking gradually eased, and the ship was still.

Scott rose slowly to his feet, watching as Demora scrambled back to her station and peered at the helm readout; a broad grin spread over her features. "We're clear."

Harriman was miraculously still at the conn. For a moment he stared at the screen, clearly amazed to find himself still alive, then punched a control on the arm of his chair. "You did it, Kirk!" He swiveled toward Demora. "Damage report, Ensign."

Demora's smile had already faded; with the efficiency of a seasoned officer, she studied her console. *A fine lass,* Scott thought; next time he saw her father, he'd be sure to tell Sulu how well she performed in the crisis. "There's some buckling on the starboard nacelle," Demora reported. She frowned abruptly and glanced up at Harriman. "We've also got a hull breach in the engineering section. Emergency forcefields are in place and holding."

Scott could not have explained then how he *knew.* Engineering covered a very large area of the ship, and dozens of areas could have been damaged without coming anywhere near the deflector room. Yet at the instant Demora said, *We've got a hull breach,* he went cold. For a moment he could not speak; when he did, he could manage no more than a single, hoarse question.

"Where?"

Demora looked at him. His expression and eyes must have betrayed him, for at the sight of his face, she seemed to realize what he was asking. Her face went slack; her dark eyes narrowed with concern. As she stared down at the console again, Harriman rose from his chair, as if he, too, suddenly shared Scott's ominous conviction.

Let me be wrong, Scott prayed, but as he watched Demora's eyes widen, then narrow again at the sight on her board, he knew he was not.

"Sections twenty through twenty-eight," Demora read dully, "on decks thirteen, fourteen . . ." She gazed up at Scott. ". . . and fifteen."

Numbly, Scott returned to the aft console and pressed the comm control. "Bridge to Captain Kirk." He paused, waited an agony of seconds, then repeated, "Captain Kirk . . . *please* respond."

An eternity of silence. Scott could not meet the gazes of all those focused on him; he bowed his head and briefly closed his eyes.

When he had gathered himself enough to speak again, he turned to Demora. "Have Chekov meet me on deck fifteen."

He headed for the turbolift, only distantly aware that Harriman followed close behind.

In sickbay, Chekov continued to help the survivors. Other than their mental disorientation, the worst wound—a facial cut, from a bulkhead fragment—belonged to the pale man who had attacked the reporter, and now lay sedated under restraints. The two journalists made fairly efficient orderlies, and it seemed the situation would soon be under control.

As he worked, he found it easier to maintain his balance, and gradually came to realize that the ship's shaking had eased. He smiled over at his two impromptu assistants, who were busily scanning patients.

"You see?" he called. "The people on the bridge can be trusted to take care of things."

The two grinned with relief. "Thank goodness," said the woman. "I was beginning to think I'd never get the chance to file a great—"

Chekov never heard the rest. The world suddenly heaved to one side, hurling him against a diagnostic bed. When the rocking subsided, he found himself on the deck atop the dark-skinned woman with the intriguing eyes. He scrambled to his feet. "Are you all right?"

She did not reply, but pushed herself to a sitting position. Her purple cap had fallen off; Chekov retrieved it and helped her on with it. She stared at him blankly as he offered her a hand, then pulled her to her feet and guided her back to the biobed.

All the while she stared, as though looking through him at another, more distant sight. And then suddenly she blinked, and seemed to see him—really see him— and gazed intently up into his eyes.

"He's gone there, now." She said it so matter-of-factly, addressing Chekov with such lucid directness that he could not help responding.

"Who's gone? Gone where?"

"To the other side." Her face grew somber with compassion. "He's gone."

Chekov glanced up as the female reporter called

jubilantly, "The shaking! It's stopped!" But only for an instant; the El Aurian woman's gaze compelled him to finish the conversation.

He was being foolish, of course, to think her words had any meaning. She had suffered a serious neural shock; she was raving. He tried to imagine how Dr. McCoy would handle this: *Now, ma'am, you just lie back and relax. . . .*

He smiled again and patted her hand. "Don't talk any more. You need to rest." Reluctantly, he turned away.

"Your friend," she said, with such conviction that he looked back. But he shook off the strange current of fear her words evoked, smiling palely at his own irrationality, and began once more to move away.

"Your friend, Jim," she said, and Chekov wheeled to face her.

"Commander Chekov." Demora's voice filtered through the intercom. Her tone seemed strained, oddly formal. "Captain Scott requests that you meet him on level fifteen, near engineering."

Still staring at the El Aurian woman's inscrutable expression, Chekov made his way through the cluster of seated survivors to the nearest comm panel. "Demora, what is it? Is something wrong?"

But she had already terminated the link.

He left the remaining patients in the reporters' care and ran to the nearest turbolift. Demora's terse message had filled him with profound uneasiness, verging on panic; even so, he did not permit himself to think, to suspect what he would find on level fifteen outside engineering until he arrived.

And saw Scott and Harriman, standing on the last few

meters of unscorched corridor, staring silently beyond a flickering forcefield and the jagged remnants of a bulkhead into open space.

"My God," Chekov whispered, as he stepped beside them. He knew before he asked what the answer to his question would be; he had seen it in Scott's defeated posture, even before he had seen his face. "Was anyone in there?"

Harriman gave him a look of such pure sympathy that Chekov's heart skipped a beat. Scott never looked at him, but gazed steadily out at blackness and stars before replying softly, "Aye . . ."

The rest of his time aboard the *Enterprise*-B was spent in a daze. He did not remember whether Scott or Harriman told him who it was that had been lost; nor did he remember returning to the bridge. But he recalled quite clearly the moment when he stood beside Scott and Harriman at the helm, and the muted anguish in Demora's voice when she said, *I've checked the entire ship and the surrounding space. There's no sign of him.*

He had looked to Scott then, unable to believe that there would not be yet another miracle, some way to pull his friend and captain from death's jaws once more. They had done it before, after all—when Kirk had been trapped in interstitial space near the Tholian border. They had thought him dead then, but he had survived. Why not now?

But Scott merely sighed as he looked at the empty command chair, then shook his head. "Just a quick run around the block," he whispered bitterly.

"No," Chekov said, and felt the sting of tears behind

his eyes as reality finally sank home. "It can't be. I never thought it would end like this. . . ."

Scott stepped over beside his friend and gently laid a hand on his shoulder. "All things must end, lad."

The two men yielded to grief for a time, unconscious of reporters and the camera's glare, until at last Harriman said quietly, "Let's go home."

And he moved over to the conn and took his place as captain of the *Enterprise*.

FIVE

☆

On the bridge of the *Starship Excelsior,* Captain Hikaru Sulu sat in his command chair gazing out at stars and darkness hurtling past on the viewscreen as he sipped his tea. At the moment, the bridge was calm as a glassy sea. The past few days had been slow enough to allow him the luxury of reflection; *Excelsior* was returning from a star-mapping expedition in the Thanatos sector. There was nothing left but the long journey home, then reassignment. And so, Sulu was left with hours to do little else but contemplate. Today, the subject was time—how, with each star streaking by, another second passed that could not be recaptured; another second that led him inexorably toward the unknown future.

Sulu smiled privately to himself, amused at his own moroseness, and decided it was directly related to the launch of the *Enterprise*-B. He'd felt both disappointed and relieved that he would not return to Earth in time to attend; disappointed, because he would have liked to share Demora's exhilaration on the day of her first mission, and see all his old friends again. At the same time, he felt relief that he would not have to be reminded once again that old times could never be revived.

And yet—it was good to be reminded of the impermanence of things. Grief was the product of useless grasping at the unattainable; happiness came from accepting the fact of change, and even one's own death. The Buddhists had a useful meditation for just that: Imagine yourself, alive and well and happy.

Now, imagine yourself—dead, your skin cold and graying, your body growing stiff.

Imagine your dead body decaying, alive with maggots, the flesh coming away from the bones as it dissolves, returns to the earth. . . .

He had contemplated his own death enough times to no longer be horrified by it. But the concept of loss still troubled him. Someday, Sulu told himself, this gleaming ship would be gone. Just as the original *Enterprise* herself was gone, destroyed as they had stood on the Genesis planet and watched her streak to her death across a twilight sky. Perhaps he would not lose *Excelsior* so violently; perhaps he would merely surrender her to another captain.

He glanced up from his reverie as his first officer, Masoud Valtane, let out a gusting sigh. A xenogeologist, Valtane had been restless of late because he had run out of new planets to play with. Sulu repressed a fond smile as Valtane, who stood in his customary place at the captain's left, began to nervously stroke his dark mustache. Valtane was not beloved by the crew, in part because of his total ineptness at social relationships and his reputation as a stickler for detail on the job. But over time, Sulu had grown to like him, because he'd learned that Valtane's social clumsiness came not from aloofness, as most assumed, but from his almost childlike lack of pretense. And maybe because his ability to take any comment literally reminded Sulu more than a little bit of another science officer.

The comm link on the command-chair arm suddenly signaled; Sulu punched a toggle with the edge of his fist, jostling the tea in its cup. "Bridge."

"Captain." Lieutenant Djugashvili's habitually calm monotone was pitched a half-octave higher than normal; her exhilaration was contagious enough to make Sulu set his cup of tea on its saucer and straighten in his chair. "Magnetic interlocks are nonfunctional; we're losing coolant. Warp breach is imminent."

Sulu glanced up at Valtane, who had stopped stroking his mustache, curved hand frozen in front of his lips. Lojur, the Halkan navigator, heard and stared over his shoulder, his family symbol, tattooed in red between his pale eyebrows, deeply furrowed. Beside him at the helm, Lieutenant Shandra Docksey turned as well, dark auburn hair swinging.

Docksey was the newest addition to the crew; she shot a swift panicked look at Lojur, who laid a reassuring hand on the back of her chair. The two had been inseparable since Docksey's arrival from Starfleet Academy only days before, with Lojur playing the role of seasoned veteran/mentor/instructor to the hilt.

"How much time do we have?" Sulu asked Djugashvili.

"Less than three minutes, sir."

Not enough time, Sulu knew from past drills, to evacuate all engineering personnel to the primary hull—

and the *Excelsior* was too far out to transport them to safety. "Evacuate everyone to the lifeboats."

"Aye, sir."

"Red alert," Sulu ordered as he severed the comm link, and the klaxon began to screech unnervingly overhead. He swiveled his chair toward the helm, so quickly that the tea sloshed over the side of his cup and spilled onto the fragile china saucer beneath. "Lieutenant Lojur. Prepare to separate from secondary hull."

"Yes, Captain." Lojur turned back toward his console and began to work.

"Docksey. Approximate distance from planets or other structures?"

The young lieutenant seemed to have recovered from her moment of disconcertment; she replied smoothly, "One half parsec to the nearest starbase, sir. No planets within a five-parsec radius."

Sulu nodded approvingly. "Stand by to take us to maximum warp, Mr. Docksey. I want at least two parsecs between us and the secondary hull when she goes. Mr. Lojur—initiate separation procedure."

"Initiating."

"Mr. Valtane—"

Valtane, who had hurried to his station the instant the red alert began, turned to reply, his restlessness replaced by the same intense anticipation shared by those on the bridge.

"—time left before detonation?" Sulu finished.

"Two minutes, six seconds, Captain."

Sulu nodded, satisfied, and waited, silently counting the seconds until at last Lojur called, "Separation procedure complete, Captain."

The view on the main screen shifted, from starry black void to the image of the secondary hull—engineering and the warp engine nacelles. Sulu watched as a swarm of tiny lifeboats erupted from the sides of the hull like angry bees spilling from a threatened hive. "Time?"

"One minute, thirty seconds, sir."

Sulu turned to his navigator. "Lojur. You've got thirty seconds to transport those lifeboat operators aboard."

"Yes, sir." With Docksey's wide, green-eyed gaze upon him, the Halkan set to work—with, Sulu noted, the faint, confident air of an old salt showing the newbie how it was done.

"Captain." Gold-and-silver hair pinned up to reveal a graceful neck, Rand turned smoothly from the communications board. Of all the bridge crew, she had the most experience; she had watched the events unfold with an unruffled, detached air. But now there was a note of curiosity in her voice that made Sulu glance at her in earnest concern. "You have an incoming personal message. From Earth."

From Demora, Sulu decided, with parental eagerness and pride; probably to give an excited report of her first day aboard the *Enterprise*-B. He was pleased she had thought to contact him, disappointed that he could not respond. "It'll have to wait."

"It's from Pavel Chekov," Rand said. Only then did her composure waver to reveal a subtle catch in her voice. "He sounds . . . I think . . . Something has happened, sir."

At first, Sulu did not comprehend; and then realized, with slow-dawning dread, that Chekov had been one of the old group who had attended the maiden launch of the *Enterprise*-B. A single thought eclipsed all others, blotting out the klaxon's wail, the frenzied activity on the bridge:

Demora . . .

He caught his breath, suddenly cold with fear.

But no—it would have been Captain Harriman's place to contact him if something had happened to her. Unless Pavel, as a friend, wanted to break it to him first.

Unless . . .

"Ask him to stand by." Sulu turned to Valtane and ordered brusquely, "Time."

"One minute, thirteen seconds to core breach, sir."

"In thirteen seconds," Sulu told Docksey, "get us out of here. Warp ten. Lojur—"

"Understood, Captain. Transporter room reports that all but seven of the lifeboat operators have been brought aboard. We'll get them all, sir."

Sulu released a small sigh, rose from his chair, and stepped over to stand beside Rand. "Put it through to this station, Commander."

She touched a control. At the station in front of her, a small viewscreen brightened in a burst of visual static, then resolved itself into the image of Pavel Chekov.

Sulu bent down, resting his palms on Rand's console to study his old friend. Chekov seemed to have aged abruptly since Sulu had last spoken with him. Yet it was not the extra gray hairs or lines etched in his face that gave that impression.

No, Sulu decided. It was the look of dazed grief in Chekov's glistening, red-rimmed eyes. That look struck the *Excelsior* captain like a physical blow; he recoiled from it, stunned.

"Pavel," he said softly. "My God, Pavel . . ." He tried to form the question that sprang to his lips, and could not; it hung unspoken between them.

Who died?

"Hikaru." Chekov's tone was dull, controlled, but Sulu heard the undercurrent of emotion that threatened to break through. "I am so sorry to be the one to tell you. During the launch, the *Enterprise*-B was trapped in some sort of . . . energy disturbance. The hull was breached—"

"Demora," Sulu said swiftly, but before the final syllable was out of his mouth, Chekov shook his head.

Behind them, Lojur called, "All lifeboat operators aboard."

"Engaging engines," Docksey reported. "Warp ten."

Sulu heard them with only peripheral awareness, as though they were suddenly far distant, the events unfolding on the bridge insignificant. The small image of his friend now consumed his attention.

"She is fine," Chekov said stiffly. "Still on duty. But . . . the captain went down to the deflector room in an attempt to rescue the ship. He succeeded, but was . . ." Overwhelmed, Chekov lowered his head. ". . . killed . . ."

"The captain?" Sulu blinked at the screen in confusion. He knew Harriman, the captain of the *Enterprise*-B, as an acquaintance; but they were not friends. Why would Chekov be calling him about—

Beside him, a small moan of despair escaped Rand's lips before she could raise her hand to them.

Sulu glanced down at her, and knew; a jolt of emotion passed down the length of his spine like pure, cold electricity. He gripped the edge of Rand's console and whispered, "The *captain* . . ."

The thought seemed impossible. He could imagine hearing such news about Scotty, or the doctor, even Chekov, but Kirk—Kirk was larger than life. A legend. Immortal. Kirk could not die. . . .

"Scott is notifying Uhura and Kirk's nephew," Chekov said awkwardly—as if searching for the appropriate words and finding them elusive. "And I will notify Mr. Spock. Starfleet is arranging a memorial service." He hesitated. "I'm sorry, Hikaru. I don't know what else to say. I can't believe this has happened. . . ."

"Pavel." Sulu touched the edge of the screen. "Pavel, my friend. Thank you for being the one to tell me. Take care. . . ."

Chekov's stricken face wavered and was gone.

Sulu placed a hand on Rand's shoulder, then turned to face his crew. "Cancel red alert." He spoke quietly, but there was a hardness in his voice that allowed it to carry over the screaming klaxon.

"Sir?" Valtane directed a questioning stare at his captain; Lojur and Docksey followed suit.

"Cancel red alert." Sulu stepped down from Rand's station and retook his chair, then hit a control on the console arm. "All hands: The drill is over." He drew an unsteady breath. "James T. Kirk died today aboard the *Enterprise*-B. I'd like to observe a moment of silence in his honor."

The klaxon ceased abruptly; the bridge went utterly still as all motion, all sound, ceased.

Along with his crew, Sulu sat and stared out at the stars, and the dark, silent future.

* * *

Leonard McCoy slipped quietly inside the interfaith chapel on the outer grounds of Starfleet's San Francisco headquarters and took a seat near the back, where sunlight filtered through tall stained-glass windows, painting the chairs, the carpet, the backs of McCoy's hands, blue, red, violet. The room was small, free of adornments, save for the large spray of fragrant calla lilies near the podium. Most importantly, it was silent, empty. The doctor had intentionally come forty-five minutes early, to have some private moments alone with his friend.

Not that Jim was here. It was a memorial service, not a funeral; Kirk had left behind no corpse, which seemed somehow fitting. The captain had simply dissolved into space, neat and clean.

McCoy settled back against the chair and released a sigh. He had slept little the night before; when he had, he had dreamt of Jim, returning to the long-distant time and place when the captain had disappeared while on the ghost ship *Reliant*. They had all thought he was dead then, too; but he wasn't, merely trapped in interstitial space.

In McCoy's dream, Kirk was there again, floating eerily in his space suit, waving his arms—just as he had done when, during spatial interphase, his wraithlike form had appeared on the bridge.

Only in the dream, Kirk wasn't gesturing for help, but waving in greeting. *Smiling,* his face split by a broad, euphoric grin. Inviting the doctor to join him. McCoy had wept with joy to see his friend happy and at peace, and had wakened with tears coursing down his cheeks.

There were times when the realization that Jim was truly gone filled him with bitter grief; yet those moments were fewer than those in which his pain was tempered by the knowledge that Jim had led a good life, an amazing life, and had accomplished more, enjoyed more, experienced more than most ever would.

The door opened softly; McCoy turned at the sound, and caught a quick flash of Spock's face in the crack. The Vulcan saw the doctor and retreated, began to close the door.

McCoy rose and stepped out into the aisle. "No . . . Don't go, Spock. Please. Come in. . . ."

Spock hesitated in the doorway. "I do not wish to disturb you, Doctor."

"If it were anyone else, Spock, I'd want to be alone. And I'd hoped never to meet you under these circumstances . . . but I'm glad you're here." The sight of the Vulcan brought a surge of fresh grief, as McCoy realized that they could never again be a trio; Jim would never be with them again. Tears stung the back of McCoy's eyes; he cleared his throat and gathered himself. He had thought he had grieved enough in private to be past suddenly welling up—and he'd promised himself firmly that he would not embarrass the Vulcan by crying in public. But he found himself fighting the urge to fall, weeping, on Spock's shoulder.

He managed an uncertain smile as Spock strode over, the rainbow colors reflected from the stained glass shifting over his solemn face. To the doctor's utter astonishment, the Vulcan paused in front of him, then intentionally offered his hand. "Doctor. I, too, regret the circumstance. But it is good to see you again."

McCoy gaped at the proffered hand a moment— Vulcans, touch telepaths, found physical contact with chaotically minded humans distressing—then gazed up at his friend and gratefully took it. Spock's grip was firm, feverishly warm, and seemed to McCoy to emanate such calm, compassionate strength that he found himself misting up again.

"I can't believe it," the doctor said, with sudden anguish. "Three days, and I just can't get used to it. I can't believe Jim is gone."

"He is gone." Spock's tone was flat, with a faint trace of bitterness. "Whether we believe it or not." He slowly released McCoy's grip, and nodded at the chairs. "Shall we sit?"

"Oh. Yes." McCoy retook his seat; the Vulcan settled beside him. For a moment, the two sat in comfortable silence, their gazes directed ahead, at the lilies beside the podium. And then McCoy said, "Spock . . . do you remember when we were in Yosemite, with Jim? When he said that he always knew he'd die alone?"

"Yes," Spock answered evenly.

"I can't help thinking I should have been there with him. I mean, I know you couldn't be—you were involved in a mission with your father—but I was simply off with Joanna watching my grandchild's graduation. I guess I could have gone to the *Enterprise*-B's christening if I had really wanted to. But . . . I didn't. I was tired of Starfleet, and, frankly, didn't want to have to waste my time aboard a ship where we weren't needed. I resented being put on display." The doctor hesitated. "I just can't stop thinking: If I'd gone with him, maybe he wouldn't have—"

"Doctor," Spock interrupted firmly, "your presence there would have made no difference. The captain would have sent you to sickbay, and he would still have gone to the deflector room. Even had you been with him in the deflector room—" He paused; the barely perceptible glimmer of sorrow in his eyes told McCoy that the Vulcan had shared the same guilt, and had logically reasoned it through. "—it would have only made things more difficult for him. He would have been concerned for your safety."

McCoy digested this a moment. "Maybe you're right . . . I guess if he had to leave us, he went the way he wanted: saving the *Enterprise.*"

Spock angled his long face toward the doctor and somehow managed to convey the notion of a smile without moving the corners of his lips a fraction of a millimeter—though, McCoy noticed, the corners of his eyes crinkled almost imperceptibly. "It is not such a bad way to die."

McCoy turned his head sharply at that. "That's right . . . you should know, shouldn't you?" The memory of Spock's agonizing death from radiation exposure was almost too horrible to bear, and still sent a shudder through him. Yet there was some comfort knowing that Jim's end had been less painful, more mercifully swift. "You know something?"

The Vulcan faced him silently, waiting.

"I feel sorry for you, Spock." He said it kindly, sincerely, without any of the acerbity he had directed at the Vulcan in the past. "Because you're gonna outlive all of us. And you're going to have to experience the loss of a dear friend over and over again." He paused, trying to keep his tone light and jesting, to keep the huskiness from his voice, and failed. "That's what you get for hanging around us humans. No *katra*s to preserve for posterity, no last-minute trips to Mount Seleya to bring us back . . ."

Sudden tears filled his eyes, turning Spock's stoic countenance into a blur. "Damn," McCoy said, as they spilled hot onto his cheeks, then swore again at the sound of his shaking voice. *"Damn.* I'm sorry, Spock." He quickly wiped them away with the outer edge of an index finger, and riffled through his pockets for a handkerchief. "I promised myself I wouldn't do this to you. . . ."

"It's all right," the Vulcan said softly. "I have served with humans for many years. I am therefore quite accustomed to emotional displays."

McCoy smiled apologetically through his tears as he continued to search his pockets. No handkerchief, but he pulled out something that made his smile grow sincere. "Look at this, Spock—I bet you thought I'd tucked this away in some drawer and forgotten about it." He held up the Vulcan mandala, its coppery finish turned green from countless fingerprints. "I carry it around with me. Call it my Vulcan good-luck charm." He managed a feeble imitation of a chuckle. "I think maybe I ought to contemplate it a bit before the others get here. My logic's not doing so good these days."

He hesitated, remembering, rubbing the metal between his fingers. "Remember the day you gave this to me?"

"Of course, Doctor."

"And Jim gave me that clock. Seems like only yesterday—but here it is already a year. I was up all last night, listening to Jim's clock strike the hours, from midnight to dawn. He gave it to me to remember the good times, he said—but all I could think about was how quickly they pass. Time just keeps moving past us, and we're helpless to stop it. You, me, even this"—he held up the mandala—"will someday be gone."

" 'Time,' " Spock quoted quietly, " 'the devourer of all things.' "

"Yes, time . . ." McCoy looked up swiftly, sudden anger in his voice. "I can't stop thinking about time. . . ."

Part Two

☆

Seventy-eight Years Later

SIX

☆

On the main deck of the *Enterprise,* Captain Jean-Luc Picard stared up at the fluttering blue-and-white banner of the United Federation of Planets and drew in a deep lungful of brine-scented air. Beneath his feet, creaking timber rocked softly to the rhythm of lapping waves; above, wind whistled through the rigging.

More than anything, he wanted to throw back his head and laugh, to revel in the perfection of the moment. Fate seemed unutterably sweet; he felt blessed to be a man who had found what he most wanted to do, what he was born to do, with his life. Yet, as he looked over his assembled bridge crew—appropriately costumed for the historical period—he kept his expression somber.

The task proved challenging, especially when he met his second-in-command's mischievous gaze. Will Riker looked amazingly at home in white breeches and dark blue waistcoat with gold epaulettes on the shoulders; but the beard and rakish tilt to his plumed hat spoke more of a buccaneer than a nineteenth-century naval officer. With a macaw on his shoulder, say, and a peg leg . . .

Picard signaled Riker with a curt nod, then looked away swiftly before his own smile gravitated from his eyes to his lips.

"Bring out the prisoner!" Riker bellowed with obvious relish.

A nearby hatch opened. Crouching to avoid losing her tricornered hat on a low-hanging beam, Deanna Troi emerged, followed by Geordi La Forge—looking distinctly un-nineteenth-century in his VISOR—and the prisoner: Worf, hatless and in shirtsleeves. Prodded by his two escorts, the Klingon moved slowly to the clank of iron chains binding his wrists and ankles.

"Mr. Worf," Picard intoned with what he hoped was convincing severity, "I always knew this day would come. Are you prepared to face the charges?"

Worf blinked and took in his strange surroundings, seemingly overwhelmed.

With mock ferocity, Troi jabbed him in the ribs. "Answer him!"

The Klingon gave her a glance at once puzzled and bemused, then gathered himself with dignity. "I am prepared."

Picard directed another nod at Riker, who produced a large scroll of parchment from beneath his waistcoat. He cleared his throat and began to read as Geordi removed the prisoner's shackles:

"We, the officers and crew of the *U.S.S. Enterprise,* being of sound mind and judgment, hereby make the following charges against Lieutenant Worf: One. That he did knowingly and willfully perform above and beyond the call of duty on countless occasions. Two. That he has been a good and solid officer on this ship for one score less twelve years. And three. Most seriously . . . that he has earned the respect and admiration of the entire crew."

As the last of the prisoner's chains clattered to the wooden deck, Riker rewound the scroll.

"There can be only one judgment for such crimes," Picard proclaimed, working hard to maintain his stern visage. "I hereby promote you to the rank of Lieutenant Commander, with all the rights and privileges thereto. And may God have mercy on your soul."

The crew roared its approval. Picard at last permitted himself to smile, and leaned forward to shake Worf's hand. "Congratulations, Commander."

Worf could not quite restrain a small smile himself. "Thank you, sir."

The captain continued to remain in the Klingon's strong, warm grip until Riker stepped between them, his eyes bright with merriment. "Extend the plank!"

The crew swarmed in to surround Worf and pushed him toward the ship's flank, where a long, narrow plank appeared over the lapping sea.

"Lower the badge of office!" Riker shouted.

Above him, a crewman who had shimmied up a yardarm lowered a rope, at the end of which hung a naval officer's three-cornered hat, complete with fluttering plume. The hat descended slowly until it dangled some ten feet above the end of the plank.

"You can do it, Worf!" Troi called, waving her own hat. "Don't look down!"

The others chimed in: "Good luck!" "Don't fall in . . ."

Picard watched with open amusement. Riker sidled up to him and said confidently, "He'll never make it. No one has."

Worf clearly needed no encouragement. With consummate determination and grace, he stepped onto the plank and inched toward the dangling trophy.

Geordi cupped his hands around his mouth and called, "That's a *looong* drop to the water!"

Riker grinned and added, in a loud stage voice, "I bet that water's freezing!"

Valiantly, the Klingon ignored his crew members' taunts, but continued his slow progress along the plank, which grew narrower with each step.

Picard watched as, nearby, a slight crease formed between Beverly Crusher's auburn brows. "Geordi." She turned to the engineer with concern. "Did you remember to engage the holodeck safety program? I don't know if Klingons can swim. . . ."

Geordi's lips curved upward in a playful half-moon as he kept his gaze on the Klingon. "I'm not sure."

The bridge grew quiet as Worf reached the end of the plank, then gazed up at the plumed hat, which dangled mere feet above his reach. The Klingon drew a breath, then gathered his muscular bulk and leapt.

Picard grinned in amazement; beside him, Riker gasped as Worf completed an impossible jeté, snatched the hat with one hand, and landed hard on the board.

For an instant, disaster seemed imminent. The wooden plank flexed, groaning mightily as Worf waved his arms in an effort to keep his balance . . .

And then he faced the spellbound audience, his countenance proud and defiant, and set the hat on his head.

The crew cheered. Picard smiled over at his second-in-command, who was applauding with less-than-sincere enthusiasm. "If there's one thing I've learned over the years," the captain said, "it's never underestimate a Klingon."

Riker did not respond. His expression remained neutral, but Picard caught a glint of humor in his eyes before Will's lids lowered subtly.

"Computer," the commander ordered. "Remove plank."

The board beneath the conquering Klingon's feet suddenly vanished; flailing arms and legs, Worf fell with a resounding splash into the turquoise sea.

Amid the renewed cheering, Picard turned to his second-in-command and said dryly, "Number One . . . it's *retract* plank, not remove plank."

"Oh." Riker's blue eyes widened with mock innocence. "Of course, sir. Sorry."

Nearby, Data tilted his head in confusion as he peered over the side rail at Worf, who was thrashing through the water toward a proffered rope ladder. He straightened and turned toward Beverly. "Doctor . . . I must confess I am uncertain as to why someone falling into the freezing water is amusing."

She looked up from the water with a toothy grin. "It's all in good fun, Data."

The android studied her blankly for an instant. "I do not understand."

"Try to get into the spirit of things." She gestured enthusiastically at the surroundings. "Learn to be a little more . . . spontaneous."

Data drew his head back and lowered his chin, processing this new information . . . then reached forward and, with only the precise amount of force necessary, pushed Beverly over the rail. He watched with a clinical air as she plummeted into the water with a shriek, then straightened to judge the reactions of his colleagues.

No one was laughing—including Picard, who had witnessed the entire exchange. However, the captain's mood was so cheerful, so expansive, that he had to force himself to repress a chuckle. He dared a peek at Riker, whose own carefully controlled expression beneath amused eyes once again forced Picard to quickly look away.

Geordi immediately hurried over to the rail, peered down, then looked up at his confused friend. "Data . . . that *wasn't* funny."

"I was attempting to be spontaneous," Data replied, his tone one of mild puzzlement. "I obviously do not understand what constitutes 'getting into the spirit of things.' Why is it that Commander Worf's fall into the water is 'good fun,' yet Dr. Crusher's is not?"

"It's . . . well . . ." Geordi sighed. "It's hard to explain, Data." He leaned forward to offer a hand to Worf, who had made it to the top of the ladder. Dripping but with soggy officer's hat proudly in hand, the Klingon stepped over the railing onto the deck. He was followed soon after by a very wet—and very unamused—Beverly Crusher.

Flanked by his second-in-command, Picard made his way up to the quarterdeck, then turned to address his crew.

"Well, now that we're all aboard . . ." He paused to smile. "Number One, bring the ship before the wind. Let's see what's out there."

"Aye, aye, sir." Will directed his gaze to Deanna Troi. "Take the wheel, Commander."

Troi quickly climbed the steps up to the quarterdeck

and took her place behind the ship's wheel as Riker shouted, "All hands make sail! Topgallants and courses! Stand by the braces!"

Picard watched with pure pleasure as his crew sprang into action, unfurling sails and trimming yardarms. "'I must down to the seas again, to the lonely sea and the sky,'" he quoted, then released a contented sigh. "Imagine what it was like, Will. No engines . . . no computers . . . just the wind, the sea, and the stars to guide you."

Riker's lips quirked with amusement. "Bad food . . . brutal discipline . . ." He paused, then delivered the killer blow. "No women . . ."

Picard shook his head, smiling; but before he could retort, the computer interrupted. "Bridge to Captain Picard. . . ."

"Picard here."

"There is a personal message for you from Earth."

Picard sighed again, this time with mild annoyance at the interruption. "Put it through down here." He turned back toward Riker. "It was freedom, Will. No ties . . . And the best thing about a life at sea was that they couldn't reach you."

He headed toward the bow, still smiling. He had no inkling what the message might be about, but whatever it was, he would deal with it quickly and return to his companions on the holodeck. He was grateful for today's festivities; they served to remind him of his great good fortune in being able to lead the life he had always wanted, that of a starship captain.

He passed a few crew members hanging high up on the yardarm, and called up, grinning: "Look alive there!" And then, as he reached the bow: "Computer, arch."

On the forecastle, an arch opened onto a bank of computer panels. Picard stepped through and cheerfully activated a monitor—without an instant's hesitation, he would remember later, or the faintest premonition of the horror to come.

It was Deanna Troi who first felt that something was wrong. She had been reveling in the good spirits shared by the crew—most notably the captain, who of everyone seemed most to appreciate the historical scenario she had suggested for the promotion ceremony, and Worf, who despite his outward Klingon reserve had been genuinely touched by his crewmates' regard.

Yet as she stood at the ship's wheel, she sensed a sudden, overwhelming surge of emotion, so raw and strong that at first she was too dazed to identify it. For an instant, she clutched the wheel and forced herself to breathe calmly; only then could she distance herself enough to analyze it.

Grief, mixed with horror. So strongly reminiscent of what she had felt when her father had died that the proximity of it was deeply disturbing.

She looked toward the bow, and saw Picard standing in the archway. At the shock on his slack, ashen face, she turned toward the crew member standing next to her and said, "Here. Take the wheel." She did not explain, but moved inconspicuously, so as not to draw attention to herself or the captain; an emotion this devastating demanded extreme tact, extreme privacy.

She hurried down the quarterdeck steps toward the arch; toward Picard, who stood staring at an invisible sight far beyond the monitor in front of him, his lips slightly parted, his eyes narrowed with unspeakable pain.

Troi hesitated at a respectful distance. "Captain," she said, so quietly that none but Picard would hear, "are you all right?"

For a moment, Picard did not answer; for a moment, he seemed not to hear. And then he seemed to retrieve his mind from a very great distance to focus it on the present place and time. "Yes," he said to the screen. "Fine." He turned blindly toward Troi. "If you'll excuse me . . ."

He switched off the screen, turned away. "Computer, exit."

The holodeck doors appeared before him. Troi watched as he headed into the corridor, carrying his grief with him.

In the meantime, Riker had headed down to the main deck and hadn't noticed the captain's reaction or Deanna's departure from her post. He was having a particularly good time, especially since he had worked the past year to overcome any lingering jealousy he had felt on Worf and Deanna's account. Apparently, they were still slowly building a relationship, though Will hadn't heard any details—and he didn't *want* to hear any details.

But after the captain had reported his experience of one possible future which led to a bitterly jealous feud between Riker and Worf, Will had been determined to change that future and regain his comfortable friendship with the Klingon.

He had succeeded. The awkwardness between them

had vanished, to the point where Riker now felt free to thoroughly enjoy hazing the new lieutenant commander.

He stepped toward Worf, still wearing his damp breeches and linen shirt—and, of course, his naval officer's hat with its soggy, drooping plume.

"Set the royals and the studding sails, Mr. Worf."

Worf turned and gazed at him blankly. "The royal . . . studs . . . ?"

Riker grinned and pointed aloft. "Well, since you've proven today that you're so good with heights . . . You see the top yardarm? Now, look to the—"

"Bridge to Commander Riker."

He broke off, turning immediately toward the direction the comm voice had emanated from. "Riker here."

"We're picking up a distress call from the Amargosa Observatory, sir. They say they're under attack."

"Red alert!" Riker shouted. Crew members immediately began running past him toward the bow. "All hands to battle stations! Captain Picard to the bridge. . . ."

On the bridge, Riker removed his plumed hat and stared at a grim sight on the main viewscreen: the battered, blackened remnants of the Amargosa Observatory against the backdrop of a yellow sun. He shook his head. "It looks like we're too late. . . ."

Still in his damp linen shirt and breeches, Worf half turned from his console. "There are no other ships in the system."

The lift doors slid open, and the captain entered—to the veiled, curious stares of all those on the bridge. Only Deanna, Riker noted from her concerned, sympathetic expression, seemed to have a clue as to what was going on with Picard. Whatever it was, it must have been world-shattering, for the captain to arrive late on the bridge during a red alert.

Picard's expression, as he moved toward his chair, was hard, utterly closed. To Riker's amazement, he did not react to the sight on the viewscreen, did not ask to be briefed. Awkwardly, the second-in-command cleared his throat, then offered: "We're approaching Amargosa, Captain. It looks like the observatory took quite a beating."

"Survivors?" Picard asked curtly.

"Sensors show five life signs aboard the station, Captain," Data responded.

"The station complement was nineteen," Riker said heavily.

Picard showed not a flicker of emotion, only rose dismissively. "Stand down from red alert." He faced Riker without meeting his eyes. "Number One, begin an investigation. I'll be in my ready room." He turned and moved away.

Riker shot a quick glance at Deanna, whose startled expression offered no explanation. "Sir?" Riker asked, not trying to hide his amazement.

Picard wheeled to face him, his tone and eyes flint-cold. "Make it so."

"But Captain, I thought you would—"

"Do it," Picard said. He turned and exited the bridge without a backward glance, leaving his crew to stare after him.

Amargosa smelled of fire and death.

The smell was the first thing Will Riker perceived of the observatory, even before his eyes refocused to see that the *Enterprise* transporter room had metamorphosed into a smoldering ruin. It was the scent of things burning that were not meant to burn: metal, synthetic compounds, flesh.

He narrowed his eyes at the sting of smoke and peered through the filmy haze. Overhead, the dying remnants of auxiliary lighting flickered, casting such feeble light that most of the wreckage lay shrouded in shadow. Riker lifted his palm beacon and swept a beam of light over collapsed bulkheads, scorched consoles—then began to pick his way carefully through the heavy debris, knowing that somewhere in the darkness and rubble lay fourteen dead. The away team—Crusher, Worf, Paskall, and Mendez—followed in silence; speaking unnecessarily seemed sacrilege, disrespectful of the tragedy that had occurred here.

The scent of destruction was fresh. The attack had occurred, Riker guessed, only a handful of minutes before. While he and his friends had been standing on the quarterdeck of the *H.M.S. Enterprise* celebrating, these people had been dying. He stopped suddenly to squint at something small and dark protruding from under a twisted metal beam: a bloodied hand. Beverly immediately stepped forward and scanned it with her tricorder, then shook her head and shared a disappointed look with Will. The group moved on.

Frowning at the scarred ruins, Worf broke the silence at last. "These blast patterns are consistent with type-three disruptors."

Brutal weapons capable of burning through skin, muscle, bone . . . "Well," Riker said with grim irony. "That narrows it to Klingon, Breen, or Romulan."

"I'm picking up life signs." Crusher's face and voice grew suddenly hopeful, animated. "About twenty meters ahead."

"That would rule out Klingons," Worf said, and when Riker gave him a curious look, added, "They would not have left anyone alive."

Beverly ignored them, moving purposefully into the darkness. "Over here . . ."

Riker followed, quickly sweeping his palm beacon over wreckage until at last the doctor paused and knelt beside a prone, still form. Without Crusher's tricorder, Riker would have taken the man for dead; the back of his Starfleet science officer's uniform had been almost entirely burned away by a disruptor blast. He turned his face from the smell of scorched flesh and fought to contain a wave of hatred for whoever had committed such an atrocity.

Seemingly immune to any emotion except determination to save the man lying before her, Crusher opened her medikit and began to work.

Riker glanced up and gestured at the three men standing nearby. "Worf, you're with me. Paskall, you and Mendez search the upper deck."

The two security guards moved off. Riker headed with Worf down a dark corridor, following the ovals of light cast by their palm beacons past more twisted, collapsed bulkheads and battered consoles. At last, a wavering arc of light played across something cylindrical emerging from the shadows: fallen ventilation tubing, Riker thought at first, until he saw the boot. Worf redirected his beacon to reveal the fallen figure of a woman; beside her lay a man. Both wore Starfleet blue.

While Worf provided light, Riker knelt quickly and felt for pulses, then shook his head, wishing the darkness had shielded him from the sight of the woman's staring face, half of which had been seared away.

At the sound of sudden banging from a distant corner, he rose, and hurried in the direction of the noise.

Worf directed his beam onto a collapsed bulkhead. "Under here . . ."

Together, both officers pulled aside the large sheet of jagged metal covering the pile of debris, then began tearing through the rubble. From beneath came stirring, and the sounds of ragged breathing. Encouraged, Riker and Worf dug faster, until at last a bloodied hand appeared and began to flail as if desperately trying to assist.

"It is all right," Worf said, with a gentleness that made Riker glance up in surprise, but not pause in his excavating. The Klingon clasped the thin, pale hand with his own great, dark one. "Do not struggle."

Where had he learned tenderness? Will wondered. From Deanna? The thought caused a flicker of jealousy; he repressed it firmly. If Worf had gotten something good out of the relationship, then so much the better.

Worf continued to hold the hand until Riker lifted and shoved aside a crushed console to reveal the head and torso of a pale-haired humanoid man. Worf released the hand, which the man lifted, shaking, to his forehead. He stared up at the two Starfleet officers with light, almost colorless eyes that were dull with shock. He seemed to Riker unwounded, although he had an old scar that ran from the center of his forehead beneath one eye and down his cheek.

"I'm Commander William Riker of the *Starship Enterprise.*"

The man blinked, struggling to make sense of Riker's words and his surroundings, to gather himself. "Soran . . ." he whispered. "Dr. Tolian Soran . . ." His eyes widened as he looked into the smoking ruins; a flicker of intense—almost insane, Riker thought— bitterness crossed his face before he lifted a hand to his eyes.

"Who attacked you, Doctor?" Riker asked with quiet firmness. He did not turn at the sound of light footsteps behind him, but watched with his peripheral vision as Dr. Crusher hurried toward them.

Soran lowered his hand and, with a disconsolate sweeping glance at the destruction around him, shook his head. "I'm not sure. . . . It happened so fast. . . ."

Beverly directed a reassuring smile at the dazed scientist and began to scan him with the tricorder. Riker watched, trying to get a fix on Soran; there was something about the man that vaguely disturbed him. The intensity in the eyes, perhaps, that verged on wildness; or maybe that the man's apparent helplessness somehow did not quite ring true.

"Commander!" Paskall called down from the upper level. "You'd better take a look at this!"

Riker directed a glance at Worf; the two strode over to the emergency ladder and crawled quickly to the upper deck, where Paskall and Mendez knelt beside another body. As Riker and Worf approached, Mendez held his beacon so that the corpse's face was clearly visible.

It was a young soldier, one who had apparently accidentally died in the falling debris. His face was bruised, smudged with smoke, but otherwise composed in death; Riker felt no surprise, only a growing outrage at the sight of the upswept eyebrows and ears, the ridged forehead. He said nothing, but let Worf give their common anger voice in a single low, disgusted growl:

"Romulan . . ."

SEVEN

☆ —————

The minute he got off duty, Geordi La Forge headed for Data's quarters. He did so partly because he felt the overboard incident with Dr. Crusher bore discussion— and partly because being around Data usually cheered him up. Amargosa had caused a strange pall to settle over the day; it seemed unfair that the earlier celebration could have been overshadowed so quickly by tragedy. But then, death interrupting life never seemed fair.

And it wasn't just Amargosa; something else bad had happened, something to do with Captain Picard. Geordi had been near the bow when the captain had retrieved his personal message. He hadn't been able to see Picard's face—not until Troi had gone over to speak with him— but even so, he had read shock in the sudden slump of the captain's shoulders.

Geordi paused in front of the door to Data's quarters and pressed the chime. The door slid open; inside, Data sat in a chair with Spot curled in his lap.

"Geordi," the android said. "Please come in. I am glad you are here. There are some questions I would like to ask—"

91

"—about the business with Dr. Crusher this afternoon?" Geordi stepped over to his friend's side as the door closed behind them.

Data's pale golden face brightened. "Precisely. I am determined to understand why her falling into the water was *not* funny, whereas Commander Worf falling into the water *was.*"

"Er, Data . . . I'm still not so sure I can explain it. Humor's pretty elusive stuff. . . ."

Data frowned faintly as he stroked the cat, who closed her eyes and purred drowsily. "Perhaps overt aggression is the key. After all, I *pushed* Dr. Crusher to make her fall, whereas Worf fell simply because the plank was removed."

Geordi shook his head. "Unh-unh. Humor can get pretty aggressive sometimes. And you didn't push Dr. Crusher hard enough to hurt her."

"Oh." Data gazed up at his friend with puzzled, golden eyes. "Is she still angry?"

"No . . . But I'd stay out of sickbay for a while if I were you." Geordi's lips curved upward in a slight smile. "Whatever possessed you to push her in the water?"

"I was attempting to . . ." Data tilted his head, searching for the right expression. ". . . get into the spirit of things, as Dr. Crusher put it. I thought it would be amusing." He frowned again, clearly troubled by his inability to understand, then lifted Spot, who emitted a displeased mew, and set her down.

Geordi watched as the android moved over to a bulkhead and activated a control panel. A small compartment slid open to reveal a tiny chip suspended in a crystalline case. It was an emotion chip made to the specifications of the android's creator, Noonien Soong. Data had long ago indicated that he had no interest in ever utilizing it; now he contemplated it with such intense interest that Geordi moved closer, both curious and apprehensive.

"Data . . . are you thinking about actually using that thing?"

"I have considered it for many months." The android focused his golden eyes back on Geordi. "And in light of the incident with Dr. Crusher, I believe this may be the appropriate time."

Geordi frowned. "I thought you were afraid it would overload your neural net."

"That is true," Data replied. "However, I believe my growth as an artificial life-form has reached an impasse. For thirty-four years I have endeavored to become more 'human'—to grow beyond my original programming. And yet I am still unable to grasp such a basic concept as humor." He turned back toward the crystalline case. "This emotion chip may be the only answer."

Geordi leaned forward to dubiously study the chip, then sighed. At worst, it could cause some annoying complications, but no permanent damage. And what right did he have to deny his friend such an experience? "All right . . . but at the first sign of trouble, I'm going to deactivate it. Agreed?"

"Agreed." Data promptly sat down, offering himself as willing subject, while Geordi moved behind him and opened a panel on his cranium, revealing the blinking circuitry within.

"This won't take long . . ." Geordi said, finishing silently to himself, *I just hope we don't both regret it. . . .*

* * *

At the same time that Geordi was performing surgery on his friend, Will Riker was standing in the captain's ready room, briefing Picard on what the away team had found at the Amargosa Observatory.

Picard's odd, distant demeanor hadn't eased. Riker wound up addressing the back of the captain's chair while Picard, hands steepled, gazed out his window at the stars.

"We found two dead Romulans aboard the station," Riker finished up. "We're analyzing their equipment to see if we can determine what ship they came from."

Index fingers resting on his lips, Picard nodded absently, then lowered his hands and asked, "There's still no indication of why they attacked the station?" His tone was one of great weariness, as though it required infinite effort for him to focus on the matter at hand.

"They practically tore the place apart," Riker said, mentally recoiling from the memories of charred bodies and the smell of death. "Accessed the central computer, turned the cargo bay inside out. They were obviously looking for something."

"Hmmm . . ." Picard fell silent and stared out the window again, for so long that Riker began to shift his weight nervously. And then the captain said lifelessly, "Inform Starfleet Command. This could indicate a new Romulan threat in this sector."

Riker did not try to keep the amazement from his voice. "You want *me* to contact Starfleet?"

Picard straightened, swiveled a quarter-turn toward his second-in-command. "Is there a problem?" he asked softly.

"No, sir," Riker said. *At least, not with me. . . .* But something very serious was troubling the captain. Whatever message he had received this morning from Earth had been devastating.

Picard continued wearily, "Thank you, Number One," and swung back toward the window.

Riker turned to go, then hesitated, awkward. "There *is* something else, Captain. One of the scientists . . . a Dr. Soran . . . has insisted on speaking with you." Anticipating a protest, he hurried apologetically: "I told him you were busy, sir, but he said it was absolutely imperative that he speak with you right away."

But no protest came; no reaction, in fact, except for the captain's faint, toneless reply: "Understood. That will be all."

He was clearly eager to be alone, but Riker decided against hiding his concern. Picard was a very private man, and Riker doubted his question would be answered—but he had to at least make the offer to help, to listen. "Sir," he asked gently, ". . . is there anything wrong?"

"No." Picard's answer was soft, but it was a softness that covered steel. "Thank you."

Riker paused a moment, then surrendered, and left his captain to his solitary grief.

With a distinct sense of unease, Geordi entered Ten-Forward, sticking close to Data's side. Maybe he was overreacting, but he couldn't shake the sense of impending disaster, despite the fact that Data seemed to be quite relaxed and enjoying himself. So far, the chip seemed to be working perfectly—so well, in fact, that the android had insisted on going to Ten-Forward for a little test run.

Nevertheless, Geordi kept his gaze glued on Data, who

was drinking in his surroundings with the wide-eyed delight of a child, gazing with hopeful interest at the bustling off-duty crowd, beaming faintly as someone at a crowded table guffawed at a joke. Even the android's movements seemed subtly altered—more graceful, more fluid, more . . . human.

The two stepped up to the bar. Almost immediately, Guinan approached, and set a flask on the counter with a determination that allowed no refusal.

Her lips curved slyly into an upward crescent. "You two just volunteered to be my first victims." She nodded at the crystal flask, which held a dark liquid aswirl with amber highlights. "This is a new concoction I picked up on Forcas Three. Trust me, you're going to love it."

She set two glasses on the counter and poured; Geordi caught a whiff of potent spirits laced with something that smelled like broccoli crossed with eucalyptus. He struggled to keep his expression neutral, so as not to influence Data, who lifted his glass, sniffed the contents, then took a large swallow.

Geordi watched intently as Data frowned down at the glass in his hand. After several seconds, the engineer prompted, "Well . . . ?"

The android glanced up, still faintly frowning, his expression one of puzzlement. "I believe the beverage has provoked an emotional response."

"Really? What do you feel?"

Data lowered the glass, clearly trying to turn his focus inward. "I . . ." He glanced up at Geordi with something very near dismay. "I am uncertain. I have little experience with emotions. I am unable to articulate the sensation."

"Emotions?" Guinan leaned forward, elbows on the counter, to direct an amazed glance at Geordi.

The engineer cocked his head to one side in a gesture that was almost an affirmation, all the while managing to keep one eye focused on his charge. "I'll explain later. . . ."

He watched as Data threw his head back and took another huge gulp—then set down the glass and curled his bottom lip in pure disgust.

Guinan turned to Geordi. "I think he hates it."

"Yes!" Data leaned toward his friends, bright-eyed, near breathless with excitement. "That is it. I *hate* it!"

The android's enthusiasm was infectious; despite his concern, Geordi felt a broad smile settle slowly over his own features. "Data . . . I think the chip is working."

As he spoke, Data rapidly drained his glass, then broke into a huge, triumphant grin. "Yes. I hate this! It is revolting!"

Guinan permitted the two men a moment more of celebration, then coyly lifted the flask, ready to pour again. "Another round?" she asked sweetly.

Aglow with happiness, Data held up his glass. "Please."

At that moment, Tolian Soran also sat in Ten-Forward, but the crowd and his table's location blocked any view of the bar; instead, he stared out an observation window at the stars—thinking of one star in particular, the one named Amargosa. "Bitter," the name meant in some Terran language or other. The bitter star; oddly appropriate, it seemed now.

Had he witnessed the exchange between the three

friends, he would have sensed precisely what was occurring—but he would not have laughed, would not have wasted upon the incident even a faint smile. He smiled at little these days; amusement did not interest him.

Only one thing mattered: his return to Leandra. Not quite a century ago, he had used the *Lakul* to return to her for a radiant, wondrous moment, only to be snatched away again by the *Enterprise*-B. That other world where she waited seemed real; the rest was all illusion, an agonizing, decades-long detour too cruel to be accepted as reality.

Once more, he was on another damnable starship called the *Enterprise;* but this one would not steal him from Leandra. This *Enterprise* would return him to her . . . if he had to kill every person aboard it.

It was, after all, not real.

Yet, real or not, in this universe, Soran knew he would have to use every bit of cunning here to return to the place he thought of as home. And the first step required manipulation of a certain starship captain.

He sat for a few moments more until he saw him: a uniformed man, lean and bald, with a lined, strongly sculpted face. Soran recognized him at once; the man's confident bearing marked him as captain of this vessel. What was the name again? Something exotically Terran. Picard. Jean-Luc Picard.

Picard made his way through the laughing crowd with single-minded intensity, and a closed expression that gave Soran pause, for it reminded him much of his own. What was it the captain was feeling? Soran's eyelids fluttered as he relaxed, allowed himself to sense his prey.

Yes. Yes . . . Offense. *We two have much in common,*

Soran said silently to the approaching human. *You, like I, are offended by what you see here: people smiling, talking, laughing, enjoying themselves, oblivious to our suffering. Oblivious to pain, to the horror that this universe truly is. But they will come to know; oh yes, they will all come to know death—their own, and those of the ones they love. No one escapes here.*

But I will. By the gods, I will, and never return . . .

Picard arrived at the table at last, and, intent, unflinching, unsmiling, gazed down at the El Aurian. "Dr. Soran . . . ?"

Soran looked up, his eyes, his gaze, his demeanor a stern mirror-image of the Starfleet officer's. "Yes, yes, Captain. . . . Thank you for coming." He extended his hand. Picard took it; firm grip, strong determination. Not an easy man to manipulate—or to read, for that matter. But there was fresh pain here, and if Soran was patient, there would soon be details that would help persuade the captain. . . .

Picard sat in the chair across from Soran, and waved away the waiter who had hurried up to take his order. "Nothing for me." All brusqueness, he turned to Soran. "I understand there's something urgent you need to discuss with me."

"Yes." Soran fixed his gaze on the captain's dark eyes. "I need to return to the observatory immediately. I must continue a critical experiment I was running on the Amargosa star."

A flicker of irritation crossed Picard's features. Soran knew exactly how it must have sounded: the eccentric scientist consumed by his work, interrupting the captain at an inopportune moment. "Doctor," Picard said, with a hint of impatience, "we're still conducting an investigation into the attack. Once we've completed our work, we'll be happy to allow you and your fellow scientists back aboard the observatory. Until then—"

Soran let some honest desperation slip into his tone. "The timing is very important on my experiment. If it is not completed within the next twelve hours, years of research will be lost." And if he did not manage to convince the captain soon, it seemed their conversation would come to a premature conclusion, before Soran could find the key, the precise words needed. Oh yes, there was definitely something here. Horrible pain. Agony. Grief . . .

But Picard was already moving to rise; with a curt, dismissive tone, he said, "We're doing the best we can. Now, if you'll excuse me . . ."

And there it was: the flames, two people screaming, dying in such abject misery that Soran drew in his breath, shuddered at the memory of his own long-ago pain. *So . . . we have more in common than I thought, you and I. . . .* And with desperation tempered by genuine empathy, he reached out and gently, firmly, grasped the captain's arm.

Picard wheeled, outraged—then was stunned to silence by the knowing intensity in Soran's eyes. Soran leaned forward until Picard's face filled his entire field of vision.

"They say time is the fire in which we burn," he said softly. "And right now, Captain, my time is running out."

Yes. He had sensed rightly. There it was again: the flames, the screams, the horror. Picard dropped his gaze, unable to meet the other man's eyes.

Soran released his grip on the captain's arm. No need

now; his words held Picard more tightly than his hands ever could. His features softened with unfeigned sympathy as he looked deep into the Starfleet officer's eyes, thinking of the Borg's death rays dissecting a malachite planet. How many nights had he lain awake imagining that final horror for Leandra, Mara, Emo, as the fiery rays streaked down from the El Aurian heavens?

You see, I too know what it is to smell the flesh of my loved ones burning. . . .

"We leave so many things unfinished in our lives," Soran continued. "I'm sure you can understand."

Picard looked away and was silent for a long moment; when finally he spoke, his voice was barely above a whisper. "I'll see what I can do. . . ."

Without a word, he turned on his heel and left before the El Aurian could reply. Soran watched with relief and triumph; he had won. He rose, then carefully pulled out the antique pocket watch Leandra had given him, a name-day present in recognition of his fascination with temporal physics. For a moment, he stared into its gilded, crystal-clad face and saw reflected there his own.

He had come to both treasure and despise Leandra's final gift to him—treasure it because it was all he had left of her, outside the nexus; despise it because it served as constant reminder of time's cruelty. In the end, time annihilated all; what was the brutally apt Terran metaphor? Cronos, eating his children . . .

Time was his enemy, now; the only solution was to sidestep it altogether, in the nexus. And, cruelest joke of all, he had only twelve hours in which to do so.

Soran moved toward the exit—then froze at the sight of a familiar face across the room, behind the bar.

Guinan. She had been among the refugees on the

Lakul the day they had encountered the *Enterprise*-B
. . . and flirted with the nexus. And if she recognized
Soran, she would at once sense his true intentions . . .
and tell the captain.

Luckily she was distracted, smiling and talking with
two crewmen; she had not seen him, and Soran was
determined to leave before she sensed his presence. He
wheeled about and, using the crowd as a shield, slipped
out the far exit.

"So," Guinan said. She bent slightly to retrieve a
dust-covered flagon from beneath the counter, then
straightened and allowed herself a small smile at Data's
comical expression, which managed to convey both
disgust and delight. "Now that you've got hate covered,
let's see if we can work on love. Aged Saurian brandy;
not quite as old as I am, but a close second. Just a little
taste, boys; this isn't synthehol, you know."

Geordi had finally relaxed enough to smile and peer at
the label. "That looks like the real thing, all right." He
drew back slightly as Guinan blew off the dust and then
began uncorking the bottle. "Data, you should test emotion chips more often. Looks like we're in for a treat."

Grinning, the android proffered his empty glass;
Guinan began to pour. At the same instant, Geordi's
comm badge signaled; he set down his own glass and
touched his insignia. "La Forge here."

"Commander Worf here. Is Data with you?"

"Yes."

"Commander Riker requests both of you report to the
transporter room immediately. I will meet you there.
Worf out."

Geordi released a glum sigh. "C'mon, Data. Let's go."

Data set down his glass and frowned. "I believe I am having another emotional reaction."

"It's called disappointment, Data." Guinan favored him with a grin as she recorked the brandy. "You'll get over it. Don't worry, this'll still be here when you two get back."

"Thanks, Guinan." Geordi waited for his now-despondent friend to rise; the two headed out into the corridor.

Guinan was watching them go when a dizzying flash of memory overtook her. Suddenly she was in the *Enterprise*-B sickbay almost a century before, in a twilight world between reality and the nexus, looking up into the dark eyes of a man she later learned was Pavel Chekov and saying, *He's gone to the other side. Your friend, Jim. . . .*

The ugliness of reality—her world, her family, her life destroyed in one brutal moment by the Borg—and the unspeakable beauty of the nexus had overwhelmed her then . . .

She tried to shake the memory off. She had not thought of the nexus—had not *permitted* herself to think of the nexus—for many years. But why . . . ?

Even before she could silently ask herself the question, she knew the answer: Someone was here. Someone who had been there that night; someone who had been to the nexus.

She whirled to face the precise spot in which she knew the person was standing.

No one. Empty carpet. Someone called her name; she gave her head a gentle shake, then turned, smiling, the memory once again submerged.

* * *

Moments earlier, in engineering, Will Riker stood beside Worf and stared at the diagram of sensor information on the monitor screen. On the console beside them, a Romulan tricorder lay attached to a diagnostic scanner.

Riker frowned at the screen and tried to make sense of the readout; he was having far better luck with it than he was in making sense out of the attack on Amargosa.

"One of the dead Romulans had a tricorder," Worf was explaining. "We analyzed its sensor logs and found they were scanning for signature particles of a compound called trilithium."

Riker lifted an eyebrow. "Trilithium?"

Worf gave a single, solemn nod. "An experimental compound the Romulans have been working on. In theory, a trilithium-based explosive would be thousands of times more powerful than an antimatter weapon. But they never found a way to stabilize it."

Let's hope that's still true, Riker thought. Aloud he asked, "Why were they looking for it on a Federation observatory? It doesn't make any sense."

Worf did not answer. Riker paused, still looking at the readout on the screen but seeing the dead on Amargosa. The terrible destruction might not make any sense, but it had happened for a reason—a reason that perhaps the survivors knew, but weren't telling.

He released a silent sigh and glanced at the Klingon. "Have Geordi and Data go over with the next away team. Tell them to scan the observatory for trilithium."

It was just as well they hadn't had time for that sip of Saurian brandy, Geordi decided, as he scanned the interior of the observatory operations room; as much as he had enjoyed his time with Data in Ten-Forward, he wouldn't want to beam down into a place like Amargosa with anything but a totally clear head.

Only the auxiliary lights were functional—just bright enough to allow humans to see, dim enough to give a gloomy, twilight effect. That, combined with the scorched ruins and utter silence, made for a decidedly eerie atmosphere, Geordi decided; or maybe it was just the fact that he knew people had died here. It was sad to see their years of work carelessly scattered, to see consoles bashed in, monitors blasted. He worked with the same hushed reverence he felt visiting graveyards.

Data, on the other hand, seemed unsettlingly cheerful, still glowing with enthusiasm for his new internal world; he smiled faintly to himself as he scanned the other side of ops with his tricorder.

Geordi peered at the tricorder readout and shook his head. "There's no sign of any trilithium in here. . . . I can't imagine why the Romulans were looking for it."

He scanned quietly for a moment longer, until Data released a soft giggle. He turned to look at his friend in perplexed amazement.

Data continued to laugh softly to himself. "I get it. I get it."

Geordi frowned; it didn't seem right to be laughing where people had so recently been murdered—but he tried not to let his irritation show. After all, Data had never before experienced fear of death, and could accept it more matter-of-factly than a human. And maybe since he wasn't used to having emotions, he wasn't that good at suppressing them, either.

"You get what?" he asked the android.

Data erupted in laughter again, then finally controlled himself enough to gasp out, "When you said to Commander Riker"—and he perfectly mimicked Geordi's voice—"'The clown can stay, but the Ferengi in the gorilla suit has to go.'"

Geordi stared blankly at him. "What?"

"During the Farpoint mission. We were on the bridge and you told a joke. That was the punch line."

"The Farpoint mission? Data, that was seven years ago."

"I know. I just got it." The android began giggling again. "It was very funny."

Geordi shot him a dubious glance before turning away. "Thanks . . ."

He headed down a short corridor that connected the main operations room with several compartments; Data followed, still chuckling softly.

Geordi stopped abruptly in front of what appeared to be a standard bulkhead. He turned excitedly to Data. "Wait a minute. There's a hidden doorway here. I can see the joint of the metal with my VISOR." He ran his finger in a vertical line over the deceptively smooth metal.

Data stepped beside him and scanned the section with his tricorder, then frowned at the readout. "There appears to be a dampening field in operation. I cannot scan beyond the bulkhead."

Geordi slung his tricorder over his shoulder and pressed his hands against the metal, trying to coax it open. "I don't see a control panel . . . or an access port."

"It appears to be magnetically sealed." Data put his

own tricorder away, then peeled back the pale golden flesh on his wrist to reveal flashing circuitry. As he spoke, he made a deft adjustment. "I believe I can reverse the polarity by attenuating my axial servo."

He finished his task, then waved his exposed circuitry over the bulkhead panel. "Open sesame."

From within the panel came a hum, followed by a loud click. The door slid open; Data turned toward his friend with a smug grin. "You could say I have a . . . magnetic personality."

I've created a monster, Geordi thought, but restricted himself to a grimace. Maybe if he ignored the android's annoying attempts at humor, they would pass. He moved quickly into the small room, which housed several probes stacked in holding racks, and began again to scan.

Almost immediately, he realized that they were very close to discovering the reason for the attack and turned to Data. "I'm still not picking up anything. Someone went to a lot of trouble to shield this room."

He put his tricorder away and moved over to the probes, ignoring Data, who was still snickering at the accumulated punch lines of a lifetime. One probe in particular—smooth and dark as polished onyx, the size of a burial tube—caught Geordi's attention.

"Data, take a look at this." He glanced over his shoulder at the android, who hurried over. "You ever seen a solar probe with this kind of configuration?"

Grinning maniacally, Data held his tricorder toward Geordi like a puppet, then opened and closed it rapidly, like a ventriloquist making a mannequin speak. " 'No, Geordi, I have not.' " He then turned the tricorder toward himself, as though it were addressing him: "'Have you?'" He shook his head solemnly, answering his makeshift puppet. "No, I have not. It is most unusual."

He burst into high-pitched laughter; Geordi felt his own expression harden. *That's it, Data; the minute I get you back on the* Enterprise, *that chip's coming out. . . .* "Just help me get this panel open," he said shortly.

Data controlled himself long enough to comply. Soon the panel swung open.

"Whoa!" Geordi recoiled. "My VISOR's picking up something in the theta band. It could be a trilithium signature. . . ."

Data erupted into giggles.

This time, Geordi made no attempt to hide his irritation. "Data, this *isn't* the time—"

"I am sorry," Data gasped between peals of laughter; his eyes were wide with alarm. "But I cannot stop myself. I think something is wrong. . . ."

His laughter soon escalated to full-blown hysteria. As Geordi watched, helpless, the android's limbs began to tremble and jerk, as if he were having a seizure. A rapid cascade of emotions convulsed his features: anger, joy, passion, terror, hate, longing, in such rapid succession that to Geordi they were a blur.

He ran to his friend's side just as Data collapsed. "Data!" He knelt beside the android and put a hand on his shoulder. "Data, are you all right?"

Data's eyes flew open, then focused on Geordi, who helped the blinking android sit up.

"I believe the emotional chip has overloaded my positronic relays," he said with mild but distinct surprise.

"We'd better get you back to the ship." Geordi hit his comm badge. "La Forge to *Enterprise.*"

No response. Geordi frowned for a split second, then realized—the dampening field, of course. But before he could react, a voice spoke softly:

"Is there a problem, gentlemen?"

He turned to see one of the observatory scientists—a thin, pale-haired civilian dressed in black—standing in the doorway. The sight startled him for a fleeting instant; the observatory had been so silent, he'd assumed no one had yet returned. Recovering, he said, "Oh . . . Doctor. Yeah, as a matter of fact, there is. There's a dampening field in here blocking our comm signal." He nodded at Data, still sitting on the floor. "Will you give me a hand?"

The scientist stepped toward them. "I'd be happy to."

He said it kindly enough that Geordi took no alarm—not until the last second, when he saw the scientist glance swiftly at the partially dismantled probe, saw the distress cross the pale man's features, saw the phaser held by the man's side.

By then it was too late. Geordi tensed, thought to make a move for the phaser; it did not occur to him to shield himself from the man's other hand. The fist caught his cheek and jaw with a resounding dull thud and sent the VISOR hurtling. There was a millisecond burst of unbearably brilliant color, then darkness—a darkness that deepened the instant his head struck the floor.

EIGHT

☆

Picard sat at the desk in his quarters and stared down at the holo in the open album before him. In the background, classical music played softly; at his elbow, a cup of tea sat cooling. But the music remained unheard, the tea undrunk; he could focus on nothing save the picture before his eyes, a scene from happier times: the Picards —René, Robert, Marie—at their family estate. Robert had presented it to him a few years ago, when he was visiting the vineyard.

Picard gently laid fingertips against a corner of the holo, as if to capture the moment pictured there. There was his shyly grinning nephew, René, flanked by his mother and father. René would be some four years older now—taller, with a deeper voice, but the same cap of golden brown hair falling in a straight fringe above the same bright, intelligent eyes full of promise. Picard remembered the moment of their first meeting, on the family estate. He had teased the boy, but only to hide his own amazement, for he had looked on René and seen himself. He'd seen, too, the gleam of admiration in the boy's eyes, and realized self-consciously that René looked up to his uncle Jean-Luc as a hero.

Marie had later confessed that René wanted nothing better than to follow in his uncle's footsteps, to become a starship captain. There she stood beside her son, golden-haired, graceful, and warm, the perfect counterpoint to her husband.

Robert stood, glowering and stiff as ever, chin tucked in, eyes narrowed and gleaming with faint disapproval at the world . . . and secret pride for his son. Dressed like a modern French peasant; always the traditionalist, Robert. A faint, fond smile played at the corners of Picard's lips. Always the conservative, who predictably raised a great hue and cry when he discovered his son's interest in Starfleet. Always grudging, always stodgy. Always. Always . . .

Time is the fire in which we burn

It was as if Soran had known.

Picard squeezed his eyes shut at the words, trying to blot out the mental image they evoked: René, Robert, screaming in final agony as flames consumed them. What had it been like in those terrible, final seconds before death? What had it been like for Robert, to see his only son burned alive, to know that they would never escape? Or had he perished first, leaving René to suffer the final torment . . . ?

Stop.

Stop.

He could not be sure it had happened that way; perhaps they were unconscious, overwhelmed by smoke. Perhaps there had been no pain. He knew nothing of the details and most likely never would. He knew nothing,

111

only what was contained in the blunt message from Marie:

Robert and René killed in fire. Memorial service Wednesday. Will understand if you can't attend.

What personal hell was she dwelling in now? She had clearly not trusted herself to send a visual or even a voice message. Picard felt a surge of guilt. He should be there now to comfort her—but duty did not permit it. Amargosa had intervened.

Yet in the hours since he had first received the news, he had found himself unable to fulfill that duty, turning everything over to Riker.

Correction: He had found himself unable to do anything save look upon the faces of the dead, who gazed back from the safety of the past. He had been too stunned even to weep.

He glanced up at the soft sound of the door chime, and realized suddenly that he was hearing it for the second time. He drew in a breath and composed his features. "Come."

The door opened; Deanna Troi stepped inside. Her movements were tentative, restrained; her black eyes somber, though she smiled faintly in greeting. She knew, of course; Picard had no doubt. Not details, but she knew. Nevertheless, he played the game.

"Counselor." He tried, but was not quite able to return Troi's smile. "What can I do for you?"

"Actually . . ." She tilted her head to one side, dark hair sweeping over one shoulder. "I'm here to see if there's anything I can do for *you.* You've seemed a little . . ." She paused, searching for the most tactful word. ". . . distracted lately."

"Oh," Picard said, feigning casualness. He could not bring himself to simply blurt it out; it would have seemed somehow disrespectful to Robert and René. "Just . . . family matters." For a moment, he struggled with the impulse to ask her to leave, to insist on privacy. But she was right; he could not keep his grief to himself forever. At some point, he would have to admit to others what had happened. He glanced down at the holo album. "You've never met my brother and his wife, have you?"

"No." Troi moved over beside him to peer over his shoulder at the album. She kept a respectful distance, still careful not to push, not to intrude before Picard was ready.

He continued, unable to keep the irony and affection from his voice as he stared down at the image of his brother. "Robert can be quite impossible. . . . Pompous, arrogant, always has to have the last word. But he's mellowed somewhat in his later years." He hesitated, realizing that he was speaking as though Robert were still alive; yet he could not bring himself to stop. "I was planning to spend some time on Earth next month. I thought we could all go to San Francisco. René's always wanted to see Starfleet Academy."

Troi leaned forward to get a closer look. "René? Your nephew?"

Picard nodded, knowing she could sense the bright glimmer of pain the image of the boy provoked; yet despite his grief, he could not help smiling fondly at the sight of the boy's face. "Yes. He's so . . . unlike his father. Imaginative, a dreamer. He almost reminds me of myself at that age."

He laughed softly, but there was no joy in the sound.

Troi faced him and asked softly, "Captain . . . what's happened?"

He tried to look away, tried to gather himself, but the empathy in her dark eyes compelled him to hold her gaze and answer. "Robert," he whispered. "And René. They're dead. They were burned to death in a fire."

She drew back, lips parted in shock and sorrow. Picard rose and moved toward the observation window to look out at the stars.

"I'm so sorry," she said at last.

"It's all right," he said tightly, clasping his hands behind him. "These things happen. We all have our . . . time. And theirs had come." It sounded like nonsense to his own ears; pointless, hollow. Meaningless. Troi would have none of it.

"No it's *not* all right." She moved slowly toward him. "And the sooner you realize that, the sooner you can begin to come to terms with what's happened. . . ."

"I know that," Picard said shortly, then caught himself and softened his tone. "But . . . right now, it's not me I'm concerned with. It's my nephew." He half turned toward her, his voice full of sudden intensity. "I just can't stop thinking about him—about all the experiences he'll never have. Going to the Academy. Falling in love. Children of his own. It's all . . . gone."

"I had no idea he meant so much to you."

Picard gave a grim nod. "In a way, he was as close as I ever came to having a child of my own."

She moved away from him then, toward the open album on the desk, and began to flip through the pages of pictures. After a time, she glanced up. "Your family history is very important to you, isn't it?"

Picard stepped beside her to stare down at the pictures. "Ever since I was a little boy, I remember hearing about the family line. The Picards that fought at Trafalgar . . . the Picards that settled the first Martian colony. When my brother married and had a son—" He broke off, overwhelmed by guilt and sorrow.

Troi finished gently for him. ". . . You felt it was no longer your responsibility to carry on the family line."

He released a great, silent sigh, and, in lieu of a nod, let his chin sink to his chest and remain there. "My brother had shouldered that burden, allowing me to pursue my own selfish needs."

Her tone became firm. "There's nothing selfish about pursuing your own life, your own career."

He did not answer, but turned again toward the observation window to gaze at the stars beyond. He agreed with her; yet he could not help feeling that he had been wrong, to think that career was everything there was to life. His career was bound to end—but loving and caring for those close to him would endure. He had always known he would retire to the family estate, and he had hoped that Robert and René—and René's children—would be there.

At last he said, "You know, Counselor . . . for some time now, I've been aware that there are fewer days ahead than there are behind. But I always took comfort in the fact that, when I was gone, my family would continue. But now . . ." He moved over to the album, and opened it to the final pages: blank, all blank.

Mindless, bitter rage swept over him. He picked up the cup of undrunk tea and hurled it across the room; cold Earl Grey spattered across the desk, across the album, releasing the faint fragrance of bergamot. The cup thudded, unbroken, against soft carpet. He stared back at Deanna Troi. "But now . . . the idea of death has a terrible sense of finality to it. There'll be no more Picards."

His outburst had startled him; but not, apparently, the counselor. Her gaze was steady, sympathetic. "Captain, perhaps we—"

She never finished, but threw up an arm to shield her eyes from the brilliant flare of light that flooded the room. Picard raised his own arm as he rushed toward the window, trying to see what had happened, but the glare was too intense, too blinding. He closed his eyes, still dazzled, as Riker's voice came on the intercom:

"Senior officers report to the bridge! All hands to duty stations!"

The disaster left Picard no choice: by the time he and Troi stepped from the lift onto the bridge, he had emerged from his grief. He stepped beside Riker and followed his second-in-command's gaze to the main screen, where the star called Amargosa was dying. To Picard's eyes, it looked as though the sun were being consumed by fire. The core was rapidly dimming, growing black as charred remains; the corona flared as it ejected flaming debris into space.

"Report," Picard said.

Riker turned his face toward the captain while keeping an eye on the screen; Picard caught the look of concern in his eye and ignored it. "A quantum implosion has occurred within the Amargosa star," Riker responded. "All nuclear fusion is breaking down."

Picard stared at the screen in wonder. He knew what stars were capable of; had watched one go supernova with his own eyes—from a safe distance, of course. But he had never seen this. "How is that possible?"

From his station, Worf answered. "Sensor records show the observatory launched a solar probe into the sun a few moments ago."

Picard frowned. The observatory . . . But there was no one there except for the away team . . . and Dr. Soran, he recalled with a chill, who had recently been given permission to return and complete his work.

Time is the fire in which we burn

Riker nodded. "The star's going to collapse in a matter of minutes." He turned as a sensor on Worf's console beeped ominously.

The Klingon looked up at the two senior officers, his eyes wide with concern. "Sir. The implosion has produced a level-twelve shock wave."

Picard said nothing, merely digested the news in stunned silence and shared an ominous look with Riker.

"Level twelve?" Troi asked, aghast. "That'll destroy everything in this system."

A voice filtered over the intercom. "Transporter room to bridge. I can't locate Commander La Forge or Mr. Data, sir."

Riker set a hand on Worf's console and leaned next to the seated Klingon. "Did they return to the ship?"

Worf ran a quick scan of the decks, then shook his head. "No, sir. They are not aboard."

Picard stepped beside them. "How long until the shock wave hits the observatory?"

"Four minutes, forty seconds," Worf reported.

Picard raised his face and shot Riker a look—a look, nothing more, but the first officer knew his captain well enough to read the order there. He gave a quick nod, then rose and headed toward the turbolift, pausing to call over his shoulder, "Mr. Worf . . ."

Then the two of them were gone. Picard stepped forward to gaze at the horrendous sight on the viewscreen, thinking again of fire and death, and the pale-haired scientist with the desperate eyes.

The smoky haze and smell of fire were gone, courtesy of the observatory's air-filtration system, but the gloom and silence had increased—or perhaps, Riker decided, it was simply the fact that he knew that, outside the observatory walls, the Amargosa star had collapsed into darkness. He turned to Worf and silently gestured for the Klingon to search the upper level of the main operations room, while he scoured the lower.

Within seconds, Worf returned, shaking his head: No sign. There was only one direction left to go in—a corridor that led to several separate cells. Riker wasted no time making his way down it, then paused at the closed doorways in front of him. One was recessed behind a bulkhead panel that had been slid back—a hidden entrance. Riker turned, nudged Worf, who followed close behind. "This one."

In the instant after the door opened, Riker got a brief impression—the stark contrast of light and dark, a spike-straight tuft of silver hair, white skin against a black tunic. In front of a rack of probes, a man sat at a console; the man he had uncovered from the rubble, the one named Tolian Soran. Soran's expression was no longer dazed, but as intense as the solar flares he watched on his monitor.

Riker opened his mouth, but never got the chance to speak. Soran whirled. Some atavistic instinct propelled Riker backward into the corridor and behind the bulkhead in the split-second before Soran fired the disruptor in his hand; the blast gouged a smoking groove into the metal doorway.

He raised his head and looked over to see Worf crouched against the bulkhead on the other side of the doorway; the Klingon had a better view of the room's interior. "What the hell's he doing?" Riker called softly.

Worf cautiously rose to peer into the room; another disruptor blast, this one going clean out into the corridor and burning a hole in the bulkhead, made him sink swiftly down again. "Lieutenant La Forge is unconscious," the Klingon whispered. "I cannot see Commander Data."

"Enterprise to Commander Riker." Picard's voice filtered clearly over Riker's comm badge. "You have two minutes left."

"Soran, did you hear that?" Riker shouted. "There's a level-twelve shock wave coming. We've got to get out of here!"

In reply, a disruptor blast angled through the open door, glancing off the doorway and searing the deck at Riker's feet. He pressed closer against the wall and grabbed his phaser—but it was no use; he could not get at the proper angle to get a clean shot at the scientist. Soran had the advantage. Riker glanced around in frustration, looking for a better hiding place . . . and suddenly noticed a figure huddled in the corner of the room.

"Data!" he called, sotto voce. "See if you can get to Geordi!"

The android looked up, golden eyes wide with terror. "I . . . cannot, sir. I believe I am . . . afraid."

Riker stared at him, at a loss, then tensed as, inside the room, a communicator beeped shrilly. At the sound, Soran leaned down to scoop up the unconscious Geordi by the collar. Riker heard the hum of a transporter beam and watched in surprise and frustration as the two dematerialized.

He hit his comm badge and said, with a sense of defeat, "Transporter room. Three to beam up."

A minute earlier on the *Enterprise* bridge, Picard was drawn away from the sight on the viewscreen—a dark, roiling shock wave, headed straight for the Amargosa Observatory—by the sound of an alarm on the tactical console. He faced Hayes just as the young ensign was swiveling toward him.

"Sir." Hayes's eyes were wide, his tone urgent. "A Klingon Bird-of-Prey is decloaking off the port bow."

"What?" Picard wheeled back toward the screen, to stare at the dying star—just as the Bird-of-Prey wavered into view on the observatory's far side.

"It's an old Class D-twelve, sir," Hayes said.

"Those were retired a decade or so ago," Picard murmured. This particular one looked like it should have stood down *two* decades earlier; the hull bore a hundred different hastily patched battle scars. To Hayes, he said, "Have they activated their weapons systems?"

"No, sir."

"Then let's—" Picard began.

"Transporter room to bridge. I have the away team aboard, sir."

Wasting no time, Picard turned to the con. "Helm, warp one. Engage. . . ."

The *Enterprise* sailed away as, on the viewscreen, the observatory dissolved into rapidly dimming flame.

Fueled by nova-bright rage, Soran made his way through dark, claustrophobic corridors, ducking to avoid overhanging cables, recoiling at the grime-smeared bulkheads, the sticky deck. The aging ship groaned and shuddered unceasingly—and stunk of warm, wet animal, making him long for the pristine, silent corridors of the *Enterprise*.

No matter. None of it mattered, none of it was real—at least, not to him—and the unpleasantness with the Duras sisters would soon be over, and forgotten eternally.

He emerged at last onto the dimly lit bridge, and at the sight of Klingons turning to regard him, his upper lip twitched faintly. They smelled the same as the ship; and though Soran had always believed himself an unprejudiced man, this particular species tested his limits. He strode past the all-male bridge crew—he was not a small man, but they dwarfed him—and paused before the two women in the command seats, who stared in amazement at the dead star on the screen.

The younger of them, B'Etor, rose to face him, her dark waving hair sweeping down over leather-clad breasts, her hideous features lit up by a leer that revealed protruding, jagged teeth. "You've done it, Soran!"

He leaned forward and struck out, full force, catching

121

her squarely in the jaw. She flailed, fell back against the console; immediately, several of the males leapt to their feet, disruptors in their fists.

"Wait!" B'Etor waved an arm as she rose unsteadily to one knee; an El Aurian woman, Soran knew, would never have gotten up from that punch. She touched the back of a hand to her mouth, frowned at the violet stain there, then glanced up at Soran.

"I hope for your sake that you are initiating a mating ritual." The edge in her tone was dagger-keen, dangerous.

Soran stood, utterly unafraid of the disruptors still pointed at him, disgusted by the thought of intimacy with this female, this . . . *primate,* clad in metal and skins and drunk with territorial power. Even if he did not completely possess the upper hand, he could not fear these creatures, could not fear death. Annihilation, simple nonexistence, did not frighten him; but life without hope of the nexus, of Leandra and the children, seemed unbearable. To be this close, *this close,* and be denied it . . .

"You got careless," he said harshly. "The Romulans came looking for their missing trilithium."

B'Etor pushed herself to her feet. "Impossible. We left no survivors on their outpost."

"They knew it was aboard the observatory," Soran countered. "If the *Enterprise* hadn't intervened, they would have found it."

The older sister stepped over to B'Etor's side. "But they didn't find it . . . and now we have a weapon of unlimited power." Her voice was calmer, deeper than her sister's, her manner more reserved—but she could be, Soran knew, just as treacherous.

His lips thinned. "*I* have the weapon, Lursa. And if you ever want me to give it to you, I advise you to be a little more careful in the future."

The last word had scarcely left his lips when B'Etor suddenly sprang toward him and secured his hands with surprising strength. An evil smile played on her lips as she lifted a double-edged Klingon dagger to his throat. "Perhaps we are tired of waiting," she hissed. Soran did not quiver, did not so much as flinch as the cool metal pressed into the tender skin of his neck, slid over his Adam's apple.

"Without my research," he said coolly, "the trilithium is worthless—as are your plans to reconquer the Klingon Empire."

B'Etor's lip curled with disappointment; Lursa reached out and patiently pushed the dagger's blade away from the scientist's throat.

Soran repressed a smile of triumph. "Set course for the Veridian system," he ordered the two women. "Maximum warp."

B'Etor said nothing, only narrowed her eyes with resentment; the implacable Lursa turned toward the helm, and issued a guttural command.

Soran had turned, thinking to head for his cramped, uncomfortable quarters, when a guard entered, dragging the unconscious Starfleet officer kidnapped from the observatory. The guard nodded at the human's sagging body. "What shall I do with this?"

"Bring him with me," Soran said. "I need some answers from Mr. La Forge."

At that moment, Will Riker was thinking of Geordi La Forge as he headed with Worf for sickbay. Clearly, Soran had committed the kidnapping with some purpose in mind—otherwise, he would have beamed away alone. But why? And why beam aboard a Klingon ship? The captain had informed him about the rattletrap of a Bird-of-Prey during the debriefing. For that matter, why destroy a star? The more Riker considered all the pieces to the Amargosa puzzle, the less sense they made.

Worf interrupted his reverie. "I have spoken to the Klingon High Council, sir. They identified the Bird-of-Prey as belonging to the Duras sisters."

Riker drew back, then shook his head with amazement. "Lursa and B'Etor? This doesn't make any sense. A renowned stellar physicist somehow uses a trilithium probe to destroy a star . . . kidnaps Geordi . . . and escapes with a pair of Klingon renegades. Why? What the hell's going on?"

Worf emitted a silent sigh. "I do not know, sir."

They rounded a corner and entered sickbay, where Crusher was just closing a panel at the back of Data's skull. The android was sitting on a biobed, scanning himself with a tricorder.

Riker caught Beverly's gaze. "How is he?"

She swept an errant strand of auburn hair from her face, which wore a serious—but fortunately, Riker knew from past experience, not grim—expression. "It looks like a power surge fused the emotional chip into his neural net."

Worf studied the android somberly. "Will that be a danger to him?"

She shook her head. "I don't think so; the chip still seems to be working." She sighed with dissatisfaction and folded her arms in front of her chest; a faint crease deepened in the pale skin between her eyebrows. "I'd feel better if I could take a closer look, but I can't remove it without completely dismantling his cerebral conduit."

Riker directed a smile at Data. "So. Looks like you're stuck with emotions for a while. How do you feel?"

Data glanced up from his tricorder, his brow furrowed, his golden eyes narrow with worry. "I am quite . . . preoccupied with concern about Geordi."

"We all are, Data," Riker said softly. "But we're going to get him back."

"I hope so, sir." The android's tone and expression remained anxious.

"Will . . ." Beverly took Riker aside and led him over to a wall monitor. "I checked into Dr. Soran's background." She pressed a control; a holo of Soran appeared, along with biographical data. "He's an El Aurian, over three hundred years old. He lost his entire family when the Borg destroyed his world. Soran escaped with a handful of other refugees aboard a ship called the *Lakul.* The ship was destroyed by some kind of energy ribbon, but Soran and forty-six others were rescued by the *Enterprise*-B."

Riker leaned forward with interest to study Soran's face. When had the holo been taken? One hundred, two hundred years before? Soran looked almost exactly the same. He wore a slight, self-conscious smile—but the intensity Riker had seen on the face behind the disruptor was still there, too. He gazed back at Beverly as her words settled into his consciousness. "That was the mission where James Kirk was killed."

She gave a single nod, then pressed a control on the monitor. "I checked the passenger manifest of the *Lakul.* Guess who else was on board?"

Riker shrugged—then did a double take as the doctor

pressed another control, and a new image appeared on the screen: the smiling face of Guinan.

"Soran?" Guinan looked up with surprise. "That's a name I haven't heard in a long time."

Picard sat beside her in her quarters, which made him feel he was no longer on the *Enterprise,* but some mysterious, long-dead world. The bulkheads were swathed in intricately patterned gold fabric, the deck covered in tile; in a far corner, an archway led to a small shrine where candles burned before a stone carving of an enigmatic goddess.

Guinan herself sat, arms clasping knees to her chest, against a stack of pillows on an indigo settee. The distant candlelight played across her broad, dark features.

"Do you remember him?" Picard asked. Soran's cryptic utterance made sense to him now; Soran *had* known about Robert and René, just as Guinan herself could know—if she wished. But Picard had forced himself to control his grief, to focus on the emergency at hand now; he could not help feeling personally responsible for the destruction of the Amargosa star. If he had simply refused Soran's request to return to the observatory—

"The outcome would still be the same, Jean-Luc," Guinan said softly. "He would have returned, with or without your permission."

Picard glanced up, mildly startled at the interruption, then returned her small, knowing smile and repeated, "Do you remember him?"

"Oh, yes. . . ." The smile faded at once. She rose and began to move about, as if trying to escape memories.

"Guinan," he said, after a moment had passed in

silence. "It's important that you tell me what you know. We think Soran's developed a weapon—a terrible weapon. It might give him enough power to—"

"Soran doesn't care about power or weapons," she interrupted, her back still toward him. "All he cares about is getting back to the nexus."

"What's the nexus?"

She moved across the room to a credenza and distractedly fingered a small sculpture there. Picard could not see her face, but he could read in her shoulders the tension, the unwillingness, there. He heard her draw in a low, decisive breath.

"The energy ribbon that destroyed the *Lakul* isn't just some random phenomenon traveling through space." She spoke with sudden rapidity, as though afraid if she didn't get the words out swiftly, they might never come. "It's a doorway. It leads to another place—the nexus. It doesn't exist in our universe . . . and it doesn't play by the same rules, either." She straightened. "It's a place I've tried very hard to forget."

"What happened to you?" Picard probed gently.

She turned to him, her expression radiant at the memory. "It was like being inside . . . joy. As if joy were a real thing that I could wrap around myself. I've never been so content." Her tone was hushed with awe.

He studied her in silence a moment, digesting the euphoria on her face, remembering the desperation on Soran's. "But then you were beamed away. . . ."

Her features darkened with sudden anger. "I was *pulled* away. I didn't want to leave. None of us did. All I could think about was getting back. I didn't care what I had to do. . . ."

She moved to an observation window and looked out at darkness and stars. "Eventually, I learned to live with it. But it changed me."

"Your sixth sense," Picard murmured, and when she did not contradict him, continued, "And what about Soran?"

"Soran may still be obsessed with getting back. And if he is, he'll do anything to find that doorway again."

"But why destroy a star?" he asked, then fell silent. He rose. "Thank you, Guinan."

As he moved to leave, she turned, her tone suddenly urgent. "Let someone else do it, Jean-Luc."

He paused to stare back at her.

"There aren't words strong enough to make you see, to make you understand. It's beyond any drug, any implant; it envelops people in the most potent narcotic there is: love and belonging." She paused, her dark eyes full of warning. "Don't get near the ribbon. If you go into that nexus, you're not going to care about Soran or the *Enterprise* or me. All you're going to care about is how it feels to be there. And you're never going to come back."

Geordi La Forge woke with a queasy headache and the distinct realization that he was aboard neither the observatory nor the *Enterprise.* He stirred, and realized that he was sitting in an uncomfortable chair aboard a vessel of some sort—the floor beneath his feet vibrated, and he could hear the groan of aging engines. The air was warm, stale, none too sweet; he could feel it on the bare skin of his chest. Someone had removed his tunic.

And his VISOR, leaving him blind. He leaned forward and groped in the darkness.

A hand reached out and grasped his. Faint laughter, and then a familiar voice, very nearby: "Looking for something, Mr. La Forge?"

Geordi drew back. The voice was Soran's, the scientist from the observatory. He remembered now: Soran had struck him—and apparently kidnapped him. But why . . . ?

"A remarkable piece of equipment," Soran continued in a cheerful, conversational tone. "But a little inelegant, wouldn't you say?"

Geordi did not reply.

"Have you ever considered a prosthesis that would make you look a little more . . . normal?"

The words angered him. *Easy,* he told himself. *He's doing it on purpose. Don't let it get to you. . . .* But he could not resist countering, "What's normal?"

"Normal," Soran said smoothly, "is what everyone else is—and what *you* are *not.*"

Geordi tried to keep the heat from his own voice, and failed. "What do you want?"

A long pause. And then Soran said, "As you may or may not be aware, I am an El Aurian. Some people call us a race of listeners. We listen." He hesitated. "Right now, Mr. La Forge, you have my undivided attention. I want to listen to everything you know about trilithium . . . and me."

It made no sense; he knew little about either subject. But he saw no reason not to comply. He thought for a moment, then replied, "Trilithium is an experimental compound developed by the Romulans. I think it's a derivative of—"

He stopped at a sharp thrill of pain near his chest, and raised his hand to the spot. Almost as quickly, the sensation disappeared; but Soran had never touched him.

"I don't want a science lecture," Soran said coldly. "You were on that observatory looking for trilithium. Why?"

Geordi sighed. This wasn't going to be much fun; he clearly knew a lot less than Soran thought he did. "I was ordered to by the captain."

"Let's try to move beyond the usual prisoner-interrogator banter, shall we? You have information, and I need it." Soran paused. "Did the captain explain his orders to you? Did he say why you were searching for trilithium?"

Geordi shook his head. "No."

Another long pause. "What about . . . Guinan? What has she told you about me?"

"Guinan?" He blinked in surprise. "I don't know what you're talking about."

Soran's tone hardened. "My instincts tell me you're lying. And I know that can't be easy for you . . . I can see you have a good heart." He gave a soft, ironic chuckle. Geordi tilted his head, puzzled at the sudden sound of ticking—like the sound of an antique Earth timepiece.

He forgot the sound as a spasm of pain gripped the center of his chest. *A heart attack,* Geordi thought, clutching his chest. *He's somehow induced a heart attack.* . . . He bowed his head at the agony, unable even to breathe.

And then the pain eased again. He drew in a great, gasping breath and began to pant.

"Oh," Soran said cavalierly. "I forgot to tell you. While you were unconscious, I injected a nanoprobe into your bloodstream. It's been navigating your cardiovascular system . . . and right now I've attached it to your left ventricle." Geordi could hear the smile in the man's voice. "A little trick I learned from the Borg."

"Yeah," Geordi gasped with irony. "They're full of great ideas. . . ."

All playfulness left the scientist's tone; with cold matter-of-factness he said, "I just stopped your heart for five seconds. It felt like an eternity, didn't it? Did you know that you can stop the human heart for up to six minutes before the onset of brain damage?"

He let the hatred he felt show on his features. "No . . . I didn't know that. . . ."

"We learn something new about ourselves every day," Soran said. "Now. Maybe I didn't make myself clear. It is very important that you tell me exactly what Captain Picard knows."

"I told you everything," Geordi told the darkness. "You might as well kill me right now."

Silence. And then he heard something entirely unexpected in the scientist's tone: genuine compassion. "I'm not a killer, Mr. La Forge," Soran said, with such honesty, such quiet shame, that Geordi believed him, and no longer feared for his life. The El Aurian sighed, and in that sound Geordi heard such unhappiness, such reluctance, such infinite weariness that, had he not known what Soran was capable of, he might almost have pitied him.

Abruptly, Soran's tone hardened once more. "Let's try thirty seconds."

Geordi heard the muted sound of fingertips pressing controls. And then he bowed his head and groaned as the chest-crushing pain seized him once more, with such mind-blotting intensity that he was aware of nothing else . . . except the soft, steady ticking of a timepiece.

NINE

☆

Other than the holodeck, one of Picard's favorite places aboard the *Enterprise* was stellar cartography. With the holographic map activated, standing on the stellar cartography deck was like lying in a country field staring up at the night sky—or better, like hanging suspended in space; one need only lean forward to touch the nearest star. . . .

At the moment, the holographic map wasn't activated; Picard stood, surrounded by computers, sensors, tracking devices designed to monitor the ship's precise position in space. Beside him, Data sat at a console, awaiting a readout. Picard gazed at the nearby bank of viewscreens, which displayed diagrams of an angry streak of ultraviolet lightning—the energy ribbon—at various times and locations.

He had used the mystery of Soran and the ribbon to focus, to extricate himself from grief. His initial fury and frustration had ebbed. There was nothing he could do to help Robert and René; but there was much he could do to help Geordi La Forge . . . and to stop whatever harm Soran planned.

Data leaned forward as the readout appeared on his screen; Picard caught the movement in his peripheral vision and turned, expectant. He was still unaccustomed to seeing the android under the sway of emotion; Data's depression showed in the slump of his shoulders, the barely perceptible downward curve of his lips.

"According to our information," Data said listlessly, "the ribbon is a conflux of temporal energy which travels through our galaxy every thirty-nine point one years." He paused and frowned, apparently having lost his place. "It will pass through this sector in approximately . . . forty-two hours."

Picard moved away and began to pace, hoping the movement might keep his weary mind and body alert; he had slept little since Marie's message. "Then Guinan was right. . . . She said Soran was trying to get back to the ribbon. If that's true, then there must be some connection with the Amargosa star." He turned on his heel and faced Data. "Give me a list of anything which has been affected by the star's destruction, no matter how insignificant."

The android did not respond, but merely stared unblinking at the glowing screen with a disconsolate expression.

"Data," Picard snapped.

Data straightened at once; Picard fancied he caught a fleeting look of embarrassment on the android's face. "Sorry, sir." He pressed several controls on the console, then looked back at the captain. "It will take the computer a few moments to compile the information."

Picard folded his arms to wait. As he watched, Data released a deep, sorrowful sigh, then leaned forward and put his head in his hands. Perplexed, the captain stepped forward and put a hand on the android's shoulder. "Data . . . are you all right?"

"No, sir." Data raised his head, revealing a tortured expression. "I am finding it difficult to concentrate. I believe I am overwhelmed with feelings of . . . remorse and regret concerning my actions on the observatory."

"What do you mean?" Picard asked gently. Neither Riker nor Worf had reported that Data had committed any unusual action.

Data sighed again. "I wanted to save Geordi . . . I *tried.* But I experienced something I did not expect." He gazed up at the captain with unmasked shame. *"Fear.* I was afraid, sir."

Picard opened his mouth to speak, and closed it again when the computer signaled. Data turned once more to his console and began to read glumly.

"According to our current information, the destruction of the Amargosa star has had the following effects in this sector: Gamma emissions have increased by point-zero-five percent; the *Starship Bozeman* was forced to make a course correction; a research project on Gorik Four was halted due to increased neutrino particles; ambient magnetic fields have decreased by—"

"Wait," Picard interrupted. "The *Bozeman.* Why did it change course?"

"The destruction of the Amargosa star has altered the gravitational forces throughout the sector," Data said. "Any ships passing through this region will have to make a minor course correction."

"A minor course correction . . ." Picard frowned as he contemplated the fact. Instinct said there was something here, some key that remained as yet elusive. He turned and headed toward the large holomap control console behind them. "Where is the ribbon now?"

Data rose and followed him to the console, then pressed a few controls. Within seconds, the room around them dissolved, replaced by a huge, twinkling map of the galaxy. Data pointed toward a red, glowing dot. "This is its current position."

Picard leaned forward, transfixed. "Can you project its course?"

Data began to respond, then hesitated; his expression suddenly crumpled with despair. "Sir . . . I—I cannot continue with this investigation."

Picard stared at him in bewilderment.

Data lowered his head in shame. "I wish to be deactivated until Dr. Crusher can remove the emotion chip."

"Are you having some kind of malfunction?"

The android shook his head. "No, sir. I simply do not have the ability to control these emotions."

"Data . . ." Picard drew a breath. Watching the android's turmoil was like gazing inward. "I have nothing but sympathy for what you're going through. But I need your full attention on the task at—"

Data wheeled on him angrily. "You do not understand, sir. I no longer *want* these feelings. Deactivating me is the only viable solution."

"Data," Picard said sternly, feeling oddly that he was speaking as much to himself, "part of having emotions is learning how to integrate them into your life. How to *deal* with them, no matter what the circumstance."

"But, sir—"

Picard straightened to his full height and summoned

his most authoritarian tone. "And I will *not* allow you to be deactivated. You are an officer aboard this ship and right now you have a duty to perform." He paused, and when no further protest was forthcoming, added: "That's an order, Commander."

As he spoke, Data's expression slowly metamorphosed from one of despair to one of stoic resolve. "Yes, sir," he said softly. "I will try."

Picard put a reassuring hand on the android's shoulder and did not quite smile. "Courage can be an emotion, too, Data." His tone grew brisk. "Now . . . can you project the course of the ribbon?"

Data squared his shoulders in such an overt display of determination that Picard struggled not to smile as the android worked the console. As Picard watched, a glowing red line appeared in the starry display, forming an arc between suns. He stepped closer, his pulse quickening. Yes, the answer was here. . . . He turned back toward Data. "Where was the Amargosa star?"

In reply, Data pressed a control; a twinkling star appeared close to the red line.

"Now . . ." Picard mused. "You said when the Amargosa star was destroyed, it altered the gravitational forces in this sector. Did the computer take that into account when it projected the ribbon's course?"

Surprise spread over Data's features as he considered this. "No, sir. I will make the appropriate adjustments."

He did so, and the single twinkling star before Picard's eyes darkened, blinked, then altogether disappeared. As it did, the glowing red line shifted to the right— changing course.

Picard glanced up, his weariness replaced by the exhilaration of discovery. *"That's* what Soran's doing—

he's changing the ribbon's course. But why? Why try to alter its path? Why not simply fly into it with a ship?"

"Our records show that every ship which has approached the ribbon has either been destroyed or severely damaged," Data offered.

"He can't go to the ribbon," Picard said, with a sudden flash of insight. "So he's trying to make the ribbon come to him." He turned to the android. "Data, is it going to pass near any M-class planets?"

Data consulted the computer once more, then looked up. "Yes, sir. There are two in the Veridian system." He touched more controls, enlarging the display of the Veridian star to reveal the four planets orbiting it.

Picard studied the red line marking the ribbon's path, which passed very close to the third planet. He pointed. "It's very close to Veridian Three . . . but not close enough."

He frowned, troubled, and gazed back at the Veridian sun. As he stared, an unbidden memory rose: the image of the fiery, dying Amargosa star, and in his mind's eye, he saw it in the healthy sun's place. A horrid revelation seized him. "Data," he said urgently, "what would happen to the ribbon's path if he destroyed the Veridian star itself?"

He knew, with unshakable conviction, exactly what would occur, even before Data worked the console controls and the display shifted once more. Before Picard's eyes, the Veridian sun dimmed, blinked into darkness. The red line indicating the ribbon's course shifted—so that it precisely intersected the third planet.

"That's where he's going," Picard said.

After a beat's silence, Data added softly, "It should be noted, sir, that the collapse of the Veridian star would produce a shock wave similar to the one we observed at Amargosa."

Picard faced him with a grim expression. "And destroy every planet in the system."

The android checked his console readout, then eyed the display with unmasked dismay. "Veridian Three is uninhabited—but Veridian Four supports a pre-industrial humanoid society."

Picard turned back to stare at the display, and the slowly revolving fourth planet. "Population?"

Data's tone was hushed with dread. "Approximately two hundred thirty million."

For an instant—no more—Picard gazed at the image of Veridian IV and tried to understand what could drive a man to destroy a world.

If you go into that nexus, you're not going to care about Soran or the Enterprise *or me. All you're going to care about is how it feels to be there. And you're never going to come back. . . .*

Picard touched his comm badge. "Picard to bridge."

"Worf here."

"Set a course for the Veridian system, maximum warp." He was already in motion as he spoke, headed for the bridge with renewed determination—and gratitude, to see Data beside him, moving with the same sense of urgent purposefulness.

On the rumbling Bird-of-Prey, Soran paused in the corridor to squint in the dimness at the face of his open pocket watch. What he saw there evoked a smile and a thrill of heart-pounding exhilaration; they should be no more than a minute now from Veridian III. Soon he would be with Leandra and the children, far away from this accursed universe where they were dead and he was trapped aboard this stinking scow of a Klingon ship.

Mr. La Forge had been of no great use. After enduring speechless agony for several seconds, he had provided no further revelations, except to confirm Soran's suspicion that the *Enterprise* captain was investigating certain pieces of the puzzle that could lead him to Veridian. Picard unsettled Soran; the captain might have been easily swayed while under the influence of fresh grief—but he was also extremely intelligent. Once that grief faded, there was a great danger that Picard would recover and apply that intelligence to learn where Soran had gone.

But he had only a minute. Soran smiled again at the thought, but the smile was not entirely untroubled. Torturing La Forge had proved more . . . unpleasant than Soran had anticipated. In fact, it had turned his stomach to think he had become like the Borg.

It doesn't matter. None of it matters. I was kind—I let La Forge live, which is more than this universe of time and death will do for him. We're all doomed here, all walking corpses.

He had restarted La Forge's heart after fifteen seconds, unable to watch the man's suffering. On his home planet, he had been a gentle man, a kind man, with no stomach for cruelty . . . certainly not murder.

The sacrifice of Veridian IV is necessary. Necessary. *It's the only way to return home. . . .*

Yet the thought of it haunted his nights.

He would do it, though. He would not falter as he had with La Forge, because what happened on Veridian IV would be distant, bloodless; he would not have to witness it, would already be in the nexus by then.

And, perhaps . . . unlikely, but just *perhaps* there might be some lucky few caught in the reverberations from the energy ribbon who would be transported to the nexus. Their bodies would perish in this universe, but their echoes would live eternally. He was doing those possible few a favor.

Nothing—guilt, outsiders, Klingons—*nothing* could be permitted to deter him now.

He repocketed the watch and stepped from the corridor onto the bridge, where the two sisters sat, gruesome leather-and-metal mirror images, at command. Lursa, the elder, husky-throated one, the one who seemed most often to have the last word, swiveled to face him. "Did you get anything from the human?"

"No," Soran said, with an inward smile. "His heart just wasn't in it."

One of the huge male helmsmen glanced over his shoulder at his mistress. "We have entered orbit of Veridian Three."

Soran glanced at the looming planet on the viewscreen with a rush of anticipation that turned his skin to gooseflesh, then turned quickly to Lursa. "Prepare to transport me to the surface."

"Wait!" B'Etor rose, distrustful and swaggering, from her chair. "When do we get our payment?"

He gazed on her, struggling to mask his hatred. He despised having to deal with such small-minded, power-hungry creatures, who would no doubt make a pitiful mess of the galaxy once he had gone.

No matter. This universe and its concerns were fast fading from his consciousness as he focused on the joy to come. These grotesque parodies of womanhood, this ship, this situation possessed no more reality than a painful dream from which he would soon wake. Lursa and B'Etor were shadows, phantoms who had sprung from the void and would soon vanish into it.

He sighed, fished a tiny chip from his pocket, and handed it to her. "This contains all the information you'll need to build a trilithium weapon," he said, as B'Etor greedily seized the deadly gift and gazed down at it with glistening, predatory eyes. "It's been coded. Once I'm safely to the surface, I'll transmit the decryption sequence to you . . . not before."

"Mistress!" the helmsman cried abruptly. "A Federation starship is entering the system!"

"What?" Indignant, Lursa leaned forward, clutching the arms of her chair. "On viewer."

On the small, dust-covered screen, a grainy, not-quite-focused image of a starship wavered into view.

The *Enterprise,* Soran knew instinctively.

The helmsman swiveled his great, dark head to peer over a leather-clad shoulder at his mistresses. "They are hailing us."

Lip curling, B'Etor growled two syllables in Klingon; her command was followed instantly by the sound of a familiar voice on the intercom.

"Klingon vessel," Picard said, and Soran closed his eyes. There was strength in the captain's tone now; he had mastered his sorrow, and become the adversary Soran had feared he might. "We know what you're doing, and we will destroy any probe launched toward the Veridian star. We demand that you return our chief engineer and leave this system immediately."

Soran felt a surge of wild, dark rage, the same fury he had experienced more than a century before toward the Borg. The situation was no different now: Picard was

Captain Montgomery "Scotty" Scott (James Doohan) is shocked at Captain Kirk's (William Shatner) refusal to attend the christening of the *U.S.S. Enterprise* 1701-B.

On the *U.S.S. Enterprise* 1701-B, Captain Kirk and Commander Pavel Chekov (Walter Koenig) prepare to greet an old friend.

Captain Kirk takes command of the *Enterprise*-B to answer a distress call.

Ensign Demora Sulu (Jacqueline Kim) and Captain Harriman (Alan Ruck) struggle to stabilize the *Enterprise*-B.

Aboard the good ship *Enterprise*, Captain Jean-Luc Picard (Patrick Stewart) and Commander William Riker (Jonathan Frakes) announce Lieutenant Worf's promotion.

Security Chief Worf (Michael Dorn) proudly accepts his promotion.

Chief Engineer Geordi La Forge (LeVar Burton)
explains to Commander Data (Brent Spiner) why they
made Worf walk the plank.

Guinan (Whoopi Goldberg) senses the presence of
Dr. Soran.

In Stellar Cartography, Captain Picard and
Commander Data investigate an interspatial nexus.

Dr. Beverly Crusher (Gates McFadden) examines
Commander Data's malfunctioning emotion chip.

The Duras sisters, Lursa (Barbara March) and B'Etor (Gwynyth Walsh) face off against the *U.S.S. Enterprise.*

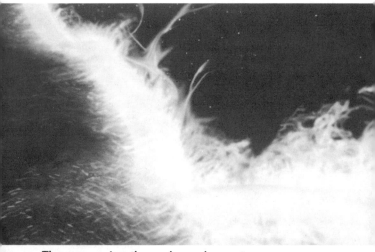

The nexus rips through a solar system.

Captain Picard asks Captain Kirk for help.

Captain Kirk fights for his life against Dr. Soran.

With First Officer Riker in command, Counselor
Deanna Troi (Marina Sirtis) takes charge of Navigation.

Commander
Data is happy to
find his cat,
Spot, alive and
well.

trying to steal Leandra and the children from him a second time.

All compassion fled Soran's soul. He would do whatever necessary—would gladly strangle Picard, the entire *Enterprise* crew, with his own hands—if it would help him return to the place he now thought of as home. Soran pulled out his watch with fingers that trembled faintly, glanced at its implacable face, then snapped it shut.

He turned to the Duras sisters. "There's no time for this. Eliminate them."

B'Etor gaped at him as though he were mad. "That is a Galaxy-class starship! We are no match for them."

Soran took a deep breath to calm himself, to dissolve the frustration that threatened to devour his reason. He would not yield. There was a solution, and he would find it, if he could manage to slow his racing thoughts. . . .

With a burst of inspiration, he pulled La Forge's optical prosthesis from his pocket, and held it before the curious women like a prize.

"I think it's time we gave Mr. La Forge his sight back. . . ."

On the *Enterprise* bridge, Picard paced as he waited for the Bird-of-Prey's reply.

"Maybe they're not out there," Riker said.

Picard kept his gaze fixed on the main viewscreen, on the darkness and stars that somewhere hid an aging vessel. "They're just trying to decide whether a twenty-year-old Klingon Bird-of-Prey is any match for the Federation flagship."

Beside him, Troi said softly, "Or perhaps they're on the surface. . . ."

Picard glanced at her. It was a possibility that had occurred to him; one that added an element of difficulty to their current predicament.

It was underscored when Worf turned from the helm to face him. "Sir . . . according to my calculations, a solar probe launched from either the Klingon ship or the planet's surface would take eleven seconds to reach the sun." He paused. "However, since we do not know the exact point of origin, it will take us between eight and fifteen seconds to lock our weapons on to it."

Picard gazed at him grimly, but said nothing.

"That's a pretty big margin of error," Riker said softly.

"Too big." Picard took another restless few steps, then swiveled toward the helm. "How long until the ribbon arrives?"

"Approximately forty-seven minutes, sir," Data replied.

The captain released a silent sigh of frustration. "I have to find a way to get to Soran. . . ." He remembered the look of desperation in the scientist's eyes—one close to madness; yet there had still been reason, there, too. Instinct said that Soran was not a willing murderer; and if Guinan had managed to adapt to life outside the nexus, then perhaps Soran could be persuaded as well.

It would not be easy. Picard had studied the scientist's biographical information; his young wife and children, all killed by the Borg. Indications were that the Borg had interrogated Soran briefly before the scientist escaped; cause enough, the captain knew, for madness . . . and for a reason to think he could get through to the scientist. He understood what it was to lose one's family in a brutal instant—and what it was like to have one's mind, one's person invaded by cold-blooded force.

He started as the helm beeped a warning.

"Captain," Worf said, "Klingon vessel decloaking directly ahead. They are hailing."

On the viewscreen, a patch of velvet blackness wavered, then transformed itself into a Bird-of-Prey.

"Onscreen," Picard ordered.

As he watched, the vessel vanished, replaced by the toothily smiling images of Lursa and B'Etor.

"Captain." Lursa's tone was one of feigned warmth. She leaned forward in her chair, her long dark hair streaming down onto metal-and-leather warrior regalia. "What an unexpected pleasure."

Picard felt his expression harden. "Lursa, I want to talk to Soran."

Her smile grew coy. "I'm afraid the doctor is no longer aboard our ship."

"Then I'll beam down to his location," Picard countered. "Just give us his coordinates."

B'Etor spoke, with the same unctuous, faintly mocking tone as her sister. "The doctor values his privacy. He would be quite . . . upset if an armed away team interrupted him."

The captain hesitated no more than a second. He had hoped to beam down armed and with communications intact, so that he could inform the *Enterprise* of the probe's location—but if that was not possible, then he had no choice but to trust the instinct that said he would be able to stop Soran on the planet surface. "Very well," he told the sisters. "I'll beam to your ship and *you* can transport me to Soran."

"Sir." Riker turned toward him, urgent. "You can't trust them. For all we know, they killed Geordi and they'll kill you, too."

"We did not harm your engineer," Lursa retorted, with such indignation that Picard believed her. "He has been our guest."

Riker faced her, his expression cold, mistrustful. "Then return him."

"In exchange for what?" B'Etor demanded.

Data looked up at the captain, his expression eager. "Me, sir."

Picard ignored him. "Me," he told the Klingon women. *"If* you let me speak to Soran."

He knew at once from their sudden, startled silence that his offer would be accepted. They glanced at each other, trying to mask their enthusiasm; B'Etor leaned over and quickly whispered something in Klingon to her sister. Lursa nodded thoughtfully, then glanced back at the screen.

"We'll consider it a prisoner exchange."

"Agreed," Picard said with relief, ignoring the look of disapproval on Will Riker's face. The screen darkened, then once more displayed the image of the Bird-of-Prey. Picard turned and headed for the turbolift.

"Number One," he said, "you have the bridge. Have Dr. Crusher meet me in transporter room three."

He left swiftly, before Riker could protest further, with determination and an odd sense of destiny.

TEN

☆ ─────────

In the humid, overheated cabin, Geordi leaned heavily against the back of his chair and awaited Soran's return. The nanoprobe's grip on his heart left him nauseated, slightly breathless, perspiring; sweat trickled down his forehead and stung his sightless eyes.

He could not quite figure the scientist out. Soran seemed mercurial, unpredictable. When the interrogation had first begun, Geordi felt certain it would end in his execution. Soran's voice held an edge of anger, pain, an undercurrent of mad desperation that said he would do anything, *anything* to get what he wanted.

Yet there had been genuine compassion in his tone when he said, *I'm not a killer, Mr. La Forge.* And in the middle of the torture, the pain had suddenly stopped.

Geordi had survived the crushing agony by forcing himself to mentally count the seconds. He had lost track somewhere after nine—when he had suddenly been overwhelmed by pain and the terrifying conviction that Soran had been wrong, that he was in fact dying. He struggled for oxygen, heard himself gasping like a struggling fish, drowning in an ocean of air. His consciousness flickered, and in his agonized, dreamlike state, he became strangely aware that Soran sensed what he felt; that Soran knew, and could not bear it.

The torment abruptly ceased. Thirty seconds, Soran had said. But the pain had stopped somewhere around fifteen.

Geordi had lifted his head, forgetting in his pain-filled haze that he was blind, that Soran still had the VISOR. *Like I said,* he had croaked, *I don't know anything beyond what I've already told you.*

Soran had not replied. In the silence Geordi had heard the scientist rise, then stand for a long moment before turning and leaving the cabin.

Maybe he had had a change of heart. Or maybe he simply didn't have the stomach for torture and had gone to get someone else. Or maybe . . .

Geordi sighed and let his head loll to one side. No point in speculating. Either he was going to die or he wasn't. The thought frightened him—but at the moment, he was too exhausted to waste much energy on worrying about it. So long as Soran left the nanoprobe alone . . .

He straightened as the door slid open with a groan, and listened intently as two—no, *three* pairs of footsteps thudded against the metal deck. One pair stopped in front of him; two behind, on either side.

"Mr. La Forge." Soran's voice neared until Geordi could sense the scientist standing directly in front of him. Soran's tone was brisk, hurried. "As much as I've enjoyed our little visit, it's time to part. Stand, please."

Geordi rose unsteadily to his feet; huge, warm hands grasped his arms just above the elbows and steadied him while another pair of hands pulled soft cloth over his head. His tunic; his arms were guided into the sleeves, and then another pair of hands placed something cool and metal over his eyes.

He blinked and touched a hand to his VISOR as the world came suddenly into focus. Soran was smiling, his blue-gray eyes bright not with desperation, but with maniacal anticipation. Even the lines and shadows beneath his eyes seemed to have lessened, making him appear a younger man. "Now, if you would be so kind as to come with us . . ."

He gestured toward the door. Geordi swiveled his head, and saw that he was flanked by two towering guards, their bronze skull ridges terminating in shaggy, waist-length manes of dark hair. *"Klingons,"* he whispered, and turned to gaze at his surroundings as the guards pushed him toward the exit. "This is a *Klingon* ship. . . ."

The quartet entered a cramped, dimly lit corridor. Soran strode in front of them, his attention focused on the hand that held the antique timepiece. "Very astute, Mr. La Forge," he murmured with a distracted, irritable air. "They do give a very thorough education at Starfleet Academy, don't they?"

Soran's intensity had so escalated that Geordi feared for a moment that he was being led to his execution; but they soon entered a transporter room.

Soran stepped first upon a pad and uttered a single command: "Energize."

One of the guards stepped behind the console and complied. Geordi tried to peer over his shoulder in hopes of spying the coordinates, but the second guard stepped behind him, blocking his view.

The transporter whined shrilly; Soran's image began to dematerialize, then reappeared with a sputter of sparks. The scientist's features darkened with rage as the guard furiously worked the console controls. Soran's form once more wavered, then dissolved, but not before Geordi read the word on his lips: *Imbeciles.* . . .

Then he was shoved upon a pad himself. The Klingon vessel faded from view and was replaced by the sleek, gleaming bulkheads of the *Enterprise.* Geordi got the faintest impression of Captain Picard dematerializing beside him, and then he was stepping forward and sinking to his knees in front of a waiting Dr. Crusher. . . .

On the surface of Veridian III, Picard gazed up at the lilac sky and thought of Eden before the creation of humankind. No sound of aircars, of industry or voices, no sight of cities or ships streaking toward the horizon; the only sounds were the stirring of small mammals in the lush foliage, of birds singing high and sweet, the only sights those of clouds, mountains, ancient trees.

He stared down and saw that he stood on the dusty clay surface of a plateau ringed by greenery. Before him, a large scaffolding had been erected against a single towering rock face—the only sign of humanoid disturbance.

On instinct, he turned and saw Soran gazing calmly at his antique pocket watch. The scientist closed the timepiece, put it away, and smiled thinly at Picard.

"You must think I'm quite the madman." He seemed outwardly composed, but there was a hint of volatility in the way the corners of his lips trembled slightly, a hint of pain in his eyes.

Picard drew in a breath, hesitated, then yielded to the truth. "The thought had crossed my mind."

Soran's blue eyes hardened faintly, though the smile did not change. "Think whatever you like, Captain." He turned and began to move away, toward the scaffold.

Picard took a step. "Soran . . . I understand you were interrogated by the Borg."

His body did not turn, but his head jerked back sharply to regard the captain with dark suspicion. "What concern is it of yours?"

"I . . . have had experience with the Borg myself." Picard hesitated, choosing his words carefully not just for Soran's sake, but for his own; speaking of the experience, even with trusted friends, still did not come easily. He could see that his words, his intensity, had impressed Soran. The scientist stared, frowning, as the captain continued: "They captured me. Made me one of their own. Used me against the Federation . . ." He paused at the painful memory. "The experience nearly destroyed me. But I survived. I had help . . . good friends. . . ." He took another step toward Soran and held out an arm. "Soran . . . don't let what happened to you destroy you. We can help—"

Such potent bitterness swept over the scientist's face that Soran could not entirely repress a grimace. "I appreciate your concern, Captain. But this has nothing to do with destroying myself. Quite the contrary, in fact." He gathered himself, managed another unheartfelt smile. "Forgive me if I don't respond to your emotional plea. You see, I don't quite believe that you've shown up because you're overwhelmed by concern for me. The only possible reason you're here is that you're not entirely confident you can shoot down my probe after all. So you've come to dissuade me from my horrific plan." He paused for emphasis, then said, with heavy irony: "Good luck."

He turned his back to the captain and strode confidently toward the scaffolding.

Picard moved to follow. A bright flash blinded him, slammed him flat on his back against rock-hard clay, shoved the air from his lungs. He gasped, struggling for an instant to catch his breath, then sat up slowly and blinked until his vision cleared.

A forcefield, of course; but it had just as quickly disappeared from view, invisibly surrounding Soran—and, Picard suspected, the scaffolding. The captain pushed himself to his feet and carefully made his way to what he hoped was the field's edge.

Beyond, Soran confidently ignored him, frowning up at the sky and then down at a padd nestled in his palm.

Picard kicked dust, and watched it glimmer briefly as the field repelled it. He was determined to get to Soran—if not through his words, then somehow, through the field.

"You don't need to do this, Soran," he called. "I'm sure we could find another way to get you into this nexus."

The scientist did not react—merely stood, pale and black-clad like a mourner, with his back to Picard, and concentrated on the data cupped in his hand. He pressed a few controls . . . and Picard started as a small probe launcher decloaked near the scientist.

Soran moved calmly to the launcher, stepped up to its control panel, and began to work. With a tone as dispassionate and detached as one scientist explaining to another how to operate the panel, he said, "I've spent eighty years looking for another way, Captain. This is the only way." He hesitated, then angled his narrow face toward Picard; an honest grin played at his lips. "Of course, you could always come with me. You fancy yourself an explorer. Here's a chance to explore something no human has ever experienced."

Picard's tone frosted. "Not if it means killing over two hundred million people."

Soran recoiled as if struck. *So,* Picard thought. *I've struck a nerve. . . .*

But the scientist quickly hid his discomfort; the calculated, calm expression descended once more over his features. "As you wish," he said lightly, and turned back toward his padd.

"Soran . . ." Picard let his voice and features soften. "I know that you lost your wife and family to the Borg; I know what it is to lose family, to feel lonely. You're not alone in that. But fleeing to the nexus isn't going to bring them back—"

Soran looked up with angry swiftness, his pale face flushed incarnadine. "You're *wrong,* Captain. You haven't been there; you haven't the slightest idea what the nexus is, what it's capable of. Everyone you've ever lost, Captain—you can have them all back. And more."

"So that's why," Picard whispered. "You're going to get them back. You would do anything, kill anyone, to get them back."

The scientist said nothing; only gazed at Picard for a fleeting second with an expression of utter vulnerability, then quickly turned his face away.

"I wonder," Picard said slowly. "Did your wife Leandra know that she married a man who was capable of mass murder?"

Soran did not glance up from his console; but Picard saw something dark and ugly flicker across his profile. The captain pressed harder.

"When you tucked your children into bed . . . do you suppose they ever suspected that their father would one day kill millions as casually as he kissed them good night?"

At last Soran stopped his work and looked up. For an instant his eyes were still vulnerable, haunted by memories. Picard felt a stirring of hope. And then the brittleness ascended upward from the scientist's hollowly smiling lips to his eyes.

"Nice try," he whispered huskily, then turned back to his work.

In the instant he woke to darkness, Geordi La Forge was seized by the unreasoning fear that he was back on the Klingon Bird-of-Prey. Soran was waiting for him in the silence laced by the ship's rumbling and the incessant ticking of a clock, and this time, all compassion was gone from the scientist's voice as he said, *I'm afraid your time is up, Mr. La Forge. Let's try for the full six minutes, shall we?*

Geordi opened his eyes with a gasp—which evolved into a relieved sigh when he saw himself surrounded by the familiar sight of the *Enterprise* sickbay. He blinked to clear the last vestiges of the dream.

He had been frightened while aboard the Bird-of-Prey—but the pain and Soran had been a distraction. Now that he was safe, the danger he had been in began to hit home. He could have easily been killed. . . .

He banished the thought as Dr. Crusher leaned,

smiling, over the biobed, and draped her auburn hair over an ear. "How're you feeling?"

He returned the smile as he realized that, physically, he felt ready to return to work. "Just fine."

She nodded. "Don't worry, there's been no permanent damage. There's only been a little arterial scarring and some myocardial degeneration. I've removed the nanoprobe and I think you're going to be fine, but I want to run some more tests."

"Thanks, Doc," he said, and pushed himself to a sitting position. He could tell from her voice and expression that he was all right and that she was, as usual, simply being very cautious.

The doctor moved away to reveal Data, who had been standing behind her.

"Data!" Geordi grinned. He had intended to ask whether the emotion chip had been removed—but the question was unnecessary. The android's eyes were troubled, his expression one of concern, mixed with remorse. "So—you didn't remove the chip after all?"

"No. It was fused into my neural net. Removing it would be quite complicated—so I am attempting to deal with the emotions." Data sighed heavily. "It has not been easy. I have been very worried about you, Geordi."

"It's okay." Geordi spread his arms wide. "I'm here, and I'm fine."

"It is more than that." Data paused, then lowered his head. "I let Soran kidnap you. I could have prevented it, but I did not. And if you had died—"

"But I didn't, Data. It's over, and I'm okay."

The android glanced up, his expression miserable. "I am sorry I let you down, Geordi. I have not been behaving like myself lately."

Impulsively, Geordi reached out and gave his friend's hand a pat. "No, you haven't. You've been behaving like a human." He paused. "I understand. When Soran tortured me, I was afraid. Dying is a very scary thing, Data. It's normal to fear it."

The android tilted his head in a puzzled gesture that reminded Geordi so much of the old Data that he smiled. "I agree," Data said, thoughtful. "But before I had the chip implanted, it would have made no sense to me." He paused. "It *still* makes no sense, even though I have experienced the emotion. What is so terrible about simply ceasing to exist?"

Geordi shrugged. "I don't know. Fear of the unknown, maybe . . . or maybe it's just that our instinct to live is so strong."

"But this is *terrible*," Data said. "I am designed to outlast everyone aboard this vessel, yet I am terrified at the thought that, eventually, one day, I will . . . cease. And that I must lose all of my friends." He shared a meaningful look with Geordi. "How do you bear it?"

He did not answer immediately. "We don't have much choice, I guess. And . . . to be honest, most of the time we try not to think about it." He hesitated. "But maybe we ought to. It'd make us appreciate each moment—and our friends"—he smiled at the android, and reached again for his hand—"a lot more."

And as he watched, the expression of dismay on Data's face slowly metamorphosed into a smile.

"I have established the link," the navigator, Qorak, said.

B'Etor shared a swift glance with her sister and smiled with relief. Until this moment, she had not trusted Soran too far; too much kindness lurked behind the madness in his eyes. Yet his intensity attracted her—despite the fact that he was a puny human, a race she had never found attractive. Physically, Soran was no exception; he was lean, wiry, short by Klingon standards. But there was something intriguing about him: the bright silver hair, cropped short, the translucent skin, the pale-colored eyes.

Those eyes . . . they held an intensity she had rarely seen, even in the most determined of Klingon males. His eyes had blazed with it when he had struck her on the bridge. She respected that intensity—for she knew few that shared it, except for herself and her sister. Her life, her being, was consumed by one passion: seeing the Duras family restored to power. Now, with Soran's help, she would see that passion consummated. And more: With the trilithium weapon, the sisters of Duras could conquer far more than the Klingon Empire that was their birthright. With such power, the entire galaxy would soon be theirs.

She had come close to killing Soran when he had struck her; but even in her anger, she was forced to bear grudging admiration for anyone who dared lash out at her on the bridge, in full view of her soldiers.

She hoped she could trust him. For if not, despite her attraction, she would personally see to his death.

"Put it onscreen," Lursa ordered.

B'Etor held her breath. Static filled the viewscreen, then cleared gradually to reveal . . . white. Nothing but white, and for an instant, she felt a stab of fury: Soran had lied, had betrayed them. . . .

And then she released her breath, gently, as she realized they were staring at a ceiling on the *Enterprise*.

B'Etor's grin returned as, beside her, Lursa said softly, "It's working. . . ."

"Where is he?" B'Etor demanded.

As if in answer, a human's face loomed large on the screen. A woman, with a face so pale and smooth, it seemed to B'Etor naked, unfinished as a gestating child's. The woman leaned over the link, smiling with abnormally even, tiny teeth, her long, fine hair hanging forward in a shining curtain.

B'Etor recoiled with a grimace. "Human females are so repulsive. . . ."

The woman began to speak silently. Lursa and B'Etor watched as the woman withdrew; soon the strange-looking android with the golden eyes appeared. He, too, silently mouthed words—and then the woman returned, and began to perform what appeared to be medical tests, until B'Etor shifted restlessly in her chair and mumbled an epithet beneath her breath.

Even so, she and her sister continued to gaze at the screen. Too much—the entire galaxy—was at stake to let vigilance lapse. At last the view switched from the sickbay to the *Enterprise* corridors. B'Etor felt a surge of hope . . . until the scene shifted to that of a luxurious cabin, and a private head. Soon the two sisters were staring at cascades of running water.

"He's taking a *bath*," Lursa growled.

B'Etor stared in irritation at the screen as a pair of dark feet suddenly peeked out from beneath sloshing water. She turned to her sister. "I thought he was the chief engineer."

"He is," Lursa replied disconsolately.

"Then *when* is he going to engineering?"

B'Etor fell silent as Lursa struck her arm with the back

of a hand to get her attention, then gestured toward the screen. The view had suddenly changed again, to one of mists and fog. B'Etor leaned forward, expectant, as a dark hand appeared from beyond the mist . . .

Then wiped away the fog to reveal La Forge's unselfconscious reflection.

She fell back in her chair and howled in frustration.

On a different bridge, Will Riker was feeling no small amount of unease as he gazed at the Bird-of-Prey on the viewscreen. He understood Picard's reasons for wanting to beam down to Veridian III, but he in no way trusted the Duras sisters. Not that he feared a direct attack—the Klingon ship was no match for the likes of the *Enterprise*—but he knew Lursa and B'Etor were capable of great treachery. And he could not shake the nagging premonition that something was amiss, something was about to go terribly wrong—and not simply with the captain.

Perhaps Deanna sensed it, too—or maybe she simply sensed his own discomfort. Either way, he was aware of her dark eyes studying him with an expression of concern; he did not meet them, but focused his attention on Worf, who studied the readout on his monitor with a decided frown.

"Any luck, Mr. Worf?" He leaned over the console.

The Klingon shook his head. "No, sir. I am still unable to locate the captain."

Riker turned as the turbolift doors slid open. Data stepped forward onto the bridge and headed for his station. The android's mood had changed radically from the last time Riker had seen him. Data's lips curved upward in a faint grin; his posture was straight, his step buoyant.

"Data," Riker said. "The sensors can't penetrate the planet's ionosphere; there's too much interference. Can you find another way to scan for life-forms?"

Data settled behind his station and glanced up at his commanding officer; his grin broadened. "I would be happy to, sir. I just love to scan for life-forms." He set at once to work, ad-libbing a merry little song: "Life-forms . . . tiny little life-forms . . . where are you, life-forms . . . ?"

Riker's lips parted in aghast amazement; he dared not turn round, for fear of catching sight of Deanna's eyes. But his gaze accidentally met the Klingon's, who shot him a look of such long-suffering martyrdom that Riker looked away quickly, before he erupted in laughter.

Atop the dusty plateau, Picard moved warily, giving an occasional surreptitious kick and noting where the pebbles bounced off the field's perimeter. Overhead, the sky still shone brightly with the Veridian sun—but not, the captain feared, for long; Soran bent, utterly absorbed, over the launcher's control panel. If he was not stopped soon—

"Soran," he said loudly; the scientist did not look up. "I can see that despite everything, you still possess compassion. You could have killed my engineer—"

Without taking his focus from his task, Soran interrupted harshly. "I didn't have the time."

"I don't believe that." Picard took a few more steps around the field's perimeter, managed another swift, unnoticed kick. Dust and pebbles collided with the field in a colorful burst of sparks, then fell to the sand. "It would have been just as easy to kill him as let him go. Soran . . . you had a wife, children. They died in a senseless tragedy. Can't you see that you've become what you most despised? What you're about to do is no different from when the Borg destroyed your world. Two hundred thirty million wives, husbands, children . . ."

Keeping his attention focused on the launcher controls, the scientist at last replied—with such soft, cool detachment in his voice that Picard shuddered inwardly. "You're right," Soran said. "And there was a time when I wouldn't have hurt anyone. Then the Borg came . . . and they showed me that if there is one constant in this universe, it's death." He paused to key in a command, then continued in the same even, conversational tone.

"Afterward, I began to realize that none of it mattered. We're all going to die anyway. It's only a question of how and when. You will, too, Captain. You might contract a fatal disease . . . you might die in battle . . ."

He lifted his face and fixed Picard with a gaze that pierced to the captain's soul. ". . . or burn to death in a fire."

Despite himself, Picard froze. Soran stepped down from the launcher and moved closer until he stood just on the field's other side.

"You look surprised," he said softly. "But you shouldn't be. I've been to the nexus, Captain. I know things about people." He leaned closer, his eyes bright with the desperate intensity Picard had first seen in Ten-Forward; his voice dropped to just above a whisper. "Aren't you beginning to feel time gaining on you? It's like a predator. It's stalking you. You can try to outrun it with doctors, medicines . . . new technologies. But in the end, time is going to hunt you down—and make the kill." As he finished, his lips twisted with bitterness.

Picard lowered his gaze. Impossible to deny the truth

of Soran's assertions; he felt the same bitterness himself, the same anger at the patent unfairness of death. He struggled to find a counterargument—but the words he chose seemed to him meaningless, clichés. "We're all mortal, Soran. It's one of the truths of our existence."

"An ugly truth," Soran said passionately. "A *hideous* truth." He paused; the anger began to ease from his features, to be replaced by dawning exhilaration. "What if I told you I found a new truth . . ."

"The nexus," Picard said.

Soran's swift smile was an affirmation. "I've spent the last eighty years speaking to other *Lakul* survivors about their experiences in it, researching it, trying to understand it. Time has no meaning there," he said, with a simple wonder that erased all trace of darkness from his features, his eyes. "The predator has no teeth. Think of it, Captain . . . the curse that has plagued the entire universe since the beginning of life—gone. No more death, no suffering . . ."

He gazed, expectant, at the sky, his face suddenly luminous with sunlight and hope. And then he turned his back on Picard and hurried back to the probe launcher.

Picard watched with a sense of defeat. He could argue no further with Soran's murderous logic; his only course lay in finding a way inside the forcefield. He glanced once more at Soran, whose attention was entirely focused on the launcher control panel, then began to pace along the field's perimeter.

He had not gone far when he spied an unusual formation within a dusty red mound: over eons, wind and water had burrowed through the ancient stone to sculpt an almost perfect archway—an opening, Picard judged, just large enough for a man to squeeze through.

He stared at the daylight beyond; if, by chance, Soran had failed to notice the gap, and hadn't accounted for it when programming the forcefield . . .

Casually, Picard bent down to retrieve a pebble and tossed it in Soran's direction. The field flashed on, revealing something that filled Picard with sudden hope: The field extended to the top of the mound, and no farther. The archway was unshielded.

As if sensing danger, Soran glanced up at the crackling sound. "Careful, Captain. That's a fifty-gigawatt forcefield. I wouldn't want to see you get hurt."

Picard's lips thinned at the irony in the scientist's tone; if all went as Soran planned, the captain would be destroyed by the ensuing shock wave. "Thank you," he replied coolly, and waited for Soran to look back down at the controls before arming himself with pebbles.

On the Bird-of-Prey's bridge, B'Etor sat scowling at the viewscreen, which revealed a roving view of the *Enterprise*'s corridors. She glanced up as her sister, who had given up in impatience and left the bridge, returned.

Lursa followed her sister's gaze to the screen. "Where is he now?"

"I don't know," B'Etor snapped. "He bathed . . . now he is roaming the ship. . . . He must be the only engineer in Starfleet who does *not* go to engineering!"

Lursa sat beside her with an unhappy groan. As she did, the view on the screen shifted as the engineer rounded a corner . . . and moved past a small bulkhead sign marked ENGINEERING.

B'Etor leaned forward eagerly in her chair. "Finally!"

They watched as the engineer approached another human—a uniformed male, who stopped and initiated a conversation. B'Etor frowned, trying to read the human's lips. Her skill in speaking Standard was formidable, and she was able to make out the words "diagnostic" and "generators."

The view shifted again, this time to something that took B'Etor to the edge of her seat: A bank of monitors, and beside them, a large graphic of the *Enterprise.* Then once more, the view began to pan to the left.

"That's it!" Lursa swiveled and grasped her sister's wrist. "Replay from time index four-two-nine."

B'Etor's fingers flew swiftly over the controls on her console arm. The image on her small monitor and the main viewscreen reversed itself to show the bank of monitors and the graphic diagram of the starship.

Lursa touched the diagram on B'Etor's small console screen. "Magnify this section and enhance."

B'Etor worked once more, enlarging the view of the *Enterprise* graphic. Lursa leaned forward until her face was a handsbreadth from the console arm, and read aloud, squinting. "Their shields are operating on a modulation of two-five-seven point four. . . ."

She rose, her face flushed, and gazed into B'Etor's eyes with triumph.

"Adjust our torpedo frequency to match," B'Etor called out, her voice rising with excitement. "Two-five-seven point four!" She returned her sister's exultant smile; for with those words, she had just secured the destruction of the *Enterprise,* and victory for the house of Duras.

ELEVEN

☆

"Sir." His cheerful expression now replaced by one of concern, Data swiveled toward Riker. "I am detecting an anomalous subspace reading in Main Engineering. It may be—"

Riker never heard the rest. The ship reeled hard to port, slamming him against the arm of his chair. He held on, managing to turn his head to look at the screen, where the bright glow of the most recent blast was fading to reveal the Bird-of-Prey against the backdrop of Veridian III. As Riker watched, another brilliantly shining torpedo emerged from the Klingon vessel and streaked relentlessly toward the *Enterprise*.

He barely had time to brace himself before the next one hit—with such thunderous force that when it ended, he felt amazed the hull above them had not been sheared in two.

Over the screaming of the red-alert klaxons, Worf called, "They have found a way to penetrate our shields!"

"Lock phasers and return fire!" Riker ordered.

On the screen, the Bird-of-Prey's shields flashed as they absorbed the impact of the starship's phaser blasts.

A no-win situation, Riker realized, even before he saw the next photon torpedo blazing toward them on the viewscreen. Without shields, the *Enterprise* would be torn apart.

The ship lurched again beneath his feet; the conn console erupted in a hail of sparks, hurling the conn officer to the deck.

"Deanna!" Riker shouted. "Take the helm. Get us out of orbit!"

Troi propelled herself from her chair and raced unsteadily across the rocking deck to the helm. Within seconds, Veridian III disappeared from the viewscreen —but the Klingon vessel was in full pursuit. Not enough, Riker knew, as he squinted his eyes at the dazzling glow of another approaching torpedo. Lursa and B'Etor had found a way to outwit the *Enterprise*'s superior firepower; it was time for Riker to return the favor.

As the ship was jolted again, Data called, his voice bright with panic, "Hull breach on decks thirty-one through thirty-five!"

"Worf!" Riker paused and braced himself as yet another hit rocked the bridge; overhead, the lights flickered. "That's an old Klingon ship. What do we know about it? Are there any weaknesses?"

Worf clutched his console and held on as the ship rolled. "It is a Class D-twelve Bird-of-Prey. They were retired from service because of defective plasma coils."

"Plasma coils? Is there any way we can use that to our advantage?"

"I do not see how," Worf replied. "The plasma coil is part of their cloaking device."

"Data." Riker wheeled toward him with sudden inspiration. "Wouldn't a defective plasma coil be susceptible to some kind of ionic pulse?"

"Perhaps . . ." Data frowned, considering it, then brightened with enthusiasm. "Yes! If we sent a *low-level* ionic pulse, it might reset the coil and *trigger* their cloaking device. Excellent idea, sir."

Worf nodded, on to the idea. "As their cloak begins to engage, their shields will drop."

"Right," Riker said. "And they'll be vulnerable for at least two seconds." He glanced at the android. "Data, lock on to that plasma coil."

"No problem," Data answered, confident. He hurried over to a bulkhead, removed a panel, and began rerouting circuitry at inhuman speed.

"Worf." Riker turned to the Klingon. "Prepare a spread of photon torpedoes. We'll have to hit them the instant they begin to cloak."

"Aye, sir." Worf began to work his console.

"We're only going to get one shot at this," Riker continued. "Target their primary reactor. With any luck, their warp core should explode."

"I have accessed their coil frequency," Data called, from his supine position on the deck. "Initiating ionic pulse . . ."

The bridge reeled once more. Riker held on, bowing his head as the aft console exploded, raining smoke and debris. "Make it quick . . . !"

A moment earlier on the Bird-of-Prey's bridge, B'Etor smiled, intoxicated with triumph, at her older sister.

Soran had proved himself a worthy ally; not only had he given them a weapon of incredible power, he had also come up with the plan which would now provide them with the added pleasure of destroying the *Enterprise*. Who would dare stand up to them now? B'Etor allowed herself a fleeting daydream: Herself, white-haired and wrinkled, telling again to her kinsmen and followers the story of how she and her late sister had, with nothing more than an ancient Bird-of-Prey, destroyed the great Galaxy-class starship. . . .

The deck rocked slightly beneath her feet. She glanced over at the helmsman, who quickly reported, "Minor damage to the port nacelle. Our shields are holding."

Her smile widened. "Fire at will. . . ."

She watched with unutterable delight as the torpedoes found their target, scarring the gleaming metal of the *Enterprise*'s hull. *You were wise to tell your captain not to trust us, Commander Riker. Are you contemplating your own words now?*

Beside her, Lursa laughed softly in pure enjoyment. "Target their bridge."

"Full disruptors," B'Etor added. They had savored their advantage long enough; time now to make a clean, swift kill.

The navigator released a soft yelp, one full of such mortal surprise that B'Etor whirled swiftly in her chair, her euphoria turned abruptly to unease.

The navigator looked up at her, his eyes wide with panic. "We are cloaking!"

"What?" B'Etor gasped.

"Mistress!" the helmsman cried. "Our shields are down!"

There was no time for her to issue an order; merely to stare, stunned, at the viewscreen, which showed a pack of torpedoes streaking toward them—then to share a final gaze of stunned defeat with her sister.

The bridge shuddered beneath the blows, which came so fast and hard that B'Etor could not keep her balance, could not remain in her chair, but fell, clawing for purchase, to the deck. Around her, consoles exploded into flame, bodies flew, men screamed; and then a rumble began, deep in the ship's belly, one that grew until the deck beneath her trembled, until the very teeth in her skull chattered. She knew by instinct that the warp core had begun to implode, that there was no chance of survival. She and the ship and everyone on it would be reduced to dust.

Even so, she felt no sorrow—it would be a good death, a warrior's death—only deep frustration at having come so close to victory, and a good amount of irritation at a human called William Riker.

Riker shielded his eyes against the blinding flash on the viewscreen as the Bird-of-Prey dissolved into spinning debris.

"Yes!" Data crowed, exultant.

Riker wasted no time celebrating, but pressed his signaling comm badge.

"La Forge to bridge. Commander, I've got a problem down here. The magnetic interlocks have been ruptured. I need to get the—"

There came a hissing sound, as if the link had dissolved into faint static. Riker frowned. "Mr. La Forge . . . ?"

In the background, he heard Geordi shout, "Coolant leak! Everybody out!" There followed the sounds of people scrambling, shouting.

"Bridge!" Geordi called in a voice sharply urgent and breathless from running. "We've got a *new* problem. We're about five minutes from a warp-core breach. There's nothing I can do."

"Understood," Riker said. He hesitated—an instant, no more—then turned toward the helm. "Deanna, evacuate everyone into the saucer section. Mr. Data, prepare to separate the ship."

He moved to the captain's chair with a sense of cold unreality, and grimly pressed the control that sounded the alarm he had hoped never to hear except in drills.

Beneath the shelter of a tree, Picard paused to make sure Soran was absorbed in his work, then tossed another pebble at the stone arch. The small stone missed its mark and bounced with a glimmer off the forcefield.

Soran glanced up; Picard sat nonchalantly on a nearby rock, and waited until the scientist's attention was once again diverted—then tossed a second pebble with the determination of a child skipping stones. This one, too, was repelled by the forcefield.

He looked up to see Soran staring at him with irritation. "Don't you have anything better to do?"

He said nothing; merely waited once more until Soran returned his gaze to the launcher control panel, then threw another pebble toward the arch.

This one did not miss. The stone struck the sand, then gave a little bounce forward and rolled beneath the arch . . . *inside* the forcefield.

Picard did not permit his expression to shift, but looked up casually as the scientist finished his work at the launcher controls.

Soran stepped down from the control panel and gazed smugly at Picard. "Sure you won't come with me?"

"Quite sure."

Soran shrugged, but there was a faint wistful look in his eye. "Your choice. Now, if you'll excuse me, Captain, I have an appointment with eternity and I don't want to be late."

He turned and began to climb up the scaffolding toward the top of the rock face.

There was no time for further appeals, no time for subterfuge. Picard dropped to the ground, rolled onto his back, and wriggled headfirst beneath the arch. He expelled all the air from his lungs, used his feet and legs to press his body as hard into the sand as he could.

There was little room. He got his head through to the forcefield's other side and slipped his shoulders beneath the arch when the field flashed blindingly in front of his chin. The jolt this time was agonizingly intense; as the field crackled, he thrashed involuntarily, then stilled himself, panting, and directed his clearing gaze upward, toward the scaffolding.

A blur of black and white, Soran paused in his climbing.

Picard pushed hard with his feet and slid forward through the sand, but it was too late. Atop the scaffolding, Soran wheeled, then pulled an object from his hip.

A disruptor, Picard realized with a rush of adrenaline. He tried to roll, tried to wriggle free. But the rock trapped his feet, and held him fast as the world around him once more faded into brilliant, deadly white.

Geordi ran through the corridors of engineering on pure adrenaline. Yet despite the chaos before him—the blur of fleeing bodies, the shouts, the screaming klaxon—he heard nothing but his own ragged breath and the pounding of his heart. His mind seemed detached from his body, which operated on pure instinct; the faster he moved, the more time seemed to slow, the more he became overwhelmed by the sense of unreality.

In his time aboard the *Enterprise,* he had lived through experiences he could not have anticipated in his wildest flights of fantasy. But in spite of all the drills, of all his preparation for this terrible moment, he had never believed it could happen: never believed that he would ever see the deadly plume of white-hot gas spewing from the warp core, that he would be the last to duck beneath the emergency isolation door as it descended.

His body was cold with fear, but his mind was utterly calm, perceiving each instant with almost unbearable clarity. He saw each millimeter of bulkhead, of deck, each console as he passed with the acute awareness that he would never see it again. He had confronted his own impermanence against a backdrop of darkness, broken only by Soran's soft voice and the ticking of a watch; and he thought himself prepared now for death—but he was not prepared for the thought that the *Enterprise* herself was mortal, that engineering, the part of the ship in which he had spent the best years of his life, was about to be destroyed in a blinding millisecond. He remembered suddenly Montgomery Scott, and how the old engineer had once spoken of the grief he'd experienced after losing the original *Enterprise*. . . .

Beyond the stream of moving uniforms in front of him, a buzzer sounded as a second isolation door began slowly to descend. Geordi forced his legs impossibly faster, knowing from years of drills that he would have seconds, nineteen seconds, to make it past to the civilian corridors beyond; in his mind, he heard the ticking of Soran's watch, and the scientist's soft voice.

Time is running out, Mr. La Forge. . . .

The burst of speed caused him to step on the heel of a dark-haired fleeing lieutenant—Farrell, with whom he'd served for years, with whom he'd joked the past fifty drills or so because somehow, they'd always managed to wind up the last two to make it out of engineering. Plus there was the fact that splay-footed Farrell ran like a duck. A running joke, Farrell had called herself last time, and Geordi had grimaced at the pun.

Farrell stumbled, half turned; there was no humor in her wide, stark eyes now. At the sight of La Forge behind her, she proffered a hand, tried to pull Geordi along with her.

"No!" Geordi shouted, waving her off. "Keep moving!" The longer they took to evacuate, the more danger the saucer would be in—if it could afford to wait.

But Farrell remained until La Forge was alongside, and they ran together at full tilt, knees and elbows pumping.

The isolation door was halfway to the deck by the time they arrived. A small group of engineers crouched there, struggling through. Geordi ducked and let himself run into them, pushing them through the vanishing doorway.

They spilled out onto the civilian corridor, where a group of five-year-olds, some of them clutching hand-made brightly colored paper mobiles, were emerging from a classroom. Some of the children were saucer-eyed, somber; others wept openly as their teachers, one male and one female, tried to comfort them. Still others cried out to their parents, who scooped up their children and dashed down the corridor. The teachers, too, picked up their charges and began running; Geordi slowed long enough to grab a round-faced, almond-eyed girl clutching a stuffed bear.

She hugged him tightly as he ran. He felt something soft brush against his back, and realized, when the girl began to wail, that she had dropped the bear.

There was no time to retrieve it, no time even to gasp words of comfort. The bear was already a part of the past, of memory, like engineering; in time, the child stopped her crying and buried her wet face in his neck. Farrell ran alongside, a stunned, silent boy in her arms; behind them, a scattered trail of colored paper fluttered to the deck.

In front, one of the teachers slowed to adjust her grip on the child in her arm and half stumbled. Geordi hurried beside her, offered his free arm. "Come on! Let's go!"

The woman began again to run, making her way with the group until they came upon a small group waiting behind others to enter an open Jeffries tube. Adults were pushing children in first; one near-hysterical father called to his uncertain child, who balked at entering the tube: "Go on, Jeffie! Crawl! I'm right behind you . . . !"

In frustration, the man finally pushed his son inside, then crawled in himself. Geordi and Farrell stepped forward and put the last two children inside the tube, then helped the rest of the adults.

And then it was down to himself and Farrell, who hesitated and motioned for Geordi to go first. Aggravated, Geordi pushed her inside, then climbed in himself. He paused to manually pull shut the hatch behind him, with the acute awareness that he was closing off what would soon become the past.

As it shut with a solid, final-sounding *clank,* he hit his comm badge. "That's it, bridge—we're all out!" And he cut off the communication abruptly, before Riker could hear his shaky sigh.

On the bridge, Riker released his own small sigh of relief after hearing Geordi's message. He turned, inadvertently meeting Troi's gaze; she was watching him tensely, waiting for the next command. Beside her, Data seemed to be in control of himself—but looked like he'd be sweating if he could. He glanced up solemnly from his console.

"One minute to warp-core breach."

"Begin separation sequence," Riker told him, then turned to Troi. "Full impulse power once we're clear."

The android began to work. Riker watched the viewscreen, which revealed an aft view of the *Enterprise* as the saucer section slowly disengaged. He began silently counting the seconds, realizing with each passing instant that they were cutting it dangerously close.

"Separation complete," Data said at last. "Ten seconds to warp-core breach."

Troi fingered her controls. "Engaging impulse engines . . ."

On the viewscreen, the image of the battle section

began slowly to recede. Riker continued his silent count-down, bracing in his chair for the explosion he knew was coming.

Despite his anticipation, he flinched at the bright blaze of light as the battle section erupted. The ship shuddered; but they were all right, Riker realized with a surge of relief. The shields had held. . . .

And then the deck lurched forward, throwing Riker from his chair. He flailed, striking the back of Troi's chair with his shoulder, and wound up on all fours. He tried to push himself up to a standing position—and was immediately thrown to his knees again. With difficulty, he crawled back to his chair, trying to interpret the strange sensation. The ship felt *wrong*. She was shuddering, rolling—not the way she did under fire. It almost felt like . . . free fall.

He caught the arm of his chair and hoisted himself up. "Report!"

He turned in time to see Troi grasp the console and pull herself back into her chair. She stared down at the helm, and a look of utter alarm spread over her features. "Helm controls are off-line!"

A sudden terrible certainty seized him, made him glance up at the viewscreen. Riker was a man well suited to command, a man who had never buckled under pressure, never allowed himself an instant's hesitation in the deadliest of situations. Yet the sight on the screen left him speechless with horror.

Troi followed his stricken gaze and saw it, too: the surface of Veridian III, hurtling toward them with impossible swiftness.

No one on the bridge uttered a sound at the sight; no

one except Data, whose spontaneous, heartfelt utterance spoke for them all.

"Oh, *shit* . . ."

As he crawled through the Jeffries tube with Farrell's shadowy form in front of him, Geordi began to feel his heartbeat and breathing return to a normal rhythm.

They'd made it to the saucer; it was beginning to look like they might live after all. But he did not slow. Evacuation procedures required that they head for the most protected area of the ship and prepare for the shock wave from the warp-core explosion.

It all depended on how much distance they managed to put between themselves and the battle section. Geordi tried to remember how long it had been since they had evacuated engineering. Three minutes? Four?

He had his answer as the tube vibrated beneath him and pitched to the right, causing him and everyone inside it to fall onto their sides and slide. It lasted a split second, no more.

Thank God, Geordi almost said, thinking it was over—that they had made it through the worst of it.

But before he could get the words out of his mouth, the ship lurched again—in a strange, accelerating movement that did not ease, only shuddered, harder and harder.

"What the *hell* . . . ?" In the dimness, Farrell's profile turned toward him.

He knew at once, with sickening, heart-stopping certainty, what had happened: The blast had slammed the ship into the nearby planet's orbit. There was a chance, if the Klingons' attack hadn't damaged the lateral thrusters, that parts of the saucer might survive the impact. Even so, many would die—and there was no way to predict who those might be.

Time is running out, Mr. La Forge. . . .

Wails and panicked murmurs rippled through the tube as those inside froze in horror; a child began to shriek. Geordi summoned the mental image of Picard at his most authoritarian, then thundered, "Keep going!"

Slowly, the dark figures in front of him began moving again. Within seconds, he was grasping Farrell's hand and emerging from the tube into the brightly lit corridor. The ship was rocking, vibrating so hard by this time that he had trouble keeping his balance; it felt like standing on the holodeck version of the nineteenth-century sailing ship—in the middle of a typhoon.

Somehow, he managed to stay on his feet, to direct the tide of moving bodies down the corridor. Before him, the two teachers hurried, crouching over their young charges, arms spread like sheltering wings, pushing them along. Geordi found the hand of the dark-haired girl who had lost the bear and ran to the front of the group, shouting directions.

"Over here!" He waved toward the nearest officer's quarters. "This way!"

He reached the entrance first and paused to let go of the little girl's hand; a teacher clasped it and hurried past, to the safety of the living room, where she braced herself and the children with her against the carpet and bolted furniture. Geordi remained in the doorway, pushing bodies through, gesturing for those still in the corridor to hurry inside. Farrell joined him and began to help directing traffic.

"Sarah!" A desperate-eyed father swooped upon a weeping golden-haired child just before she was shoved inside the quarters, and carried her away.

Geordi and Farrell kept working until all the corridor was clear, then ran inside themselves to huddle with the crowd of adults and children. Geordi fell onto the nearest spot of bare carpet, and found himself staring over at the glistening, tear-filled eyes of the teddy-bear girl, who lay beside him. Her face was flushed, damp, her dark, straight hair tousled; but it was the misery in her dark eyes that filled Geordi with a compassion that made him forget his own fear and see only hers. He reached for her small, dimpled hand, leaned close to her ear so that she could hear him above the klaxons and the shuddering ship. "It's all right. It's going to be all right. Just hang on and don't let go. . . ."

"My mommy," she whimpered. "I don't know where she is. . . ."

"Where does she work?" Geordi asked.

"Engineering."

"Then she's okay." He patted her silken hair. "Everyone made it out of engineering. I made sure of it."

"But where *is* she?" Tears spilled onto her full cheeks. "I couldn't find her. . . ."

"I bet I know where she is," he said, and almost smiled at the sudden hope on her face. He stroked her hair once more. "Somewhere nearby, worrying about you."

"Are we going to die?" she asked suddenly, with such matter-of-factness that he was taken aback.

"No," he said, feigning confidence. "This is the safest part of the ship. It's going to be all right."

It was a lie, of course; whatever happened would *not* be all right. But there was nothing more he could do to help the children or himself; they were all entirely at the mercy of forces greater than themselves. His fear gave way to acceptance. He settled down onto the soft, shuddering carpet with a deeply weary sigh, and waited.

TWELVE

☆

On the bridge, Deanna Troi pressed her upper body against the shaking helm console and gripped the edges with all her strength to keep from being thrown forward. The ship's rocking had become so intense that she clenched her jaw to keep her teeth from chattering. Yet she felt oddly calm, detached; the dizzying sight of Veridian III rushing toward them evoked a terror so primal that it was entirely physical. Her skin was cold, damp, her pulse racing like the ship—but her mind was too numbed to register fear.

Save for the screaming red-alert klaxon and the rumbling of the ship, there was silence; all on the bridge waited as Data worked his console in an attempt to slow the *Enterprise*'s momentum. It was, Troi knew, the difference between annihilation and survival, and the tension in the android's face reflected that. She pushed herself up far enough to study his shifting expression. It was like focusing in on everyone's emotions: fear, repressed panic, determination, faint hope . . .

She glanced behind her at Worf, who did not allow himself to meet her gaze. Troi understood; she sensed no fear emanating from the Klingon, only resolve to meet death bravely, and a stirring of pride. If death came, it would be an end fitting for a warrior. He would waste no time in remorse—but Troi could not help feeling disappointment that there might be no more time for them.

She turned her head then, and shared a look with Will. At the sight of her face, he allowed his command demeanor to soften for a fleeting instant. She did not quite smile; she could read his expression so well that it was hardly necessary to read his emotions. There was regret in his eyes, and a light that said he would have liked to have had the time to prove Picard's vision of the future wrong.

That future certainly seemed wrong now, in the face of one that said they might all die together. Impact would pulverize the ship unless something could be done to ease it. Yet that future, too, seemed wrong.

Data looked up from his console at last, and the faint trace of relief on his fear-stricken face gave her an inkling of hope.

"I have rerouted auxiliary power to the lateral thrusters," he called to Riker. "Attempting to level our descent . . ."

"Will it be enough?" Riker shouted.

"Uncertain, sir. The thrusters have sustained minor damage. There is no time to assess it and attempt repairs. I estimate a forty-percent chance that they will fail. . . ."

"And sixty percent that they'll hold. I'll take those odds." Riker leaned to one side, struggling to hold on with one hand while the other pressed the comm control. "All hands brace for impact!"

Troi glanced up for one final look at the viewscreen,

and recoiled in surprise. Veridian III's green and blue surface could no longer be seen—only lavender sky.

She leaned forward onto her console. The ship's shuddering increased until she could no longer think, could scarcely even draw a breath—could only hold on blankly, mindlessly, as around her, consoles erupted into flame. . . .

At a sudden, high-pitched screaming, she tried to raise her head; gravity pressed it back down. She pressed one cheek against the console and turned her face in the direction of the shriek—an almost humanoid cry.

Amid the vibrating, smoking blur that was the bridge, she saw the scream's source: a far bulkhead crumpling, like paper being slowly crushed. It was the sound of metal buckling, of the ship screaming. She looked at the viewscreen and saw a jumble of green and brown.

The jolt began at her feet, as intense, as icy-hot as lightning, and spread upward to her skull. Impact, she realized, and at the second the thought occurred to her, it was almost instantly blotted out, shaken loose from her stunned brain and replaced by darkness as she hurtled up and forward, toward the screen. . . .

Soran raised his disruptor and squinted at the cloud of dust and smoke rising from the collapsed rock archway where Picard had wriggled beneath the forcefield. The scientist jumped down a level, weapon ready, his mind full of fury; there was no time to deal with distractions! He should have killed the human outright, when he first came, to save himself the annoyance now.

But no, you had to be softhearted. And why? You'll soon have the blood of two hundred thirty million on your head. . . . What's one more?

A breeze stirred, dispersing the haze to reveal a scorched hole gouged in the earth where the captain had lain.

But no Picard. . . .

Frustrated, Soran peered around him at the shifting wisps of smoke. No sign of the captain. . . .

But the sky above his head glimmered, with a sudden, distantly familiar splendor that made Soran catch his breath and look up.

A snake of brilliant rainbow light thrashed across the sky, so bedazzling him with its promise, its beauty, that his wide eyes filled at once with tears.

No time. There was no time to search for Picard, no time to do anything save scramble up the scaffolding and prepare himself for escape from this temporal hell.

Soran climbed, eyes blinded by the ribbon's blazing glory, by tears. His heart, once heavy at the thought of the deaths of Veridian IV's inhabitants, of Picard, of those aboard the *Enterprise,* now seemed light, absolved of any wrong by the coming wonder of what he was about to embrace.

Leandra . . .

What was the Terran parable? A jewel, a pearl of great price. Worth anything, everything, to possess. Surely he, above all others, understood the tale. The nexus was worth any number of lives; who could put a price on eternal paradise? He smiled thinly as he pulled himself up onto the next highest peak, and stepped quickly onto the narrow metal scaffolding that bridged two plateaus.

Soon; soon he would be with Leandra, and as he pulled out his pocket watch—the only tangible remnant he had of her in this hellish universe—he stared into its blank, crystalline face and instead saw hers.

Halfway across the scaffolding, he glanced up, startled —not into his dead wife's face, but Picard's.

With pure, mindless instinct, Soran raised the disruptor to fire, but Picard moved faster, with a desperation that came close to matching Soran's own vicious need. The captain seized the wrist of the hand that held the disruptor and smashed it fiercely once, twice, three times against the cool metal railing, until Soran's own hand betrayed him and surrendered its grip. The disruptor hurtled downward, coming to rest several meters below.

Soran never noticed what became of the watch; rage and hatred and desire galvanized him. He had never been a man given to personal violence, but now he struck out at Picard with brutal, killing force, slamming his fist into the captain's jaw hard enough to break them both.

Again. Again. Again he struck, each time astounded to find his target still standing, and striking back.

But Picard's blows were tempered with reason, compassion; they were, Soran realized with irony, the blows of a man who was determined not to kill.

And that would be his undoing. Pity, compassion. What use did they serve in a universe intent on devouring its own children?

Soran struck out again with unrestrained fury, shrieking at the unfairness of the situation, at the implacable passage of time. His fist once again connected with the captain's jaw. This time the air rushed from the human's lungs with an audible hiss as Picard was hurled backward against the metal scaffolding.

Victory, Soran thought, and moved in for the final blow—only to stagger backward and drop to his knees when Picard lashed out with legs and feet.

And with a swift, rolling movement, the captain was standing before him again.

Soran looked at him with infinite hatred. Eighty years he had waited to get to this moment. *Eighty years* . . .

As Picard lunged at him again, Soran embraced him; together they moved in a brief, deadly dance upon the slender, shuddering scaffold. And then Soran embraced him more tightly, drawing him forward, and slammed his own forehead against the captain's.

Picard lost his balance and fell. Soran drew back, breathless at the sudden triumph, and clung to the railing as the human dropped several meters down into a sandy crevice.

Alive, Soran judged, but stunned. All fury in him evaporated at once, replaced by a dawning euphoria.

He gazed up at the ribbon of light crackling through the sky—a great serpent, but one that would lead *to* paradise—and listened to the distant hum of the launcher as it prepared to send the probe to its final destination.

Seconds now. Only seconds.

Leandra, my darling . . .

Soran moved swiftly across the bridge toward the higher platform he had placed with infinite care, at the precise spot the ribbon would intersect Veridian's mountains.

Movement beneath him: He glanced down to see Picard lift his head and gaze up at the coming splendor. The captain stirred feebly, then sagged once more, while beneath them both the launcher whirred as the probe slid into position.

There came a sudden roar as the probe thundered, like a great sleek black bird, into the sky.

Out of time, Picard. You, me, the universe . . . we've all run out of time . . .

Soran stared after it, speechless with joy.

* * *

Picard stared after it, too, kneeling in the sand beside the launcher. The probe arced in a perfect trajectory upward, toward the shining sun; Picard shaded his eyes and watched until it disappeared from view, then pushed himself slowly to his feet.

He did not intend to die on his knees.

Bitter enough to face his own death, so close to the loss of Robert and René; but to know that he had failed his crew, who might be caught by the coming shock wave, and two hundred thirty million unknowing souls on the next planet . . .

Overhead, the sky faded to the odd, faux-twilight gray of a solar eclipse. The trees surrounding them, which had rustled with animal life, went abruptly silent; a solitary bird released a tremulous cry that echoed off the nearby mountains, then fell quiet. As Picard stood gazing upward, Soran reclimbed the scaffolding against the backdrop of darkening sky, streaked with jagged, writhing energy. Once atop the pinnacle, the scientist raised his face toward the heavens; the glow from the ribbon lit his features, revealing the ecstatic, beatific expression of a saint.

In the gathering gloom, the wind picked up quickly and began to whip up dust. The ribbon neared, illuminating the plateau with unearthly light, filling the air with a strangely electrical charge, one that smelled of a recent lightning strike, one that made the hair on the back of Picard's neck rise. He instinctively backed away until his back pressed against the scaffolding.

There was nowhere to run, nowhere to flee. He shut his eyes, grimacing at the airborne sand that stung his face, at the piercing crackle of the ribbon, at the light so dazzling, so colorful, it pained him despite his closed eyelids.

And then the ribbon intensified beyond all human capacity to bear; he cried out in agony at its deafening roar, its sheer brilliance, its blinding beauty.

And just as suddenly, there was no Picard, no Soran, no Veridian, no self or other. Only darkness . . .

Deanna Troi inhaled a lungful of smoke and coughed, then winced at the sudden spasm in her ribs. The sharpness of it helped clear her head; she stirred, and realized that she had been thrown from her chair and now lay atop the console, with her arms and shoulders dangling over. Data sat slumped forward over the navigation console beside her, his hands still gripping her legs; obviously, he had kept her from flying into the viewscreen. Her movement seemed to revive him; he straightened, released his hold, and helped her from the console.

"Counselor? Are you all right?" Data seemed unharmed, but his hair was tousled, his eyes wide with shock.

She nodded, even though her legs trembled beneath her, and grimaced at another stab of pain in her rib and the complaints issuing from torn muscles in her shoulders. Blessedly, the ship was silent and still, the ground beneath her feet solid.

The bridge was veiled in smoke from smoldering consoles but, strangely, no longer as dark. She squinted at the glare, and realized that rays of light filtered through the haze. At first she thought that auxiliary lighting had miraculously been restored; and then she gazed upward, beyond the layer of smoke, at the sunlight shining through the shattered dome above the bridge. As she watched, two birds perched on the edge and stared down at those below.

"I think we've landed," Troi whispered—to no one.

Data had already moved off and was helping others to their feet. She turned and saw Worf behind her, pushing himself to a sitting position on the deck; clearly, he had been thrown over the tactical console.

And then she saw Riker, lying faceup and motionless on the deck near the overturned command chair. His head was cocked at an odd angle, his eyes open and staring blankly up at the shattered dome.

"My God—Will!" She ran to him, seized by the dreadful certainty that he was dead, and fell to her knees.

"I'm all right," he croaked. "Just enjoying the view . . ." He sat up slowly, gingerly. "Report . . ."

Data emerged from the haze, with Worf beside him. "All systems are off-line, sir," the android said. "I do not know how the rest of the ship has fared. But there are no casualties on the bridge. Only minor injuries."

"Good," Riker said. He reached for the back of the overturned command chair and, ignoring Data and Troi's offers of assistance, pulled himself up. "Evacuate the bridge and organize all able-bodied personnel into search-and-rescue parties."

"Aye, sir." Data turned and headed for the emergency exit; Worf and Troi followed . . . and paused as the sunlight faded, and the bridge began to grow ominously dark.

Sunset, she thought swiftly; perhaps it was only the approach of night. But the darkness descended too suddenly, unnaturally, and as she hesitated, the ground began to rumble beneath her feet.

"Soran," Will whispered, with such defeat, such bitterness that it stole Troi's breath.

The shock wave, she realized. Soran had succeeded in launching the probe. They had endured the crash and survived, only to be killed in the shock wave.

"So," Worf said quietly beside her. "The captain was right; the future *is* changed." He paused. "It is not a dishonorable way to die." He turned to Troi and said, even more softly, "If you are to die, I am glad to die with you."

"Same here." Riker forced a smile, but his eyes were hollow. "I wonder if the captain . . ." He let his thought trail, unfinished.

She tried to return his smile, to look into the eyes of her friends one last time, and could not; the darkness grew, shrouding his face and Worf's until she could see them no more, until the bridge was veiled in blackness.

The rumbling grew until it felt like a mighty earthquake. She staggered, reached out and clutched Worf's arm to steady herself. He put it around her and held her tightly.

"But this isn't right," she said suddenly, with inexplicable conviction—the same conviction she had felt when Picard had told her his experience of the future: her death, and the years of enmity between Worf and Will. She had known in her heart that that future would not, could not come to pass.

Just as certainly now, she knew that this future was simply *wrong,* that she and the *Enterprise* crew had never been meant to die together like this. . . .

"It's not right." Her words were swallowed up in the shock wave's deafening roar. The earth swelled like a wave, pitching her and Worf to the deck.

"It's not right," she repeated, even as the ship around them began to vibrate and the ground beneath grew hot. It was her last thought, even as the bulkheads around her began to glow and her uniform burst into flame.

It's not right
It's not right
It's not right. . . .

THIRTEEN

☆

Darkness. Picard drew in a breath and gathered himself; for a moment of dizzying disorientation, he could not remember who he was, where he had come from. Soran, Veridian III, the energy ribbon—the memories seemed as distant to him as an ill-remembered dream.

Most disorienting of all, he did not know where he was. He was not blind; his vision was obscured by what felt to be a simple cloth blindfold, which he could not remove because someone—with a warm, gentle touch—held his arms.

Smaller hands tugged at his uniform at the waist, at the knees, leading him slowly across thick carpet. He knew at once by the smell, by the feel of the floor beneath his boots that this was not the *Enterprise.*

Yet he felt as comfortable here as there; perhaps more so. Despite his confusion, he felt no fear.

A heavy door creaked open, releasing with it a waft of scented air. Picard filled his lungs with it, savoring, identifying: Pine. Nutmeg. Apples. Cinnamon. And a smell he had not experienced since his childhood: A roasting goose. . . .

He was guided forward a few more steps; then, abruptly, the hands released him. He paused, wavering.

"What's going on? Where am I?" There was no indignation in his question, only curiosity.

A tug at the back of his head. The blindfold dropped. Picard blinked at the kaleidoscopic blur of color and light as his surroundings came into focus.

It was a large, high-ceilinged family room, twenty-fourth-century French from the looks of it, and in its center was a huge Christmas tree asparkle with light. Picard gaped in pleasure. Clustered beneath the tree—which towered at least a meter above him—lay presents of every conceivable size and shape, wrapped in gleaming gold and red and green foil. Branches of fresh holly garlanded the wooden staircase banisters and the stone mantel above the hearth, where a decorated Yule log blazed.

And in the midst of this holiday splendor, five children stood, smiling and expectant, their bright gazes all focused on him.

Picard looked at each of them with wonder. These children were strangers; he had never seen them before, and yet . . . he knew them. Two girls and three boys, each of them staring lovingly back with *his* eyes, his chin, his smile . . .

Here was Olivia, the eldest at thirteen, grown suddenly tall and willowy this past year; and here was Matthew, just seven, still chubby-cheeked, with his mother's brilliant mind for mathematics. And here was Madison, aged ten, with his father's dark hair and love of military history, and Thomas, his twin—and Mimi, the baby at five, the much-adored apple of her father's eye.

He stared at them in awe and realized that this was *his*

home, these were *his* children, and that he loved each of them with an intensity and tenderness he had never before known.

"Go on. . . ."

A soft voice at his elbow took him aback. He whirled, and saw his gentle captor—golden-haired, straight, slender—smiling at him with the same indulgent love in her green eyes.

He had never met her; yet he knew that this beautiful creature was Elise, his wife of the past sixteen years. And she had spoken to him in French.

"Say *something*," Elise urged, with fond impatience, and rested a hand lightly upon his shoulder. "They're waiting."

He released a breath, overwhelmed, and then a soft, uncertain laugh. "I . . . I don't know what to say. . . ."

Olivia—known, for good reason, Picard knew, to her brothers as "Bossy"—spoke up. "Say Merry Christmas, Papa!"

"Merry . . ." He faltered as his gaze swept around the room. ". . . Christmas . . ."

The youngest, Mimi, let out a cry of pleasure and began to applaud. The other children followed suit; Elise leaned over and kissed him gently on the cheek. Dazed, he let her lead him to a large, overstuffed chair—a respectable copy of Robert's chair at the family estate, the one he never permitted anyone else to sit in, not even René . . . and certainly not his brother, Jean-Luc. Picard had privately sworn to himself that, when he retired, he would have a similar chair made, and put in his living room.

And here it was.

He settled into it with a satisfied sigh—it was every bit

as comfortable as he had imagined—and watched as the children dashed over to the tree and began noisily distributing presents.

This one's for you. . . .

Where's mine?

I hope this is the book I asked for. . . .

Take this one to Papa. . . .

Contentment covered him like a blanket. He shared a blissful look with Elise, then gazed back at the bustling, laughing children with a sense of such complete joy that a smile spread, unbidden, across his lips.

Little Mimi bounded over to him, her round face flushed, her long golden curls bouncing, and put a dimpled hand upon the arm of his chair. "Isn't the tree *beautiful,* Papa?"

Picard reached out and stroked her impossibly soft hair. "Oh yes," he answered, surprised at how easily—how naturally—the words came to him, at how utterly natural it all seemed, as though he had spent every moment of the last sixteen years in this house with this woman, as though he had loved this child from the day she was born. "Yes, it's astonishingly beautiful. All of it."

As he spoke, the other children gathered round; Matthew, standing with almost military stiffness, produced a beribboned package from behind his back and handed it to his father. "This is from all of us."

"Thank you," Picard said, with genuine sincerity. "I can't imagine what it is. . . ."

He pulled off the ribbon, tore away the paper wrapping, and opened the box. Inside, cradled in tissue, was a curved instrument of gleaming polished brass. Picard lifted it carefully and held it to the light. It was a beautiful piece, one that had been used by some nineteenth-century sailor to navigate by the stars; no question of it. A grin of pure delight spread slowly over his lips.

"It's a sack-tent!" Thomas cried excitedly.

Picard chuckled. "You mean a *sextant.* And it's a handsome one at that . . . from about eighteen-twenty, I'd say. Wherever did you find it?"

Mimi tilted her head coyly. "It's a secret."

"Oh, a *secret.*" Picard's smile grew conspiratorial. "Well, that makes it a *doubly* special gift." He shared a look with each child. "Thank you. Thank you all. . . ."

Impulsively, Mimi crawled into the chair and hugged his neck. The others swarmed in to bestow what hugs and kisses they could manage.

Merry Christmas, Papa.

I love you, Father.

Merry Christmas . . .

Joy enveloped him, saturated him, so completely that it seemed tangible, something he could reach out and grasp hold of. . . .

It was like being inside joy. As if joy were a real thing that I could wrap around myself. . . .

Guinan's image flashed in his mind. They had been talking long ago, in some other universe, about someone, about . . .

Soran.

He pushed the thought away immediately, forced himself to return to the present, to the love and happiness that surrounded him.

Mimi scrambled from his lap and hurried with the

others back toward the sorted piles of presents. Smiling at the scene, Elise stepped beside the arm of his chair.

"I'll go get dinner ready. They'll be starving in a minute." She turned, then swiveled her head to speak over her shoulder. "Besides, Robert and the others are due any second."

Picard glanced up sharply. "Robert . . . ?"

She gave him a mildly curious look. "Of course. It wouldn't be Christmas without one of your brother's famous *buche de Noel*s."

Sudden tears stung his eyes; he blinked them back, swallowed hard, found his voice. His heartbeat quickened with abrupt anticipation. "And René. Will he and . . ." He paused, marveling at the memories that came from some mysterious place outside his own recollection. ". . . Katya be coming?"

Yes, Katya. That was her name; a tall, red-haired young woman with striking Asian features. He had attended their wedding two years before; Mimi had been flower girl.

"Of course. Marie says they have a surprise they'll be sharing with us."

Mimi glanced up from the mound of shredded Christmas wrapping at her feet. "A surprise? More presents?"

Elise directed a grin at her daughter. "Oh, they'll bring presents, young lady, don't you worry. But the surprise . . . I'm afraid you'll have another eight months or so before you get to play with that one." She shot Picard a knowing smile and wink before leaving.

He settled back into his chair and watched the children playing with their new toys. The pleasure was intoxicating; he wanted nothing more than to sit and revel in this scene for the rest of eternity. Everything his gaze rested on brought delight; there was Mimi enjoying the interactive handheld encyclopedia he had chosen for her, and wrapped with care. There, too, beneath the tree was the tiny gold-foil box Elise had not yet discovered, the one he would present to her tonight after the children were asleep, the one that contained his grandmother's heirloom diamond pendant.

And the sparkling tree—each ornament hanging there had a history of its own. There were many priceless antique decorations from his parents' tree; Robert had finally been coaxed into parting with a few, he could see. He smiled at the reminders of his boyhood. There was the old-fashioned silvered-glass Papa Noel, with the same small chunk that had been missing from his nose ever since nine-year-old Robert had, in his excitement to get to his presents, inadvertently toppled the tree. And there were Maman's white doves, made from real feathers, with holly sprigs in their beaks.

And there . . .

He blinked and leaned forward to better see an ornament near the top of the tree, one he did not recognize. It was a hollow glass ball, lit internally by what appeared to be a tiny star in its center. As he watched, the tiny star flickered, dimmed, then darkened altogether, radiating a wave of shimmering light outward.

Picard stiffened in his chair.

The shock wave. He was safe now, but somewhere, the Veridian star had been destroyed, and hundreds of millions had died in the resulting shock wave.

Perhaps even those aboard the *Enterprise*.

The thought so disrupted the tranquil joy of his surroundings that it seemed unbearable. To escape, he rose and walked over to a nearby window. Outside, snow fell steadily, quietly, from a leaden sky, blanketing the French countryside in white. He let the sight soothe him for a time.

And then his eye caught sight of it again, reflected in the windowpane: the dying star inside the glass sphere.

He could not escape it. As much as he wanted to merge again with the sense of utter belonging, utter happiness, he could not ignore the fact that it had been purchased with blood.

Two hundred thirty million lives—because he had failed to stop Soran.

"No," he said, to the seductive tug that pulled him back toward the children, toward joy. "This isn't right. This can't be real. . . ."

"It's as real as you want it to be."

He started at the sound of a voice—a truly familiar voice, one he had known from another reality. He wheeled and saw Guinan, looking much as she had the day he had questioned her about Soran.

"Guinan . . . what's going on? Where am I?" It had occurred to him that this was a strange mental state induced by dying . . . but he was not dead. His flesh seemed to him perfectly solid.

Her answer was the one he expected. "You're in the nexus."

"This . . ." He swept his gaze over the family room. ". . . is the nexus?"

"For you," she said. "This is where you wanted to be."

He shook his head. "But I never had a wife, children, a home like this. . . ."

A knowing smile spread across her lips. "Enjoy them, Jean-Luc."

"Guinan . . ." He frowned at a sudden realization as the memory of his former life came flooding back. "What are *you* doing here? I thought you were on the *Enterprise.*"

"I *am* on the *Enterprise*. I am also here." At his puzzled look, her smile widened. "Think of me as . . . an echo of the person you know. A part of her she left behind."

"Left behind . . . ?"

"When the *Enterprise*-B beamed us off the *Lakul*, we were partially in the nexus. The transporters locked on to us . . . but somehow everyone left a part of themselves behind."

"Soran . . . ?" Picard asked.

"All of us," she said softly.

"Where is he now?"

"Wherever *he* wanted to be. . . ."

"Papa!"

Picard turned at the sound of Thomas's voice. The boy was constructing a building out of small interlocking blocks—a toy his father had played with for many happy hours as a child. "Papa, help me build my castle."

He sighed, tempted to return to the fantasy's warm embrace, but gathered himself. "In a few minutes," he said, smiling at his son.

He turned back to Guinan and said, awed, "These are my children. *My* children . . ."

She eyed them fondly. "Yeah. They're great, aren't they? You can go back and see them born . . . go forward and see your grandchildren. Time has no meaning here."

Elise poked her head in the room, then disappeared

just as quickly. "Dinner's ready! Let's go! Your aunt and uncle and cousins are here, and they're hungry!"

Happy shouts came from around the tree; toys were dropped, crumpled paper kicked carelessly aside as the children scrambled toward the dining room.

Picard glanced toward the adjacent room and caught a glimpse of shadowy figures moving toward a long table. One of them laughed—an abrupt, deep, throaty sound.

Robert. He closed his eyes, struggled to compose himself.

He was in the nexus; which meant that two hundred thirty million innocents had died. And for what? None of this was real. Robert and René were not really here, really alive. In reality, he would be assumed dead, destroyed in the shock wave. And Lursa and B'Etor might very well possess the ability to cause such massive destruction again.

The youngest boy, Matthew, lingered, and took his father's hand in his small warm one. "Papa . . . are you coming?"

Picard gazed down into his child's earnest, delicate face. A rush of tenderness overwhelmed him, filled him with a contentment, a peace beyond that induced by any drug. He turned his back to Guinan and let Matthew lead him one step, another, toward the laughter and happy voices emanating from the dining room.

On the way, they passed the tree. Once more, the flickering light inside the glass globe caught his eye.

He stopped in midstride. Matthew looked up at him, quizzical.

"Is something wrong, Papa?"

"No." Picard bent down toward the boy and rested a hand briefly, lightly on his cheek. "I'm fine, Matthew. I just have to . . . hide Maman's present so I can give it to her after dinner. Go on. Go on without me. . . ."

Matthew's hazel eyes, so like his father's, held such innocence, such loving concern that for an instant, Picard faltered, tempted.

And then he straightened, and took his hand away. Matthew bounded off into the other room.

Picard turned. "Guinan," he said with sudden urgency, "can I leave the nexus?"

She blinked, astounded. "Why would you want to leave?"

"*Can* I?"

"Yes," she allowed slowly. "Where would you go?"

He hesitated, confused. "I don't understand."

"I told you, time has no meaning here. If you leave, you can go anywhere . . . any time."

A faint smile spread over his face. "I know exactly where I want to go—and when. Back to that mountaintop on Veridian Three—before Soran put out the star. I have to stop him." He hesitated. "Only tell me before I go . . . Only a part of you is here. So you're also on the ship. If you're still here . . . then the ship is all right, isn't it? It must have outrun the shock wave."

All traces of the smile ebbed from her face; she gazed at him solemnly a time before answering, "No, Jean-Luc."

He closed his eyes again as the sound of Robert's laughter wafted from the dining room once more. When he could speak again, he whispered, "Then it's done. I'm going back."

She laid a hand gently on his forearm. "What makes you think things will be any different this time? What if you fail again?"

"You're right." He straightened, squared his shoulders. "I'll need help. Guinan—will you come back with me? Together, we could—"

"I can't leave. I'm already there, remember?"

He bowed his head in frustration, casting about for some other option, some other way; when he looked up, Guinan was smiling enigmatically.

"But I know just the guy. . . ."

"My God," McCoy breathed with delight, peering through the cracked doorway. "They're all out there, Jim. It looks like a Starfleet retiree convention."

James Kirk gazed another second through his transparent bedroom wall at the glittering view of San Francisco Bay at night. Boats twinkled as they skimmed across the water, which lay black against an indigo sky. He turned, smiling. "Spock made it?"

The doctor, his nose pressed to the crack in the door, wore the expression of kid sneaking a peek at the presents under the tree before Christmas morning. He seemed to have grown younger in recent years; grandparenthood and retirement sat well with him. His hair was still completely silvered, but the shadows beneath his eyes seemed to have eased, the lines on his brow to be less deeply etched. "He made it, all right. Sitting right up front. Scotty's there with him—and Uhura and Chekov." He crinkled his forehead, squinting. "But who's the woman sitting on his other side?"

"Woman?" Jim strode over to the doctor's side. "You're kidding. . . ."

"Tall woman. Reddish hair. You mean she's no relation?" McCoy angled aside to let Jim take a look.

He put one eye to the crack and stared. Beyond, the

spacious living room had been cleared of its usual furniture and garlanded with white roses and gardenias; a small podium had been set at one end, and in front of it stood rows of chairs—all of them occupied. It was a room he had also loved, but had never appreciated as much as this moment, when it was filled with those who were most important to him. He grinned at the sight of his friends in the front row; all of them looked as rested and content as McCoy. Even Spock, who appeared as always ageless, without a single wrinkle or strand of gray. The Vulcan sat one seat from the aisle, with Scott on one side—and the mysterious woman on the other. She was human, striking, lean and light-eyed, with a long veil of copper-gold hair that fell straight to her shoulders. As Jim watched, she leaned over and whispered something into Spock's ear; the Vulcan listened attentively, impassively, then nodded.

"I'll be damned," Jim said softly, and grinned with pure pleasure. "He asked if he could bring a friend. . . ."

"A *friend?*" The doctor pushed him aside in order to take a second look. "You mean he brought a *date?*"

"I didn't say that," Jim protested, quite unable to erase the smile on his lips—not just because of Spock and the woman, but because of everything: the fact that it was his wedding day, and he was here with McCoy, in this wonderful place. . . . "You're jumping to conclusions, as usual. Maybe she's a . . . fellow scientist."

"In a pig's eye." McCoy glanced up from the doorway and looked up at Jim with bright blue eyes—eyes happier and more mischievous than Jim ever remembered them being. He looked the way Jim felt—intoxicated with pure joy, delighted by everything surrounding him—even though each of them had only had a sip of the vintage Dom Perignon the doctor had smuggled into the room. "Never thought I'd see the day—Spock bringing a date. I'm gonna tell Carol to throw him the bouquet."

"She's not carrying a bouquet," Jim said.

"She ought to. There are enough flowers out there. She could impro—" McCoy started as the door was pushed partway open from the outside. "Well, I'll be. The preacher's finally here."

He stepped back to permit Hikaru Sulu into the room.

"Captain." Jim clasped the uniformed younger man's forearm and rested a hand on his shoulder. "It's good to see you again."

Sulu revealed a crescent of white teeth. His golden-skinned features were almost as unlined as Spock's, and his black hair had barely begun to silver. "Sorry about the delay, sir. I got held up by a little . . . company business."

"No problem." McCoy picked up his sweating champagne flute from a nearby dresser and lifted it waggishly. "We were enjoying ourselves so much we didn't care if we ever got around to the wedding part."

"Speak for yourself," Jim said.

Sulu laughed. "Well, I think we can get started when-ever we want. Everyone's all here." He paused. "Are you sure, sir, that Mr. Spock doesn't mind my performing the ceremony? I just thought—"

"You should know by now you can't insult Spock," McCoy hurried to answer, with a gleeful look at Jim. "Besides, he's got a date."

Sulu's eyebrows rose swiftly in surprise. "A *date?*"

"A *date,*" the doctor answered, at the very instant Jim corrected:

204

"A *friend.*"

Sulu glanced dubiously from McCoy's face to his former captain's. "Ah. Well . . . the universe never ceases to amaze me." He gestured toward the door. "Gentlemen . . . shall we?"

McCoy threw back his flute and took a quick gulp, then set it down with a definite *clink.*

"Let's get out there," Jim said.

He followed Sulu and McCoy out the door and over to the podium, pausing to nod at each of his friends—at Scott and Chekov, Uhura, and especially Spock, whose stoic expression dawned into the palest ghost of a smile as his gaze met Jim's. And there were his brother Sam with his wife, Aurelan, and their son, Peter, tall and bearded and looking impossibly adult in his Starfleet uniform . . . and Will Decker and his father, Gary Mitchell and his family, and two dozen other dear faces, the sight of which filled him with a joy almost impossible to contain.

He felt not even the slightest flicker of nerves, only elation as Sulu took his place beside the podium. With McCoy beside him as witness, Jim stood in front, then turned to face the assembled group—and smiled down the aisle at the sight of Carol, who emerged from the opposite end of the room.

She wore white, like the roses that lined the aisle, like the gardenia and baby's breath tucked into her hair. Her cheeks were flushed pink, her eyes radiant, shining, her arm twined around that of her escort.

In the instant before she met Jim's gaze, she laughed softly at some comment whispered in her ear, and looked up at her golden-haired witness—her escort, her son—with frank love and happiness.

For an instant, David returned his mother's gaze; and then he lifted his face and looked down the aisle at those waiting there—at Sulu, McCoy, his father.

In the brief time he had known his son, Jim had been struck by the anger that seemed permanently etched in the young man's features. David had always been intense, restless, inexplicably furious at his father.

But there was no restlessness, no anger in David's blue eyes now. He grinned and shot Jim a knowing, impish look, an affectionate look that could only be shared between two men who loved the same woman.

Then Carol looked up, and smiled. . . .

"Stop," Jim whispered, feeling a surge of heart-pounding euphoria so great he could no longer bear it. He closed his eyes. "No more. . . ."

It was, of course, the way things should have happened, the way they should have been. He could no longer remember when it had first begun, but he had learned to stop questioning it, and now freely amused himself by going back to correct the past. Every crew member he had lost was now saved, every wrong decision righted, every opportunity missed, taken. Every iota of pain he had ever caused a lover was erased, replaced by happiness.

Sometimes the woman was Carol; sometimes, Ruth. Once he had returned to the far past, to Edith Keeler, and done the impossible: spared her life, without disturbing history's flow.

Through it all, he was consumed by joy.

Though he could not remember how long ago the universe had turned magical—it could have been a year, a century, a millennium—he still had vague memories of another reality, a true, concretized past. He remembered the *Enterprise*-B, and his last few moments there, rerouting the deflector circuitry, hurrying back down the corridor. And, of course, the explosion.

When he first appeared here—wherever "here" was, for it constantly shifted—he thought himself dead, died and gone to some enigmatic heaven. After a time, he decided he had been blown into some strange temporal anomaly, courtesy of the energy ribbon.

Either way, it didn't matter. He no longer wondered; he simply accepted, and enjoyed.

"No more," he whispered, and even as he spoke, he felt the floor change beneath his feet, from soft carpet to hard-packed earth, felt the air against his skin grow bracing cold.

He opened his eyes to snowcapped mountains, vast against brilliant blue sky, and smiled.

FOURTEEN

☆

But I know just the guy, Guinan said, and Picard glanced over his shoulder and up at a shrill, sudden cry. Against a backdrop of bright, cloudless sky, a hawk circled overhead, casting a shadow of its great spread wings over the frozen ground below.

Picard breathed in cold, pristine air scented with pine as he looked back, frowning, mouth open to ask Guinan what had happened to his children, to his home—and found himself alone, in a small valley surrounded by spectacular snow-laden peaks. Earth, instinct said, yet unlike the home he had just left, this place sparked no sense of familiarity.

He folded his arms against the chill and turned slowly, taking in the entire view. Behind him, nestled against a rocky berm, stood a rustic cabin. He had begun to circle it, wondering whether he should find the front door and seek its occupants, when he heard a nearby knocking sound, emanating from around the corner of the house.

No. Not knocking. Chopping; the sound of someone chopping wood.

Picard quickly rounded the corner—and stopped

abruptly in his tracks, releasing a silent gasp that hung as mist in the cold air.

It was, indeed, a man chopping wood. A Starfleet officer in a century-old uniform, to be more precise, who had removed his outer burgundy jacket and rolled up the sleeves of his shirt in order to more comfortably wield the axe. But not just any Starfleet officer; this one had thick chestnut hair streaked with silver, hazel eyes full of quicksilver intelligence, and a broad, handsome face—a face that Picard immediately recognized from the countless holos he had seen in classes at the Academy.

"James Kirk," he breathed, not realizing until after the words were out of his mouth that he had spoken. His mind could not digest the fact that this legend was actually standing before him. But how . . . ? Kirk had died three-quarters of a century ago. . . .

Then he remembered: The *Enterprise*-B. Soran. the energy ribbon . . . Then Kirk had not actually died in the explosion, but been transported directly to the nexus, just as he, Picard, had been.

Kirk hefted the axe over one shoulder; the blade swooped down in a gleaming silver arc and split the log at his feet with a loud *thunk*. And then he paused, and raised his flushed, sweat-beaded face to study Picard with eyes full of radiant wonder.

Picard knew the look; it was the same he supposed his own face had worn, when he had gazed upon Elise and his five children around the sparkling Christmas tree.

"Beautiful day, isn't it?" Kirk's question was not an attempt at polite conversation; he gazed up at the clear sky, at the mountains, the tall evergreens with such joyous appreciation that Picard was almost caught up in the euphoria again.

"Yes. Yes, it is. . . ." He forced himself to ignore the dazzling surroundings and focused his mind on those who had died to bring him here: the crew of the *Enterprise,* and the millions on Veridian IV.

Kirk pointed cheerfully to a log on a nearby woodpile against the house. "Do you mind?"

Picard blinked, momentarily confused. "Oh . . ." He went over, retrieved the log and set it on the block at Kirk's feet.

"Captain . . ." He paused, searching for the most potent, direct words to explain himself and his need for Kirk's help, to dissolve the nexus's seductive hold on the famous captain. "Do you realize what—"

"Wait a second!" Suddenly galvanized, Kirk glanced at a point beyond Picard's shoulder. "I think something's burning!"

He dropped the axe and began to run.

Picard pivoted. Smoke was billowing out one of the house's open windows. Kirk rushed inside, leaving the back door open behind him; Picard followed, then paused in the open doorway, feeling suddenly awkward about barging into a strange house—even if that house happened to be the construct of James Kirk's imagination.

The door opened onto a kitchen—nineteenth-century American West, Picard judged, with a few twenty-third-century touches thrown in for good measure. Copper pans hung above an antique cast-iron stove, upon which rested a dented, well-worn teakettle; nearby stood an outdated computer console, upon which rested a padd and a communicator of the sort Picard had only seen in the Starfleet museum.

The source of the smoke was a large cast-iron frying

pan on the stove. Kirk reached for it, swore and yanked his fingers away, then found a nearby dishtowel. He swathed his hand in it, successfully grabbed the pan's handle and, waving the smoke away from his face, dumped the pan and its contents into the old-fashioned sink.

"Looks like someone was cooking eggs," Kirk mused to himself, then glanced up and caught sight of Picard in the doorway. He smiled. "Come on in. It's all right." He gestured at their surroundings. "This is my house—or at least, it used to be. I sold it years ago."

Picard entered, and decided to broach the matter directly. "I'm Captain Jean-Luc Picard of the *Starship Enterprise*."

As he spoke, a timepiece chimed the hour, making him think at once of Soran. Distracted, Kirk moved over to a nearby shelf and gazed in surprise at the sound's source, an antique mantel clock with a gleaming gold face.

"This clock . . ." Kirk whispered, entranced, and ran his fingers admiringly over its polished dark cherry surface. "I gave this clock to Bones. . . ." A beatific smile spread over his face as he turned toward Picard. "He said it was the best present anyone ever gave him—with the exception of his grandchildren."

"Captain," Picard said sharply, hoping to pull Kirk from his reverie. "I'm from what you would consider the future. The twenty-fourth century . . ."

Kirk gave a vacant nod to indicate he had heard, but the lure of his surroundings held his attention fast. He started at a sudden sharp bark, then broke into a wide grin as a great dane bounded through the open back door and ran toward him, tail wagging.

"Jake!" Kirk crouched down and embraced the animal, who gave his master's cheek a thorough licking, then sat and grinned, tongue lolling. "Jake, you miserable old mutt . . . how can *you* be here?" He looked over his shoulder at Picard as he scratched the dog's head. "He's been dead seven years."

Frustrated, Picard opened his mouth to speak, but another voice—a woman's, firm but playful, filtered down from somewhere upstairs.

"Come on, Jim, I'm starving. How long are you going to be rattling around in that kitchen?"

Kirk rose and turned in the direction of the sound, his lips parted in amazement. "That's Antonia," he murmured to himself. He glanced over at the stove and the scorched pan in the sink, frowning faintly as inspiration came to him. "Wait a minute. . . ."

He moved over to a drawer and pulled it open as he spoke to Picard. "The future. . . . What are you talking about? This is the *past.*" As if offering proof, he produced a horseshoe, adorned with a small red ribbon, from the drawer. "This is seven years ago. The day I told her I was going back to Starfleet."

He raised his face and looked beyond Picard, at some invisible distant memory, then stepped over to the sink and grasped the handle of the frying pan.

"These were Ktarian eggs. Her favorite." His expression dimmed, grew somber. "I was cooking them to soften the blow . . . and I gave her this." He lifted the horseshoe in his other hand.

Picard stepped forward, impatient. "I know how real this must seem to you," he said, thinking of Elise, of little Mimi, her face reflecting the glow of the shimmering tree. Seeing someone else seduced by the nexus was a revelation; now that he was distanced from his own

212

fantasy, he could see clearly now just how illusory, how false it all was. "But it's *not*. This isn't really your house. We've both been caught up in some sort of temporal nexus."

"Dill weed," Kirk replied, with sudden excitement. He pointed at the pantry to Picard's left. "There's a bottle of dill weed on the second shelf to the left, right behind the nutmeg."

And he promptly set down the horseshoe and scraped out the ruined eggs, then switched on the stove and set the pan on a flaming burner.

Picard faltered, uncertain. Recruiting Kirk was proving more difficult than he expected. He was tempted to refuse to cooperate, to insist that Kirk pay attention to him *now*—yet instinct said to be patient. He was, after all, not losing any time by playing along; Guinan had said that he could always return to the precise moment before Soran launched the probe.

He released a small sigh and fetched the dill weed, then handed it to Kirk. He paused, watching as Kirk pulled two fresh eggs from an old-fashioned refrigeration device and cracked them open on the now-sizzling skillet, then lifted a spatula from a nearby drawer and began to stir.

"How long have you been here?" Picard asked conversationally. Perhaps if he could integrate himself into Kirk's fantasy, he might meet with more success.

Kirk sprinkled dill weed over the cooking eggs. "I don't know." He frowned faintly, remembering. "I was on the *Enterprise*-B . . . in the deflector control room . . ." He broke off and handed Picard the spatula. "Keep stirring these, will you?"

He moved to a cabinet, opened it, and began setting

plates on a breakfast tray. With mild amusement at himself, Picard repressed the surge of indignation that rose at yet again taking orders from another captain, and obediently stirred the eggs.

"The bulkhead in front of me disappeared," Kirk continued casually, as though he were relating an everyday occurrence. "Then I was out here, chopping wood." He smiled. "And I've also been a few other thousand or so places since then. I could hardly believe it at first . . . but I've gotten used to it." He moved back to the stove and took the pan from Picard. "Thanks."

"History records that you died saving the *Enterprise*-B from an energy ribbon eighty years ago," Picard said. He expected a reaction at that, but the oblivious smile remained fixed on Kirk's lips.

Kirk glanced up, faintly amused, but not in the least bit distracted from his enjoyment of the moment. "So you're telling me this is the twenty-fourth century . . . and I'm dead?" As he spoke, he removed the pan from the stove and scooped the eggs onto the plates, then set a small vase of flowers onto the tray.

"Not exactly. As I said, this is some kind of . . ."

"Temporal nexus." Kirk's smile widened as he worked. "Yeah, I heard you." He set the hot pan in the sink, then turned back and frowned down at the tray. "Something's missing. . . ."

As if on cue, two pieces of toast popped up from an antique toaster on the counter. Kirk grinned at them with delight, set one on each plate and headed out of the kitchen with the tray.

Picard followed, suddenly desperate as he felt his chance slipping away. "Captain," he said, as urgently as he could manage, "I need your help. I want you to leave the nexus with me."

Kirk said nothing, merely headed through a spacious, rustic living room toward a wooden staircase. Picard kept up alongside, though it was clear that Kirk would have preferred to shake his uninvited guest.

"We have to go back to a planet called Veridian Three," he continued, "and stop a man from destroying a star. There are millions of lives at stake."

The nonchalance in Kirk's expression chilled him. The captain shrugged and said lightly, "You said history considers me dead. Who am I to argue with history?"

Picard let the anger through in his voice. "You're a Starfleet *officer,* and you have a duty to—"

Kirk stopped abruptly at the foot of the staircase and faced the other captain, his voice and expression hard. "I don't need to be lectured by you. I was out saving the galaxy when your grandfather was still in diapers. And frankly, I think the galaxy owes me one." He paused, struggling to master his indignation, lest it overwhelm the euphoria of the experience. "I was like you once," he said, and for the first time, he seemed to see—*really* see—Picard. "So worried about duty and obligations that I couldn't see anything past this uniform. And, in the end, what did it get me? An empty house." A shadow flickered over his features; he glanced toward the top of the stairs. "Not *this* time."

He brushed past his companion. "I'm going to walk up these stairs, march into that bedroom, and tell Antonia that I want to marry her. This time, things are going to be different."

And he strode up the stairs and disappeared behind a

bedroom door, leaving the younger captain to look after him.

Picard took in a determined breath and followed, hesitating only an instant at the closed bedroom door before grasping the knob and yanking it open.

He froze in the doorway. Beyond lay not a bedroom containing the mysterious Antonia, but an old barn, sunlight streaming through its wooden slats, pitchfork and shovel hanging against the opposite wall. Picard stepped forward onto the dirt floor, scattered with straw, and drew in the scent of farm animals.

In front of him stood Kirk, sans breakfast tray, looking every bit as amazed as Picard felt.

"This doesn't look like your bedroom," Picard said dryly.

"No," Kirk replied. A slow smile dawned over his face. "No, it's not. It's *better.*"

"Better?"

"This is my uncle's barn in Iowa." Kirk moved to the far end, to a group of stalls containing horses. One of them, already saddled, with a coat the color of gleaming coal, snorted in recognition as the human reached up to stroke its neck. "I took this horse out for a ride nine years ago . . . on a spring day." Inspired, he hurried to the barn door and swung it open, revealing a green, sunny landscape outside. "Just like this. If I'm right, this is the day I met Antonia."

He turned toward Picard. "This nexus of yours is very clever. I can start all over again, do things right from day one."

Kirk hurried back to the horse, swung up into the saddle, and galloped out of the barn. Picard watched the receding figures of horse and rider for only an instant—

216

then took a saddle from the wall and found a mount of his own.

This time he followed on an intelligent, cooperative steed, over rolling green countryside, riding hard to keep within sight of Kirk: across a clear-running stream, through a copse of ancient oaks, out onto a grassy plain. From a distance he watched as Kirk spurred the American saddlebreed toward a wide ravine, never once slowing pace. At the last possible instant, the horse made a beautiful, arcing leap and landed on the other side, its hind hooves barely clearing the edge.

Kirk slowed at once; then came to a complete stop and paused to gaze at the ravine behind him. He frowned, then wheeled his horse around and galloped back for a second try.

Kirk made the jump a second time; yet this time, the older captain reined his animal to an immediate stop and sat, frowning, as Picard rode up beside him.

Kirk looked once again at the ravine, his expression saddened, confused—for the first time, free of any trace of the euphoria induced by the nexus. Picard felt a stirring of hope, but remained silent as the other man sorted through his feelings.

"I must have made this jump fifty times," Kirk finally said softly. "And every time, it scared the hell out of me. But not this time. Because . . ." He paused, clearly pained by the words that followed. ". . . it's not real."

He lifted his hand to shade his eyes, and stared at something moving down a distant hill. Picard followed his gaze and saw a small, slender woman leading a horse.

"Antonia?"

Kirk nodded, wistful. "She's not real either, is she? Nothing here is . . . nothing here matters. . . ." He looked around at his surroundings with sorrow. "It's kind of like . . . orbital skydiving. Exciting for a few minutes, but in the end, you haven't really done anything. You haven't made a difference." And then his gaze fell upon Picard—and for the first time, he seemed to really see the man in front of him.

"Captain of the *Enterprise,* huh?" He shot the other man a look of pure camaraderie and did not quite grin, but the corners of his eyes crinkled.

"That's right." Picard smiled with relief, surprised that Kirk had even registered the information.

"Close to retirement?"

"I hadn't planned on it."

"Well, let me tell you something," Kirk said, with a sudden passion that told Picard he was at least seeing the *real* man. *"Don't.* Don't let them promote you, don't let them transfer you, don't let anything take you off the bridge of that ship. Because while you're there, you can make a difference."

"You don't need to be on the bridge of a starship," Picard countered firmly, grateful that at last his words were being heard. "Come with me. Help me stop Soran. Make a difference again." He paused, his own tone rising with a fervor that matched Kirk's. "You're right; nothing here is real, nothing matters. But the two hundred thirty million who died when the Veridian sun was destroyed —*they* were real. So was my crew—"

Kirk leaned forward, his expression intense. "The crew of the *Enterprise*-D?"

Picard dropped his gaze, nodded somberly. "All killed when the ship was caught in the resulting shock wave."

Kirk turned his face away, toward the woman walking down the distant hill, and was silent a long moment.

And then he looked back at Picard, and a smile spread slowly over his features. "How can I argue with the captain of the *Enterprise*?" He paused, and an amused glimmer very like the one Picard associated with Will Riker shone in his eyes. "What was the name of that planet? Veridian Three?"

"That's right," Picard said, with utter relief at the realization that he had at last succeeded.

"I take it the odds are against us, and the situation is grim?"

"You could say that," Picard allowed.

Kirk gave a small, resigned sigh. "Of course, if Spock were here, he'd say I was being an irrational, illogical human for wanting to go on a mission like that. . . ." He grinned suddenly, brilliantly. "Sounds like fun."

And he turned and went with Picard without a backward glance at the approaching woman.

FIFTEEN

―――――― ☆ ――――――

"Now, if you'll excuse me, Captain, I have an appoint-ment with eternity and I don't want to be late," Soran said.

Picard cast a swift glance at his surroundings. A millisecond before, he had been astride a horse, beside James Kirk, looking out at a gently rolling plain. Now he was once more atop the dusty plateau, seated on a rock in the shadow of a great tree, his hand full of pebbles; overhead, the Veridian sun shone down, radiating gentle warmth upon his skin.

James Kirk was nowhere to be seen.

Before him, Soran—pale face aglow with maniacal anticipation—turned and began to climb the scaffolding toward the top of the rockface.

There was no time for further appeals, no time for subterfuge—no time to peer anxiously about to see whether Kirk had indeed gone through with his decision to leave the nexus. Picard dropped to the ground, rolled onto his back, and wriggled headfirst beneath the stone arch, praying silently all the while that he would not be doomed to see history repeat itself.

There was little room. He had gotten his head through to the forcefield's other side and slipped his shoulders beneath the arch when the field flashed blindingly in front of his chin. The jolt was agonizingly intense; as the field crackled, he thrashed involuntarily—knowing that Soran would see, that the disruptor blast would be sure to follow—then stilled himself, panting, and directed his clearing gaze upward, toward the scaffolding.

A blur of black and white, Soran paused in his climbing.

Picard pushed hard with his feet and slid forward through the sand, knowing that it would be too late, preparing himself for the inevitable. Atop the scaffolding, Soran wheeled, then pulled an object from his hip.

A disruptor, Picard knew. He drew a breath, squeezed his eyes shut, and lay still. . . .

Soran raised his disruptor and squinted at the cloud of dust and smoke rising from the collapsed rock archway where Picard had wriggled beneath the forcefield. The scientist jumped down a level, weapon ready, his mind full of fury; there was no time to deal with distractions! He should have killed the human outright, when he first came, to save himself the annoyance now.

But no, you had to be softhearted. And why? You'll soon have the blood of two hundred thirty million on your head. . . . What's one more?

A breeze stirred, dispersing the haze to reveal a scorched hole gouged in the earth where the captain had lain.

But no Picard.

Frustrated, Soran peered around at the shifting wisps of smoke. No sign of the captain. . . .

But the sky above his head glimmered, with a sudden, distantly familiar splendor that made Soran catch his breath and look up.

A snake of brilliant rainbow light thrashed across the sky, so bedazzling with its promise, its beauty, that his wide eyes filled at once with tears.

No time. There was no time to search for Picard, no time to do anything save scramble up the scaffolding and prepare himself for escape from this temporal hell.

Soran climbed, eyes blinded by the ribbon's blazing glory, by tears. His heart, once heavy at the thought of the deaths of Veridian IV's inhabitants, of Picard, of those aboard the *Enterprise,* now seemed light, absolved of any wrong by the coming wonder of what he was about to embrace.

Leandra . . .

What was the Terran parable? A jewel, a pearl of great price. Worth anything, everything to possess. Surely he, above all others, understood the tale. The nexus was worth any number of lives; who could put a price on eternal paradise? He smiled thinly as he pulled himself up onto the next highest peak, and stepped quickly onto the narrow metal scaffolding that bridged two plateaus.

Soon; soon he would be with Leandra, and as he pulled out his pocket watch—the only tangible remnant he had of her in this hellish universe—he stared into its blank, crystalline face and instead saw hers.

Halfway across the scaffolding, he glanced up, startled —not into his dead wife's face, but that of a stranger.

A stranger, but somehow vaguely familiar, making Soran think he had seen his holo somewhere before. A human, hair chestnut shot with silver, wearing a Starfleet uniform Soran had not seen in almost a century. . . .

"Just who the hell are you?" Soran whispered, but he knew the answer even before a voice replied behind him:

"He's James T. Kirk. Don't you read history?"

He whirled to find Picard standing behind him—then turned back again to gape at the grinning impossibility in front of him.

Yes, this was Kirk all right: the captain who had died when the *Enterprise*-B was trapped by the energy ribbon. *Supposedly* died—but clearly, Kirk must have been transported into the nexus instead. But what was he doing here, now. . . ?

Soran knew he had a choice. He could try to pull out the disruptor and kill one of them, permitting the other to tackle him. Or he could flee and kill them one at a time.

He grabbed the metal rungs with both hands and propelled himself upward, onto the rocks. As he scrambled away, Picard said below him:

"I've got to get to the launcher; the ribbon will be here in a minute."

"I'll take care of Soran," Kirk's voice said.

The conversation between the two prompted a jolting thought: Picard had somehow been to the nexus, solicited help, knowing that he could not both reprogram the launcher and distract Soran. But how could Picard have gone to the nexus, unless . . .

Unless he, Soran, had been successful. Unless he had already found his way back to Leandra's arms. Grief pierced him as he scrabbled over rocks and sand.

He would feel no pity for either of them. They were trying to steal his very life from him, just as surely as he would now claim theirs.

Pain and madness heightened his agility and his

senses; he moved quickly, easily over the rocks, and so silently that soon he detected Kirk's stertorous, gasping breath nearby, on the other side of a giant rock.

He ran around it smoothly, pulling out his disruptor just in time to aim it cleanly at Kirk's head. The human gazed at him with greenish-brown eyes that were intense, wary, but oddly free of fear.

"Actually," Soran said, not bothering to keep the exultation from his tone, "I *am* familiar with history, Captain. And if I'm not mistaken, you're dead."

He had intended to squeeze the trigger at that moment—but at the instant the word *dead* had slipped from his tongue, his eyes had caught a blur of movement to one side.

Picard, leaping down from atop a rock.

The distraction allowed Kirk to rush Soran, who bellowed at the realization that there was no time to take aim, nothing to be done except to hurl himself backward against Picard—and send him rolling down a nearby slope.

The odds were better, but even so, the supposedly dead captain never allowed Soran the opportunity to recover and fire the disruptor. Instead, Kirk threw himself upon the scientist, coming dangerously close to knocking the weapon from Soran's hand.

Soran struggled with a madman's intensity, a madman's strength, merely to hold on to the disruptor, but this aging dead human who fought with an odd glimmer of humor in his eyes was more than a match. Soran cried out, kicked out, lashed out—and yet Kirk shook off each blow and replied with one of his own. And at last he struck Soran's chin with such force that the scientist almost fell onto the cliffs below, managing at the last instant to clutch the chain-metal railing as his lungs emptied with a hoarse rush of air. His fingers nearly lost their grip, then through some miraculous intervention, managed to clasp on to the weapon.

Yet when he attempted to raise it and fire, Kirk struck out again—this time causing Soran to stumble, and step out upon empty air.

Mindlessly, he clung to the disruptor as though it could save him and, for a brief, breathless millisecond, clawed one-handed in midair for purchase, seeing before him in the wide sky another dazzling streak: the promise of the future, lost. Then came another instant of grace as he swiped at the chains, the railing, the bridge itself, and his hands came away with a thin lifeline: a rope.

Soran fell.

As he fell, he slid down the rope, one palm and the crook of one elbow burning as they gripped the lifeline, his knees and shins and feet slamming against the hillside. Above him, Kirk and Picard and the scaffolding receded with dizzying speed.

Abruptly, Soran bore down against the rope with his knees, and came to a lurching halt; there he dangled but a second, thumping against the red rockface, disruptor still in his tenacious grip, before he realized what he had to do.

Picard and Kirk had run off the bridge and were moving down the rocks. Soran did not care if they moved toward him; his greater concern was the launcher. And so he carefully replaced his disruptor in his belt, then reached for the remote launcher control pad. Balancing his feet against stone, he pressed the appropriate control, and permitted himself a grimly hopeful smile.

* * *

Seconds earlier, as Picard approached Kirk on the scaffolding and the two of them watched Soran's strange descent, Kirk spoke with what appeared to be good-natured annoyance.

"I thought you were heading for the launcher."

"I changed my mind," Picard said. "Captain's prerogative." He did not care to admit the truth: that he had had a sudden overwhelming premonition that the legendary captain needed his help. There had still been enough time before the probe's launch, so he had yielded to instinct. Certainly, the *real* James T. Kirk would not have required help in his lifetime; then again, this was not the living Kirk, but one who had been dead some three-quarters of a century. Picard could not help thinking of him as old, *ancient,* from a bygone era, though clearly the hard-breathing, ruddy-cheeked man who stood before him, hair tousled, eyes shining, seemed as vigorous and powerful and purely *alive* as anyone Picard had ever met.

Kirk said nothing, but wore a slight, cryptic smile as the two of them moved down the hillside toward Soran —and the launcher.

And then, as Picard glanced over at him, the smile transformed into a frown: Picard quickly followed Kirk's gaze, and saw what had provoked the change.

The plateau that had borne the sleek black rocket and its launcher now stood empty.

Some distance away, dangling from the side of the rockface, Soran smiled in evil triumph, and lowered a small black device in his hand. Yet his gloating expression soon turned to one of panic as the rope suddenly gave way with an audible snap.

Still clinging to it as it undulated serpent-like above

him, the scientist slid downward, accompanied by a cascade of pebbles and soil and rising clouds of red dust. Yet Soran's luck—and the rope—held fast once more, as the end of the rope tangled then caught on the overhead trestle.

Soran came to a stop so abrupt the control fell from his hand and tumbled downward, coming at last to a clattering stop on a metal bridge spanning two steep hillsides.

"We need that control padd," Picard said, to himself as much as to Kirk; before the words left his mouth, he was running at full speed toward the bridge, with the vague realization that Kirk was beside him, matching stride for stride.

Yet as he ran, an ominous sense of danger came over Picard, the same one he had felt when first he'd tried to leave Kirk alone to fight Soran. Instinct drew his eyes back toward the rockface, and the dangling rope that had saved Soran from death.

Now the rope hung, empty.

"Captain, look!" Picard shouted, coming to an abrupt halt, and lifted an arm to point to the rope. He scowled, scanned the red rock for their foe's slender, dark form, and found nothing. "Where's Soran?"

Beside him, Kirk stopped, kicking up a small cloud of dust, and gazed up at the deserted, dangling rope. Just as suddenly, he surged forward, toward the bridge . . . and the control padd.

Picard hung back, held by a sense of foreboding and responsibility to keep watch over the man he had dragged from paradise. He raised his face and squinted once more in a strong Veridian sunlight at the unrevealing hills.

A swift, bright blaze of light dazzled him, leaving its blinding yellow imprint upon his retina; he turned, blinking as the afterimage faded, to see Soran behind them with the disruptor.

Another brilliant blast: This one struck the bridge dead center—a hand's breadth from where Kirk now stood—filling the air with the stench of scorched metal. The scaffolding groaned, then shuddered as it erupted in flames, limned by black smoke; Picard ran toward it as the other captain stumbled, then grabbed the railing as the bridge gave a deep sigh and broke in two.

Amazingly, Kirk clung fast to the edge that hung nearest Picard; beyond him, a streak of roiling energy undulated in the sky. Beneath him, a deep ravine waited ominously.

Picard moved to the edge and knelt, reaching out a hand toward the captain. Kirk was gasping, his face crimson, gleaming with sweat and smudged with soot, his legs kicking against empty air for purchase, but the determination never left his eyes. He pulled himself toward Picard and cautiously extended one hand.

Picard leaned precariously close to the abyss, reaching, straining toward Kirk's outstretched fingertips. He had not turned his back on paradise and convinced Kirk to do so as well just to fail. Only millimeters between them now. If Kirk could slide only a few millimeters, while maintaining his one-handed grip . . .

Kirk slid closer; the bridge shuddered as he did, causing him to lose his precarious hold on the railing.

In that split second before he could plummet downward, Picard reached still forward and, impossibly, maintained his balance as his hand caught the other captain's. He gave a mighty backward lurch, ignoring the screaming protest from offended arm and shoulder and back muscles.

He fell backward, but soon righted himself again to see Kirk pushing himself to his feet. Together they moved away from the scaffolding, toward level ground; a sudden play of light above them made them both gaze upward, at the jagged streaks piercing the bright sky.

"We're running out of time," Picard said, fighting a surge of despair. Yet at the instant he said it, his eye caught something to ease that despair: On the ravine's opposite side, half of the bridge still stood, suspended in midair.

And upon it lay Soran's small, black device.

"Look!" He pointed. "The control padd—it's still on the other side." A quick glance around them showed that there was no way through the impassable peaks to the bridge's other side. The only way to reach it was to climb down the dangling edge he had just rescued Kirk from . . . and jump across.

"I'll get it," Kirk said, obviously having come to the same conclusion, for he was already moving back toward the dangling bridge. "You go for the launcher."

"No," Picard countered firmly. The scaffolding's supports were clearly in danger of giving way entirely—and he had no desire to be responsible for Kirk's dying a second time. They had already come uncomfortably close enough to that. "You'll never make that by yourself. We have to work together."

He moved to turn; Kirk stepped into his path, and with a warmth usually reserved for very old friends, put his hand on Picard's shoulder and said, "We *are* working together. Trust me. Go."

Picard's first instinct was to refuse, to insist on helping

retrieve the padd—but he knew that Kirk was right: Time had grown short, and he could no longer afford the luxury of watching over Kirk to be sure the Starfleet legend came to no harm.

At the same time, he could not shake the unsettling premonition that Kirk was in mortal danger; and so he, Picard, would have preferred to go after the padd himself. But both he and Kirk knew that a twenty-third century captain was no match for twenty-fourth century technology. And so he released a barely audible sigh and surrendered to the inevitable as he said softly, "Good luck, Captain."

Kirk grinned; the act lit up his face with a brilliance that matched the writhing sky. "Call me Jim."

And as Kirk stepped back onto the broken bridge, he found himself remembering a part of his life he had not thought of in . . . eighty years, was it? It scarcely seemed that long ago, when he had wakened, sweating, from the dream of falling down the sheer rockface of El Capitan.

That's right; in reality, Spock had rescued him. But in the dream he had fallen endlessly, eternally, with no Spock, no friend, no one to save him. . . .

And the day he had been aboard the *Enterprise*-B—the day he had been oddly overcome by a premonition of his own death; the day, according to Picard, that he had indeed died—he'd experienced the same sensation.

He felt it again now, the instant his foot stepped onto the metal bridge: emotional free fall, the sheerest terror and bliss. Terror, because he knew Spock would not be there to catch him; bliss, because he was once again doing what he had been born to do—make a difference. There was no time for thought, for reflection, only for pure mindless action.

There were two hundred fifty million lives at stake—and those of a well-trained, loyal *Enterprise* crew. Surely the lives of those shipmates alone were worth the sacrifice of his; he had seen their captain, and if Picard was representative of twenty-fourth-century Starfleet, then these were exceptional individuals indeed.

What was it Spock would have said?

It is merely logical, Jim: The good of the many outweighs the good of the one.

This half of the bridge sloped dangerously downward. He took mincing half-steps, half-walking, half-sliding as he clutched the rails with both hands, his eyes fixed on the remote device, which lay on the opposite half of the broken scaffolding, the half that still remained standing.

Control padd, he reminded himself, trying to overcome the fear with amusement. *You've got to remember these things if you're going to live in the twenty-fourth century. Maybe I'll get the chance to know what Gillian felt like . . .*

I wonder if Spock's still alive?

Suddenly the sole of his boot slipped against the slick metal, and he was sliding downward, flailing frantically and shouting: "Whoa! *Whoa. . . !*" A small, noisy avalanche of sand and pebbles followed, pelting his head and shoulders, stinging his eyes.

Somehow he managed to grasp the chain railing and regain his footing, but behind him came ominous groans: the sound of bolts, which supported the scaffolding, working their way free from the rock.

And for a moment he was back on the *Enterprise*-B, his heart pounding, his breath coming in gasps, knowing that the fear did not matter. For the first time in an eternity, he felt truly alive.

And he could feel the bridge supports giving way. A glance behind him at the bolts in the rockface confirmed it; he did not have much time.

Beyond, on the other side of the bridge, lay Soran's device.

Kirk drew a breath and leaped toward the other side, thinking of anything except the gaping ravine that lay beneath him; thinking of Spock, of McCoy, of Carol and David, of Picard and those last moments aboard the *Enterprise*-B.

Astoundingly, he did not fall, but caught the very edge of the jagged metal and hoisted himself up. The bridge trembled beneath him, sagging lower, lower—but it held just enough for him to crawl toward the small black device clattering against the metal.

A shriek as metal chains and bolts snapped and gave way. The bridge lurched ominously downward. Kirk reacted with pure instinct, reaching with one hand to swipe the remote the instant before it clattered off the side and down into the abyss. With the other, he grabbed the bridge itself and held on through adrenaline's grace.

There was no time for thought, for reason, for anything other than pure inspiration. Mindlessly, he glanced down at the control in his hand and with brilliance born of necessity, found the proper control and pressed it.

Below him, safe upon the plateau, Picard rushed up onto the now-visible platform that revealed the dark probe and its launcher.

"Aha!" Kirk breathed, exultant, and grinned gently. This was what he had sought in every experience in the nexus; this was what had convinced him to leave it, and brought him here to this place and this moment, to the aid of strangers.

The bridge shuddered again, this time swinging downward, slamming him against the rockface before the failing metal gave one final agonized scream.

He held fast as he closed his eyes and told himself, *The good of the many* . . .

And when the last bolt freed itself and the last support gave way, sending him hurtling into the abyss with a thundering cascade of rocks and sand, he felt no fear, no regret, only a glimmer of gladness that a planet and starship crew were safe, and would continue without him.

And then there was silence, and the beginning of the ultimate, infinite freefall . . .

Only heartbeats before, Picard had dashed up onto the launcher platform and gone to work; he had not dared to look back at Kirk's precarious situation. He could only feel a surge of deep gratitude and pray that, somehow, the bridge would hold and the captain would find a way to cling to it . . . and that he, Picard, could avoid Soran and his disruptor long enough to reprogram the launcher.

He had heard the distant sound of tumbling rocks and screeching metal; still, he could not permit himself to look up from his task. The control panel was labeled in utterly alien hieroglyphics—El Aurian perhaps—and a half-dozen screens displayed meaningless visuals and graphics. He had no choice but to start randomly pressing controls.

The main screen flickered, changed to an image of the Veridian sun, caught in the center of a crosshair. He kept touching controls; the image changed again, again, to distant stars, to the roiling sky—and at last to the image of the rocket itself, encased in its launcher.

This was the key.

With a thrill of exhilaration, Picard drew in a breath and began testing other controls.

"Picard!"

Soran's shrill voice echoed off the surrounding cliffs. At the sound of it, Picard forced himself not to look up for a half-second, forced himself to keep his eyes on the screen and find the command he sought. He could not read the script, but he understood the visual graphic well enough: It showed two large forcefield locks encircling the rocket.

He selected the command in a half-second, no more, then glanced up to see Soran striding swiftly toward him over the rock-strewn clay, arm extended, disruptor aimed at Picard's heart.

"Get away from that launcher! *Now!*"

Picard lifted his hands and backed carefully away, then turned and leaped from the platform as Soran approached.

He took cover behind a rock and watched as the scientist climbed up to scowl at the launcher control panel.

Soran hunched over the launcher panel as, overhead, bolts of prismatic lightning streaked through the blue Veridian sky.

Not long. It would not be long now—only seconds away from Leandra and the children, so long as Picard had not, in his moralistic idiocy, altered the rocket's course.

With the trembling fingers of one hand, he pressed the control and stared uncomprehendingly at the message that appeared on the screen:

Locking clamps engaged.

In disbelief, he gazed up at the sky, at the promise of paradise, lost. The ribbon was here *now,* and the time for the probe to be launched was *now,* not two seconds from now, or five, the time it would take him to correct Picard's intrusion.

Leandra . . .

He would join her, yes—but not in the manner he'd hoped.

He thought of the watch she had given him, ticking relentlessly against his heart.

Out of time, my darling. You and I are out of time . . .

Zero hour. The rocket strained to launch against its restraints. Soran knew full well what was coming, yet refused to yield to instinct, to fling himself from the platform. Instead, he held fast to the panel, embracing the explosion when it came to take him out of time . . .

Leandra . . .

Heat. Pain. Blazing white. And then the darkness . . .

Overwhelmed by grief and remorse, triumph and exhilaration, Picard knelt beside Kirk's body. The bridge had plummeted into the ravine, and the captain had been buried beneath the resulting avalanche of metal and stone; now he lay motionless beneath a large rock, his face pale, his lips stained with blood. Picard hastened to move away stones and fragments of twisted metal; although it was too late to help, the least he could do was give Kirk a burial befitting a hero.

The legendary captain was finally, truly dead. The fact

filled Picard with strange sorrow; despite the fact that he had always relegated James Kirk to the past, despite the brevity of their encounter, he felt a deep kinship with the man.

And then Kirk's eyes flicked open; he drew a ragged, hitching breath.

"Did we do it?" he whispered. "Did we make a difference?"

"Oh, yes." Picard released a sigh that caught in his throat. "We made a difference. Thank you."

"Least I could do . . . for the captain of the *Enterprise.*" Racked by a spasm of pain, he coughed, a deep gurgling sound emanating from his lungs. Fresh blood flecked his lips. Yet before Picard could urge him to remain quiet, he continued, a weak smile playing at his lips. "It was . . . fun."

He stared sightlessly up at the sky, a pane of sunlight illuminating his features. All suffering seemed suddenly to leave him; his expression grew reflective, peaceful. In the distance a lone bird burst into song.

And then the faint smile abruptly vanished, replaced by a look of infinite amazement, infinite wonder. "Oh *my,*" he whispered, eyes wide.

Picard glanced up at the sky, expecting to see a rescue craft or some equally inspiring sight—but there was nothing overhead save blue sunlit sky.

When he looked down again, Kirk had gone.

Deanna Troi inhaled a lungful of smoke and coughed, then winced at the sudden spasm in her ribs. The sharpness of it helped clear her head; she stirred, and realized that she had been thrown from her chair and now lay atop the console, with her arms and shoulders dangling over. Data sat slumped forward over the navigation console beside her, his hands still gripping her legs; obviously, he had kept her from flying into the viewscreen. Her movement seemed to revive him; he straightened, released his hold, and helped her from the console.

"Counselor? Are you all right?" Data seemed unharmed, but his hair was tousled, his eyes wide with shock.

She nodded, even though her legs trembled beneath her, and grimaced at another stab of pain in her rib and the complaints issuing from torn muscles in her shoulders. Blessedly, the ship was silent and still, the ground beneath her feet solid.

The bridge was veiled in smoke from smoldering consoles but, strangely, no longer as dark. She squinted at the glare, and realized that rays of light filtered through the haze. At first she thought that auxiliary lighting had miraculously been restored; and then she gazed upward, beyond the layer of smoke, at the sunlight shining through the shattered dome above the bridge. As she watched, two birds perched on the edge and stared down at those below.

"I think we've landed," Troi whispered—to no one. Data had already moved off and was helping others to their feet. She turned and saw Worf behind her, pushing himself to a sitting position on the deck; clearly, he had been thrown over the tactical console.

And then she saw Riker, lying faceup and motionless on the deck near the overturned command chair. His head was cocked at an odd angle, his eyes open and staring blankly up at the shattered dome.

"My God—Will!" She ran to him, seized by the

dreadful certainty that he was dead, and fell to her knees.

"I'm all right," he croaked. "Just enjoying the view . . ." He sat up slowly, gingerly. "Report . . ."

Data emerged from the haze with Worf beside him. "All systems are off-line, sir," the android said. "I do not know how the rest of the ship has fared. But there are no casualties on the bridge. Only minor injuries."

"Good," Riker said. He reached for the back of the overturned command chair and, ignoring Data and Troi's offers of assistance, pulled himself up. "Evacuate the bridge and organize all able-bodied personnel into search-and-rescue parties."

"Aye, sir." Data turned and headed for the emergency exit; Worf and Troi followed.

In midstride she hesitated, dizzied not by the physical aftershock from the collision, but by the mental ghost of a separate present. Reality wavered; in her mind's eye, the bridge abruptly darkened.

The shock wave, she thought, with sudden swift panic, hearing in her imagination a silent rumble, and raised her face toward the shattered dome.

Birds warbled, basking in the warm sunlight; the sky was bright and still. She drew a breath and shuddered, releasing the phantom image and the fear. For some incomprehensible reason, she felt as she had when the captain had first told her grimly of a future which excluded her: that she had been given a second chance at life.

"Deanna?" Will took a step toward her, his smoke-smudged brow furrowed. "Are you all right?"

Worf and Data stopped, turned to look back at her.

She gazed at them, seeing the concern in their eyes, in

Will's, and was overwhelmed with gratitude to be alive and surrounded by the friends she loved; overwhelmed by the preciousness of the moment.

"Yes," she answered softly, when at last she found her voice, and smiled. "Yes, Will . . . everything's just fine."

Kirk he buried beneath the shade of an ancient tree, in a spot with a view of the jungle and the sky. By the time he set the last rock atop the captain's grave, that sky had reddened, and deepened to purplish twilight; against the tree- and mountain-studded horizon, the flaming Veridian sun had slipped low, its streaming rays painting the graves' white stones tiger-lily orange.

The long task done, Picard retrieved Kirk's command insignia pin from his pocket and set it reverently at the head of the grave.

In the first moment he had realized Kirk was dying, he had felt almost unbearable guilt; it was he who had urged Kirk to give up eternal happiness in the nexus in exchange for death. Yet he knew, from meeting the captain, that Kirk would have chosen no other course.

And Kirk's sacrifice, offered so cheerfully, so easily, had freed Picard from any lingering desire to return to Robert and René, and his fictional wife and children. He recalled the anger on Guinan's face:

I didn't want to leave. . . . All I could think about was getting back. . . .

But as he stood at attention in front of James Kirk's grave, staring into the striking Veridian sunset above the darkening landscape, he felt only relief to have escaped back to reality. Kirk had understood; such an existence would have been meaningless in the extreme. Eternal, yes; real, no. And while life outside the nexus was a temporary, fleeting phenomenon, did that not give each moment more value, more poignancy?

Picard stood several moments in the cooling air, reflecting on the debt he and millions of others owed James Kirk. And then he lifted his gaze overhead at the sound of a droning engine, and spied something pale and blinking streaking through the deepening sky.

The *Enterprise* shuttlecraft. It settled gracefully, softly in a clearing at the far end of the mountaintop, without stirring up dust. Picard strode quickly past trees to meet it, and arrived just as the hatch slid open to reveal Worf and La Forge.

Worf jumped out first, narrowing his eyes at the growing dusk to study his commanding officer. "Captain, are you all right?"

"Yes," Picard said wearily.

"What about Dr. Soran?" La Forge asked, lingering in the doorway.

Picard hesitated, thinking of the two graves behind him, hidden by trees and brush. No doubt in the future he would report the precise details of what had occurred to him here on the plateau, and in the nexus, with James Kirk and Soran . . . but at the moment, he wanted only to return to the ship, and rest. "You needn't worry about the doctor anymore."

He moved to enter the shuttle . . . and paused, squinting in the failing light at the small bandage on Geordi La Forge's brow, at the tear in Worf's uniform, at the scorched dents in the side of the shuttlecraft.

"Was there a problem with the Klingons?"

La Forge shared an ominously reluctant look with Worf; for an instant, neither officer replied. And then

Geordi said, with a gusting sigh, "You could say that. . . ."

"Captain's log, Stardate 48650.1.

"The *Starship Farragut* has arrived in orbit and has begun to beam up the *Enterprise* survivors for transport back to Earth.

"Our casualties were light . . . but unfortunately, the *Enterprise* herself cannot be salvaged."

Picard paused in his recording to gaze out the open doorway at the stream of personnel moving past—some carrying what personal effects they had rescued from their quarters, some hauling undamaged equipment, still others evacuating the wounded on stretchers. Lit by emergency beacons, the corridor led to an open hatch; beyond lay sunlit sky and the lush greenery of the Veridian jungle.

"Computer," Picard said, swiveling in his chair to stare out the hatch at the distant mountains, "end log. I'd like a cup of tea. Earl Grey. Hot." He rested his elbows against the gleaming surface of the conference table. The ready room had been reduced to virtual rubble; he had had no time thus far to sift through the wreckage, but had instead been busy here, at one of the few places on the ship where communications and the computer functioned.

"That selection is not currently available," the computer droned. "Choice of teas is limited—banchu, blackberry, or Thirellian mint."

Picard sighed. "Never mind."

A sudden shadow fell across the table. He glanced up to see Guinan, smiling in the doorway.

"I'm glad to see you again." She seemed unharmed,

unruffled, entirely untouched by the chaos surrounding her.

"I'm glad to see you, too." He returned the smile. "I had a question to ask. . . ."

"I know." Her expression grew teasingly enigmatic. "And I wanted to apologize for underestimating you, Jean-Luc. For being afraid that you wouldn't come back."

"I had good reason. Veridian Four. This crew . . . and you, Guinan." He hesitated. "Why didn't you tell me about all this?" He spread his hands, gesturing at the damaged room, at the scene beyond the open door.

She did not answer immediately, but paused to listen to the sharp, silver song of a bird outside. She turned her face toward it, and said, "Some things are *meant* to be. Like your saving the Veridian star. And this . . ." She glanced around her. "This was meant to be, too."

"But crew members died," Picard said heavily. "We lost seventeen."

"Yes . . ." Guinan gave a single, solemn nod, her dark eyes ashine with empathy. "And that's as it *should* be. Death isn't always defeat, Jean-Luc. It's part of birth, the way of the universe." She paused. "I've been places where they weep at births and celebrate deaths. I think it's not such a bad idea; keeps things in perspective."

"So I was meant to save those on Veridian Four, and most of the crew," Picard said. "But not those seventeen . . . ?" He shook his head faintly. "If you had told me about them—"

She interrupted. "—you would have gone back earlier in time to save them anyway. I know. That's why I didn't tell you." She gave a soft, wistful sigh. "It's not easy knowing things, sometimes." She raised her face and gazed at her surroundings. "I'm going to miss this ship. . . ."

Picard nodded. His deep relief at saving the population of Veridian IV and his crew had been overshadowed by the loss of the seventeen, and the *Enterprise* herself. He mourned her—not with the intensity he did Robert and René, but there was grief nonetheless.

Yet he did not feel the rage, the fury upon hearing of that loss as he had when learning of his brother's and nephew's deaths. His experience with the nexus and Kirk had changed his perspective; had helped him to value what was temporal, fleeting—precisely *because* of its impermanence.

"I want to thank you," he told Guinan, "for helping me in the nexus. For introducing me to Kirk." His tone softened; and he told her what he had revealed to no one else. "He returned here, to this planet, with me; he was killed helping me stop Soran."

"I know," Guinan said, very quietly; this time, there was no amusement in her gaze. "That was meant to be, too. Sometimes, the universe can be very fair. He died the way he wanted to: making a difference."

Picard raised his head sharply at that, remembering Kirk's final question; then his lips curved upward, very faintly. "I hope, when my time comes, that the universe is as kind to me."

She reached across the table, and set her warm hand upon his. "I suspect it will be, Jean-Luc," she said, and smiled. "I suspect it will. . . ."

SIXTEEN

☆

Deanna Troi stood amid the ruins of a cargo bay, scanning with a tricorder for signs of life.

More than anyone else, she was keenly aware of how very near they had all come to dying; images of what might have been—the same images that had haunted her on the bridge soon after the collision—still visited her dreams, with terrifying reality.

At the same time, she felt liberated, rejuvenated by the close brush with death. It had helped her to remember what was most important, to give up her anxiety over Worf and Will and what the future might hold.

She had spoken with them both, and discovered they both felt as she did—simply grateful to have survived, and willing to let any relationships unfold naturally.

She had spoken with countless crew members since the crash, trying to help them sort out their emotions. Surprisingly, the captain seemed reborn; Troi had expected that the loss of the *Enterprise* would come as a double blow, but Picard took it well, and appeared to have resolved his grief over the deaths of his nephew and brother.

She was far more concerned about Data. At the moment, she stood near him, gazing out at piles of collapsed bulkheads and bared, twisted circuitry.

The android's expression was faintly anxious but composed as he aimed his tricorder at a pile of rubble. "I would like to thank you, Counselor, for helping me with my search. It is very kind of you."

"It's no problem, Data." She looked up from the tricorder readout to smile at him. "I've already cleared out what I can from my quarters. I'm afraid there wasn't much left."

"You are dealing with your loss very well. Certainly better than I seem to be. . . ." He sighed glumly as he moved over to a new area and began again to scan.

"That's different, Data. I lost only *things*. . . . Besides, I'm quite impressed with how you're handling this."

The android nodded, and said, with the faintest trace of ingenuous pride, "It has been difficult, but I believe I have the situation under control."

"So you've decided not to remove the emotion chip?"

"For now," Data said, gazing out at the wreckage. "At first I was not prepared for the unpredictable nature of emotions . . . but after experiencing two hundred sixty-one distinct emotional states, I believe I have learned to control my feelings." He squared his shoulders with such touchingly innocent determination that Troi repressed a smile. "They will no longer control me."

"Well, Data," Troi replied approvingly, "I hope that—" She broke off as her tricorder beeped, and stared down at the readout. "Over here!" She gestured excitedly at the android. "I think I've found something."

Data hurried over to her side, his eyes wide with hope.

Troi held up the tricorder so he could read it. "One life sign, very faint."

He handed her his tricorder and dashed over to the source of the reading: a fallen bulkhead, which he pulled aside with preternatural strength. Beneath it lay metal fragments and the scattered contents of storage containers—shredded uniforms, boots, food, medical supplies—all of which Data dug through with eager swiftness, until he arrived at a piece of plating.

He flung it aside to reveal Spot, wedged safely beneath the rubble. She gazed up at the android and released a throaty, plaintive yowl.

"Spot!" Data crouched down, scooped up the cat, and buried his face in her striped red fur; she immediately began purring, so loudly and enthusiastically that Troi released a soft, delighted laugh.

"I am very happy to find you, Spot," Data murmured, cradling the animal against his chest.

"Another family reunited." Troi could not repress a huge grin. She picked her way through the debris and stood beside the crouching android, bending down to give Spot a pat.

Data turned, revealing golden eyes ashine with tears; Troi's smile faded at once.

"Data," she asked softly, surprised and touched at the sight, "are you all right?"

He gave a small, sheepish shrug, causing a single glistening drop to spill down his pale cheek. "I am not sure, Counselor. I am happy to see Spot . . . and yet I am crying. The chip must be malfunctioning."

Troi gently placed a hand on his arm. "No, Data. I think it's working perfectly."

He looked up at her and smiled through his tears.

In the wreckage of the ready room, Picard bent low, sifting through the remnants of the past.

He had learned from Soran the foolishness of grasping at what was gone and could not be regained, at what was by its very nature impermanent. There were many belongings here that had been destroyed; things that he had valued, that he would miss. Yet they seemed now unimportant in the light of his experience in the nexus. And they were, after all, only things, even if some of them were unique and could not be replaced.

Only one of those things mattered to him now. He would accept its loss, if he must; but the rest he would let go willingly, even cheerfully, if this one could be retrieved. . . .

"Is this it?" Riker called.

Picard turned to gaze over at his second-in-command, who stood in the midst of the overturned furniture and scattered personal effects, holding up a large dust-covered binder.

"Yes," Picard said; the word served as a sigh of relief. "Yes, Number One. Thank you."

He and Riker picked their way to each other. Picard took the album gratefully. The embossed cover had been torn, but it appeared otherwise unharmed; he brushed away the dust and opened it reverently to the last few photos of his grinning nephew.

Riker stood beside him, hands on hips, looking out at the devastation. "I'm going to miss this ship. She went before her time."

Picard glanced up from the album, closed it carefully, and followed Riker's gaze. "It's not how many years you've lived, Will . . . but how you've lived them." He paused. "Someone once told me that time is a predator that stalks us all our lives. But maybe time is also a *companion* . . . who goes with us on our journey, and reminds us to cherish the moments of our lives—because they will never come again. We are, after all, only mortal."

For a time, Riker did not speak; and then the familiar impish glint came into his eyes. "Speak for yourself, sir. I kinda planned on living forever."

The captain smiled at him as they stepped from the ready room onto the wrecked bridge. A shadow passed over Riker's features as he looked at the captain's chair.

"I always thought I'd have a crack at this chair one day."

"You may still," Picard said. "Somehow, I doubt this will be the last ship to carry the name *Enterprise*." He hesitated a moment to give the bridge a final glance, to fix it forever in his memory, then touched his comm badge.

"Picard to *Farragut*. Two to beam up."

He straightened at the transporter's gentle whine, and stood very still, watching, as the past dissolved.

BEHIND THE SCENES OF
STAR TREK® GENERATIONS™

A Special Report by Judith and Garfield Reeves-Stevens, Authors of *The Making of Star Trek: Deep Space Nine*®

When Ronald D. Moore and Brannon Braga, the script-writers of STAR TREK GENERATIONS, walked into Rick Berman's office for a mysteriously scheduled meeting in February 1993, they thought they were going to be fired.

At the time, both were writers and producers for the STAR TREK: THE NEXT GENERATION television series, for which Rick Berman was executive producer. Moore had been writing for the show since his first spec script sale ("The Bonding") to the series, in the third season, and Braga since joining the series as a summer intern in the fourth season. (He earned his first script credit for the series working with Moore on "Reunion.") *The Next Generation* was halfway through its sixth

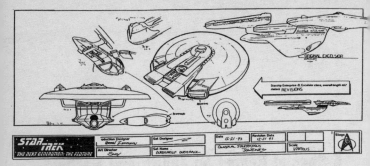

From December 1993, this preliminary blueprint of the *Enterprise*-B shows some of the modifications that were made to the original *Excelsior* model to transform it into a state-of-the-art starship, *circa* 2295. Note the unwieldy working title of the movie at this time.

season that February, with most people involved with the series anticipating that it would last until its eighth.

But Ron Moore and Brannon Braga felt they had no assurances that they would be there to continue with the show's success. As Moore says, "There was just no reason for the meeting at that time. Rick Berman just doesn't 'meet' with you and 'chat.' So, Brannon and I started thinking that we were being fired, and that the show was canceled."

Things didn't get any easier once they walked through the door of Berman's office, either. As Moore recalls with a smile, "Rick likes to milk these things for all they're worth. So we sat down and he was very serious and he was up and he was pacing as he said, 'Well, boys, I've been in three months of negotiations with the studio. . . .' And I thought, Oh, my God, we're fired, the studio is going to cancel the series, and it's over. It's really coming to an end. But *then* Rick said, 'And I'm

252

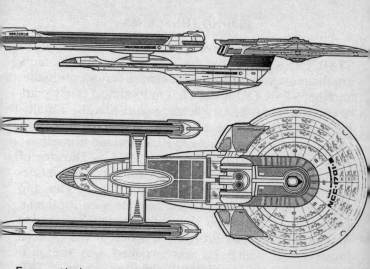

From artist's concept to computer diagrams . . . these plans show another view of the modifications that turned the *Excelsior* model into the *Enterprise*-B. The original *Excelsior* was designed by Bill George and was built at Industrial Light and Magic.

going to produce the next two STAR TREK films and I want you guys to write one of them.'

"Well, we just stared at him slack-jawed because we had no response." After that first meeting, Moore remembers, "We walked out of the building and we walked around the Paramount lot three times just saying, 'This happened? This really happened?' And from that point on we started working on the story."

Of course, Moore's and Braga's surprised response to Rick Berman's announcement was not just relief to be keeping their jobs, but excitement because they were being asked to take part in *The Next Generation*'s next incarnation. The idea of there being a *Next Generation* movie was really not a surprise to anyone involved in STAR TREK, given that the first six STAR TREK films are the most successful science-fiction series ever made, and that STAR TREK itself has in its almost thirty years of entertainment history become quite literally a multi-*billion*-dollar franchise. Much of that ongoing success in recent years is attributable to Rick Berman himself.

Berman came to Paramount in 1984 as Director of Current Programming, with responsibility for oversee-ing the hit Paramount sitcoms *Cheers, Family Ties,* and *Webster.* By May 1986, he had become Vice President, Long Form (Hollywood jargon for made-for-television movies) and Special Projects, and one of the "special projects" to which he was assigned was the just-announced new syndicated television series, STAR TREK: THE NEXT GENERATION.

After about two weeks in his new role as a liaison between the series' production team and the studio, Berman was asked to lunch by STAR TREK's creator, Gene Roddenberry. So well did the two men get on that Berman characterizes the meeting as "love at first sight." Roddenberry's response was more to the point—the next day he asked Paramount if Berman could come work on the show as a producer. Berman recalls that, "over the first three-month period, I went from produc-er, to supervising producer, to co-executive producer, and by the middle of the first season I was running the show with Gene." Though none could know it at the time, Gene Roddenberry had taken the first step in preparing to pass the torch of STAR TREK's steward-ship.

However, in the years since Roddenberry's death, Berman has become far more than just a steward of

Roddenberry's creation. In addition to his role as executive producer for all current STAR TREK television projects, and producer of the new movie, Berman is also the co-creator of both new STAR TREK television series, STAR TREK: DEEP SPACE NINE and STAR TREK: VOYAGER, and shares story credit on STAR TREK GENERATIONS.

Given his success in expanding an already successful franchise to even greater heights, just as it was inevitable that a *Next Generation* movie would be made it was inevitable that Rick Berman would be the person Paramount would ask to make it. The making of the film would be part of the studio's continuing, long-term management of what Paramount executives refer to as "the crown jewel" of all their entertainment properties.

Rick Berman describes Paramount's overall strategy of development and production, into which the movie fits, as beginning even earlier than the start of his three months of negotiations. "Brandon Tartikoff, who was running the studio at the time, first came to me more than three years ago, to ask me to develop a new series, which became *Deep Space Nine*. The plan was that *Deep Space Nine* would go on the air, that it and *Next Generation* would overlap by about a year and a half, and that *Next Generation* would end after its seventh season. One of the reasons it would end was so that we could make a film. That's a decision that was put in the works, I believe, by Stanley Jaffe, who used to be the head of Paramount Communications."

As for the genesis of the film itself, Berman recalls that "Sherry Lansing, John Goldwyn, and Don Grainger came to me around Christmas '92 and asked me to create and produce a STAR TREK: THE NEXT GEN-ERATION movie for them. What I decided to do, because writers are so hard to find, was to get two scripts going simultaneously. I would cowrite stories with two different writers, and then they would go on to write two screenplays and the better would go first. In other words, the script that did not go first would not necessarily be tossed in the trash. It would be positioned to be renurtured into a second movie."

The Paramount executives were enthusiastic about Berman's plan, which led to his mysterious invitation to Ron Moore and Brannon Braga to come to his office for a "chat." At the same time, Berman also called in writer and producer Maurice Hurley, a good friend and someone with whom he had worked for two years on the *Next Generation* series.

For the next seven months, at the same time he was working as executive producer for both *The Next Generation* and *Deep Space Nine,* in ultimate charge of every aspect of their production, Berman worked with Moore and Braga, and with Hurley, to develop two different *Next Generation* scripts suitable for the big screen.

"In both scripts," Berman explains, "the stories that we developed, at my request, were stories that entailed to different degrees members of the original series along with *The Next Generation.* First, we went through the story development on both, and both stories were submitted to the studio. We got a lot of notes from the studio, the stories were revised, and then we went to first draft on both. Eventually, it became quite obvious that the studio and I were both leaning toward Ron's and Brannon's script. That's not to say that Maury's script wasn't terrific, it just was far less advanced by the time we really had to make a decision." Berman goes on to add that Hurley's script will continue to be developed as the potential second *Next Generation* movie. "It's a great script," he says.

But long before the decision was made as to which of the two scripts would become the first *Next Generation* movie, the stories themselves had to be developed. Anticipating the broader scope of a motion picture after seven years of working within the constraints of television's tight schedules and tighter budgets, Berman says, "We immediately set out to write a story that had an epic quality to it."

He explains that in his initial meetings with his writers, "My mandate was that it be a story that start in the twenty-third century, and then follow through to the twenty-fourth century. The script with Ron and Brannon had that. The script with Maury was a little bit different, but it did include Captain Kirk. And past that, basically, the sky was the limit. Our attitude was that we were not holding ourselves back to the limitations that normally one takes as rote when you're in development on a television script."

Ron Moore also remembers the storytelling freedom that the script assignment brought with it. In the first meeting he and Braga had with the studio executives who would be involved with the project, "Their instruction to us was: 'Go make a good movie, guys.' It was that simple. They just said: 'You know what you're doing, we trust you, we like your work, you guys know the show. We want to make this a successful franchise. Give us a good movie.' And that was that."

Then the story-development meetings began in earnest. As Brannon Braga recalls, "We worked for several weeks just talking. You have to remember we were producing the series at the same time, so any chance we'd get, we'd just brainstorm. Which is really the most fun. Conceiving the whole thing."

During this brainstorming phase, Moore adds, "We started talking about *The Original Series'* characters, whether they were going to be in our film or not, or if they would be in the other script that was being developed. Somehow, through the mix of it, we decided that was something we wanted to do, and we ran through a lot of different options. For a while, we were intrigued with the 'poster' image that we wanted, which was the two *Enterprise*s fighting each other. We thought that would be really cool: Kirk versus Picard! But we just couldn't come up with something where it was plausible that they would both be at such odds that they'd be fighting against each other, and the audience is still rooting for them both. It just had too many difficulties to set in place, so we abandoned it. And then it was Rick who came up with the format of 'how about a mystery that starts at the time of *The Original Series*—fade out—and then pick up *The Next Generation.'* That is, a mystery that spans the two generations. Once we had that in place, then we started looking for ideas—what story it was going to be in. How would the two crews meet? Would there be time travel? Do the *Next Generation* characters go back? Do *The Original Series* characters go forward? Is it something else?"

Eventually, Berman, Moore, and Braga decided that they didn't want to use time travel to bring the crews together, which led to a new series of questions as they tried to arrive at some "neutral ground" where the long-anticipated meeting of the generations would take place.

"That's how the nexus came about," Moore says. "It was someplace where they both could go, that's neither in the past nor the future."

But though the eventual meeting between the *Starship Enterprise*'s two greatest captains had been long awaited, the result of that meeting is likely to be a surprise to many. If you haven't yet seen the movie or read this book, this might be a good place to stop reading until you do.

Generations' most dramatic story development is, of course, the heroic death of Captain Kirk—certainly a key incident in the almost thirty-year history of the STAR TREK universe. But as Rick Berman recalls, there was no one precise moment when the idea for showing Kirk's death in the movie came to the writing team.

"I think we sort of took it for granted," Berman says, "that if we were going to somehow bring Kirk into the twenty-fourth century, he was going to die. It was something that was *a priori* from Day One because we were facing three choices. One was sending Kirk back after he and Picard had stopped the madman. One was keeping him in the *Next Generation*'s present, alive. And the other one was killing him.

"Keeping him in the present, alive, seemed a little silly. Sending him back didn't really fit well into the story, considering that going back meant returning to an earlier death that's seen in the beginning of the movie [when Kirk apparently dies saving the *Enterprise*-B]. So it seemed appropriate to let him die at the end of the movie, although some are going to accuse us of symboli-

Twenty-eight years after he first appeared as Captain James Tiberius Kirk, William Shatner returns to the Paramount sound-stages to reprise his role for the final time. But then, didn't Mr. Spock die in the third STAR TREK movie, only to be . . . Naw. It couldn't happen again, could it?

cally having Picard bury Kirk as being some kind of metaphor for *The Next Generation* burying *The Original Series*. That was totally unintentional. It'll be interesting to see how people comment on that."

Brannon Braga, however, feels that the emotional power of Kirk's death will not be cause for contention. "It just felt like the right thing to do," he says, "kind of passing the baton. And certainly just the image of having Kirk die in Picard's arms and Picard burying him at the end of the movie has an eloquence about it, and will speak to every STAR TREK fan."

Perhaps the second-biggest surprise in the new movie is what Ron Moore calls "the big 'wow' sequence of the film"—the spectacular scene at the end when the main section of the *Enterprise*-D is destroyed and the saucer section crash-lands in the jungles of an alien world. Unlike the death of Kirk, this plot development pre-dated even the most preliminary discussions of the film.

"That was actually an idea we originally had for the season-six cliffhanger," Moore explains. "It was something that Brannon and I and Jeri [Taylor] had pitched to Rick and Mike [Piller]. We had a plot line where the *Enterprise* was recalled to Earth, where it was going to become the honorary *Queen Mary*-type of starship, a diplomatic showboat going round and round the solar system. The crew was going to be split up and it was the end of the mission. In fact, the title for the episode was going to be 'All Good Things' [which was the title used for the *Next Generation*'s final episode].

"On their way back to Earth, of course, they're sidetracked, and the *Enterprise* saucer separates and crashes on the planet's surface. That was going to be the cliffhanger as it went crashing down into the atmosphere. Unfortunately, production said there was no way we could crash the saucer section with a television budget. It would just look too cheesy and too cheap on what we can afford to do. 'You'd hate it,' they told us."

But the *idea* of crashing the saucer section remained intriguing, and with the budget for the *Next Generation* movie being about ten times more than the budget for an individual episode, Moore and Braga suggested that the sequence be incorporated into the story. Berman agreed, and the rest is future history.

On the bridge of the *Enterprise*-B, Scotty struggles at the controls as Kirk rushes to the Deflector Relay Room. This behind-the-scenes photo shows one of the advantages of a motion-picture budget over a television-episode budget — *two* cameras and film crews on the set to simultaneously record the action from multiple viewpoints.

Of course, just as Berman is concerned about what fans might think about the symbolism of Picard burying Kirk, Brannon Braga wonders about his and Ron Moore's approach to storytelling as illustrated by the destruction of the *Enterprise.* "I don't know how else to say it except our dictum from the studio was to have fun. So we did. We had fun destroying things. I don't know what that says about us. But then," he adds with a smile, "that *Enterprise* has been on the screen for seven years.

I'm ready for a new one. I think that will make the second movie all the more fun."

Traditionally in Hollywood, writers are encouraged not to hold back when writing a first-draft screenplay. They should never limit the story they want to tell by worrying about budget or the ability of visual-effects wizards to create the most amazing and complex images the writers can imagine. However, as the start of production looms closer and the writers begin working on second, third, and fourth drafts, as a rule the practicalities of the business aspects of moviemaking take on more importance. STAR TREK GENERATIONS was no exception to that rule, either. Rick Berman remembers that the first time the script was subjected to a cost breakdown, the figures came in about eighty percent over what the movie was intended to cost.

Fortunately, however, when the hard choices about what to cut back on were being faced, Berman and his production team drew on their seven years' worth of television-series expertise in squeezing every last penny out of a budget and putting it on the screen.

With a touch of justifiable pride, Berman says, "I think no one but we could have turned in a movie of this magnitude for this budget, simply because of our experience with continual penny-pinching. Being television action-adventure people, which is kind of rare today, we know how to do things cost-effectively. And that enabled us to do a movie that I think is going to look ten million dollars more expensive than it was."

Of course, not all of the changes to the script came about because of cost concerns. From the moment the words FADE IN are printed on the page, the primary responsibility of everyone connected to the production of a feature film is storytelling. And some of the story-

Aboard the *Enterprise*-B, Captain Kirk rips open a wall panel in the Deflector Relay Room to discover . . . a camera crew? In the parlance of moviemaking, this kind of camera angle, in which the character is seen from a viewpoint *inside* a piece of equipment, is known as a "refrigerator shot," for obvious reasons.

telling aspects of the first *Next Generation* movie were unique.

As Brannon Braga explains, "The film still needs to be accessible to those people who have never heard of STAR TREK in their entire lives. So we wanted to make it a broader storyline, with a bigger action plot. Our episodes tended to have a great deal of character, and I think you'll find this picture is more plot-driven than an episode. Not that the movie does not have character, of course. There are core emotional arcs. But we needed a big, throbbing action plot to carry the picture. The action had to be bigger. The humor had to be bigger."

Ron Moore agrees. "We knew from the get-go that we couldn't depend on a lot of backstory that we had established in the series. You couldn't just start picking up plot threads from 'Descent,' or from any of the other episodes, because you just can't depend on the audience being aware of them the way you can on the television series, with dedicated viewers. Yet we didn't want to have to walk around explaining what starships are. We had to go with the idea that STAR TREK is sort of an icon. You kind of know what the *Enterprise* is even if you've never watched the series. You kind of understand the universe in which it takes place. But for the audience that really doesn't understand, let's make casual reference somewhere to the fact that Data's an android, Troi has empathic powers, the thing on Geordi's face is a VISOR, and Worf is a Klingon. We tried to work in little clues like that for the nonviewer throughout the picture."

Another area in which the writing of the movie differed from the writing of an episode is in what could be done to the characters. In television, there is the need for characters and key situations to remain the same week after week. But with a movie, all that changes.

"For instance," Braga explains, describing yet another surprise development from the film, "we gave Data emotions. That is something we never would have done on the series because the second you do that, you've inexorably altered the character. In fact, you've eliminated his quest altogether. But in the movie, we had to do something that big. Or, we wanted to. Because that was our first chance to do something really major. Now, in a second film, you'll see a very different Data. But because the films conceivably will be spaced out every couple of years, you can take those kind of chances."

The decision to give Data emotions—by way of the "emotion chip" made for him by his creator, Noonien Soong—was not lightly taken, and it led to what Braga calls the scene with the greatest controversy: "The Spot scene at the end, where Data recovers his cat and sheds a tear."

Braga explains that he, Ron Moore, and Rick Berman thought the scene was very poignant. "We wanted Data to think he had his emotions under control, but then experience one of those emotions which really no one can explain—crying when you're happy. So Data finds his little cat and he doesn't understand what's happening to him. He says: 'I'm happy to see Spot, yet I'm crying. The chip must be malfunctioning.' But Troi says, 'No . . . I think it's working perfectly.'"

The controversy over this scene stemmed from actor Brent Spiner's concern that having Data actually produce tears would be too much of a change in his character, and his fears that it would come across as too "schmaltzy." Braga is quick to agree that Spiner had a point but, in the end, "we decided that the film could use a little schmaltz, if you will. We'll just see what the audience thinks."

Eventually, the written word must be transformed into the visual image, a process that begins in the preproduction phase, when the film's director begins to conceptualize the scenes that will be brought to life. It is at this point that the production designer joins the team. For STAR TREK GENERATIONS, the production designer in question had considerable experience in

Part of the challenge of creating a fully realized future environment for a STAR TREK movie can be seen in this collection of preliminary costume sketches for STAR TREK® GENERATIONS™. Thanks to the holodeck sequence in Picard's time, costume designer Robert Blackman's work had to span more than five hundred years of human history, with a few detours into alien realms of apparel for good measure.

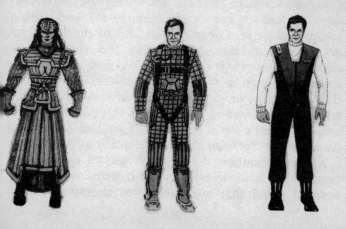

bringing the future to visual life. He is Herman Zimmerman, and he had been on STAR TREK teams many times in the past.

The production designer for a film is, in Zimmerman's words, "the person responsible for everything you see on the screen—except for the acting." This responsibility requires an intricate meshing of technical knowledge about everything from film stock and camera lenses to visual effects, wardrobe, set and prop design, all combined with the eye of an artist.

Zimmerman first joined the STAR TREK television team when producer Robert Justman brought him in as production designer for *The Next Generation*'s first season. After that, Zimmerman returned to film work, including *Star Trek V* and *VI*. Today, his work can be seen each week on STAR TREK: DEEP SPACE NINE, one of the most visually striking shows on television.

Because of the quick pace of television production, Zimmerman usually begins work on any given *Deep Space Nine* episode when there is just a story or a first-draft script to refer to. But in the case of *Generations,* he had the luxury of beginning his work with a completed script. Given the breadth of the visual requirements of the script—from the twenty-third-century *Enterprise*-B to never-before-seen areas of the *Enterprise*-D, from the near-mystical environments of the nexus to the jungles and deserts of Veridian III—it's hard for those not in the business to understand how anyone begins a job of that scope. Fortunately, Herman Zimmerman has been around the galaxy a few times.

As he remembers, his first job was to upgrade the original, made-for-television *Next Generation* sets. "The level of detail that is necessary to photograph for a motion-picture screen as opposed to a television screen requires elaborating on your good ideas," Zimmerman says. "What I hope we have accomplished is to raise that level of detail in those original sets and make the audience feel when they see it on the big screen that: 'That must have been what it looked like all the time, but we just didn't see it because we were looking at it on a video screen instead of a thirty-foot-high, seventy-foot-wide cinemascope screen.'

"For example," Zimmerman continues, citing just a few instances of the myriad details he creates and oversees, "on the bridge we've beefed up the ceiling trusses. When I first did STAR TREK: THE NEXT GENERATION, we had some budget limitations that kept me from doing all of the sculptural things I would have liked to have done in the ceiling. The ceiling is a particularly interesting design on the bridge, and it always came across on television, to me, as a little less than easily understood. The beams that defined the ceiling didn't always read as well as they might, because it's really quite a beautiful design. So I took the opportunity in the feature to make them about seven and a half inches wide, instead of just three inches. That change in size makes a big difference in the statement the ceiling makes when you see it."

As for other changes to the bridge, Zimmerman says, "We raised the captain's and mates' area by putting a platform under them, and that gave the captain and the mates a little more importance on the bridge. It also brought them closer to Worf, who was always standing behind them at the weapons console, so it was easier to photograph them and make the interplay between the actors happen more readily.

"We also installed, to the right and left of the wishbone railing, a new set of computer consoles so that we could have a larger staff on the bridge. We have some very exciting scenes that take place on the bridge under very extreme duress, and the presence of the extra crew members heightens the drama."

In fact, the addition of new computer console stations on the bridge had been suggested to the studio earlier, as a proposed change for the television series. However, since the new stations would require additional actors to be present during the filming of almost all bridge scenes, without necessarily adding to the series' story possibilities, the extra stations were rejected for the series as too expensive an addition.

Of course, there was a bittersweet feeling about upgrading the existing *Next Generation* sets for their first motion-picture appearance, because it was also their *last* motion-picture appearance. During the climactic crash-landing sequence, the sets were literally ripped apart. Brannon Braga says matter-of-factly, "It was really interesting to walk onto these sets you'd been working on for so many years. They just blew them to pieces." When asked to describe his feelings at that time, Braga simply says he found the destruction of the sets both unbelievable and very satisfying at the same time.

After modifications to the original sets, Zimmerman turned his attention to the new areas of the *Enterprise*-D that the movie required. "Stellar Cartography is probably the single most important set in the film because without the understanding of what goes on in it, you won't be able to follow the storyline very well," Zimmerman says. This set is where Picard, Data, and the audience figure out what Soran's plan is, and realize they have to stop him.

Like the movie's writers and producers, at times Zimmerman had to rethink his plans carefully in order to get the most effective results from the money he had to work with. Yet as Rick Berman noted, his production team's years of television experience in making the most of limited resources guarantees that the *Generations* audience won't be shortchanged.

"We didn't actually cut numbers of sets," Zimmerman says. "Instead, we sharpened the pencil on the ambition of some of them. For example, where the script might call for a hundred-foot-long corridor, we settled on a fifty- or sixty-foot corridor. We did need to keep the budget under control, but the requirements for the sets remained the same all the way through and I think the overall result of the economies hasn't hurt the picture."

But money is only one of the valuable resources to be carefully apportioned during movie production. The other is time. And as production began, time became an issue in the area of production design.

Though set construction was on schedule, Zimmerman says, "The exterior locations were not selected by the time we started principal photography. We had only one out of seven that we knew for sure we were going to use. So the director, and myself, and the location manager literally spent every weekend while we were shooting, up until about two weeks before we went to the 'Valley of Fire,' which was the very end of the schedule, in a helicopter, looking for the other locations that hadn't been blocked in. That was unusual, and it was exhausting. But it really didn't impact on the stage work, which is the bulk of the work that has to be done on a STAR TREK feature."

As the director of STAR TREK GENERATIONS (as well as the director of the pilot episode of STAR TREK: DEEP SPACE NINE, and many STAR TREK: THE NEXT GENERATION episodes since the third season), David Carson was also deeply involved in guiding and establishing the overall look of the film. Thus, finding the right exterior locations was extremely important to him.

"STAR TREK movies have a scale that is more on the epic side than on the naturalistic side," Carson says. "They have an almost operatic quality about them from time to time. That's why we chose to film it in anamorphic, which is the wide screen, to give the audience all that immense scale. I think that when you make a STAR TREK movie, you have to go for that sort of scale so you can entertain the audience to the best of your ability. You have to go for the oddest desert and the most peculiar mountain, and instead of building a sailing ship on a soundstage, you have to get a real one and go out to sea. All of which are extremely difficult to do, particularly on a very tight schedule, which we were on."

As Zimmerman has mentioned, the Valley of Fire location was one of the most difficult to find, and to shoot. In keeping with his own desire to maintain the immense scale of a STAR TREK movie, David Carson recalls that in trying to find the perfect site for Soran's compound, "We looked for an extraordinary mountain that was close to the sky and would give us a feeling of being in an alien place with a full three-hundred-sixty-degree view without any civilization in it."

But when Carson, Zimmerman, and the location

On location in Marina Del Rey for the opening holodeck sequence in the era of *The Next Generation*, director David Carson confers with Patrick Stewart before a shot. Later, when an urgent call to action causes the crew to rush to the bridge of the *Enterprise*-D without changing costumes, Brent Spiner commented that when he sat down at his Ops console in his old-fashioned uniform, he felt like Liberace.

manager finally arrived in the Valley of Fire, they had to do more than just *look* for a mountain. "Herman and I climbed about eleven of these huge peaks," Carson says, "and late in the afternoon we came to this particular area where the location manager suggested we go up this hill. So we climbed up and I looked across from the top of the hill and I saw the mountain that we eventually

Soran's compound on Veridian III was actually located in the Valley of Fire, about an hour and a half out of Las Vegas. Note the trucks in the distance. All the equipment, props, and set-building material had to be carried to this mountaintop prior to filming.

used. I said, 'How about we go there?' And they all looked at me as though I were crazy. But Herman and I climbed it and it was a wonderful location where you could see for three hundred sixty degrees with no civilization anywhere, just plateaus. It is quite an extraordinarily beautiful location."

Beauty, however, does not come easily, and finding the right location was only the first step toward actually using it. The next step was working out a way to bring an entire film production crew to this site in the remote desert.

"At first," Carson continues, "it looked as though we wouldn't be able to film there because we were so far away from the road. When we went back to the rangers and told them we wanted to use this place they said, 'Well, we're not going to allow you to go across the desert floor with all your trucks and things.' And even then, we were going to have to climb up a good quarter of a mile or more. So, we came back with a helicopter to scout around it, and because I had to film helicopter shots around the thing. As we were flying around, we noticed that there was an old trail from the road leading halfway up this mountain. You couldn't see it from the road, but from the air you could see it quite clearly. Very, very ancient it must have been because it was completely blown over. But you could see that once upon a time there had been a trail there. So we got the ranger to come up in the helicopter and showed him. And he said, 'Oh, well, since it's there, let's make a case for it.' And that's how we got the location—the helicopter showed us the way."

Another key exterior location is Kirk's log cabin on Earth. As Zimmerman says, "It's an important part of the story because that's where Kirk and Picard first meet." He recalls the challenge that location presented. "We had difficulty finding the cabin because the script calls for the Northwest United States, the Cascade range, and there's very little within a hundred-and-fifty-mile radius of Los Angeles that you could say would pass for the Cascades. Finally, we were fortunate enough to find a cabin up near Mount Whitney that, I think, makes a very good approximation for what the script called for.

On location near Mount Whitney, William Shatner and Patrick Stewart share a light moment.

But we didn't find that cabin and lock into it until probably two weeks before we had to go there and shoot it."

That figure of one hundred and fifty miles is not some magical Hollywood distance, but it is extremely important in determining the cost of shooting on location. The farther away from Los Angeles the company moved, the more costly it was to pay for travel time, or for hotel rooms and expenses. At the beginning of the search for exteriors, Zimmerman says, "the key distance was thirty miles." Then he laughs. "Believe it or not. But because we exhausted all the possibilities within thirty, we went then for a hundred, and then we went for a hundred and fifty, and finally we did connect with everything that we needed within that radius, except for the 'Valley of Fire,' where Soran's launcher facility was built. To find that location, we flew to Las Vegas and drove another hour outside of the city."

Of course, many of the locations needed for a STAR TREK movie cannot be found even within a billion miles of Los Angeles. Starships, space stations, vast tracts of alien jungles—all those exist only in the writers' imaginations. To film them, therefore, requires the expertise of a whole different category of artists and technicians—the visual-effects team.

For STAR TREK GENERATIONS, the key visual-effects team is considered by many to be the best in the movie business: Industrial Light and Magic, the company founded by George Lucas to create the effects for *Star Wars,* and which has since gone on to constantly redefine the state-of-the-art in films such as *Terminator 2* and *Jurassic Park.*

In the case of *Generations,* the ILM team was brought

on board early in the preproduction phase as consultants. Bill George, visual-effects art director for ILM and *Generations,* explains that the first step to this process is a face-to-face meeting about the script. "In the beginning, I talked to the director, David Carson. We have what's called a creative team here at ILM, which consists of the visual-effects supervisor and the art director. And we go down and try to feel out Dave Carson, Rick Berman, to get their ideas and their vision for what the project is. Then we come back and we do design work: illustrations, sketches, storyboards, whatever. Then we come back and present it to them, they react, and we come back and do some more work. So it's a real back-and-forth process."

Alex Siden, ILM's visual-effects supervisor on the *Generations* film, describes the process in terms even more apropos for a STAR TREK project. "When we're working on a movie like this, we've got to figure out a way to enter into a creative partnership with the producers, where we can sort of do a 'mind-meld' with them and pick up on what it is that they're trying to go for."

What the producers were trying to go for, of course, in the best STAR TREK tradition, was something that had never been seen before. Chief among the groundbreaking effects they envisioned for the film was the mysterious Nexus.

In the script, the Nexus is simply described as "a HUGE RIBBON OF CRACKLING ENERGY." But as Alex Siden explains, "The nexus is probably the most important effect in the movie. It's central to the plot and all the big effects sequences. So we really wanted to get a cool look for it." Early on in the planning stages, it was obvious that, to show what had never been shown in a STAR TREK movie before, it was going to be necessary to use a technology that had never been used in a STAR TREK movie before, either—computer modeling.

Computer-generated images—or CGI—*had* been used in prior STAR TREK films, but never to the extent to which they will appear in *Generations*. In the past, the most notable examples of STAR TREK CGI was the unparalleled "Genesis Effect" sequence from STAR TREK II: THE WRATH OF KHAN, and the spectacular explosion of the Klingon moon and the resulting shock wave in STAR TREK VI: THE UNDISCOVERED COUNTRY. However, both of these sequences were clearly not depicting objects intended to be taken as "real." On the other hand, in *Generations* there will be times when everything we see onscreen will be computer-generated—*including* both the *Enterprise*-B and the *Enterprise*-D.

Interestingly enough, today there is little cost difference between creating a visual-effects sequence of, for example, a starship flying across a starfield, either by traditional motion-control photography of a model, or by CGI. However, in the case of STAR TREK, where excellent models already exist, motion-control photography is generally the preferable approach.

But, in *Generations,* for those scenes in which starships must appear with the glowing tendrils of energy formed by the nexus, ILM quickly determined that CGI was the only technique that would yield acceptable results.

Bill George explains. "The reason why we created the *Enterprise*-B in the computer was for those scenes in which it encounters the nexus, which is very, very volatile—full of lights flashing, with all these energy tendrils lashing out toward the ship. Now, combining a traditional model that we would shoot onstage with the computer-graphic element like the nexus would create difficulties in matching the lighting. Because we would have to, onstage, put in those flashes where a tendril would jump out at the ship. Whereas when we do them both in the computer, we can tell the computer to increase the light level on the ship when a tendril gets close. So in other words, the tendril actually lights the model. That was the reason we decided to do the ship in the computer—for the interactive light effect."

However, the *Enterprise*-B will not always be depicted by CGI throughout *Generations*. The sleek new starship is actually a modification of the existing, seven-foot-long stage model of the *Excelsior* starship which first appeared in STAR TREK III: THE SEARCH FOR SPOCK. With extra propulsion ports and other details added as shown in the illustration accompanying this report, the *Enterprise*-B is clearly an *Excelsior*-class vessel, exactly as it has been depicted among the models in the *Enterprise* 1701-D conference lounge.

Of course, if ILM went to the trouble and expense of creating a CGI *Enterprise*-B, an obvious question is, Why was a traditional model needed at all? Bill George has the not-so-obvious answer. "Computer graphics work best when they are far away. For instance, in *Jurassic Park,* the dinosaurs that are farther away from the camera in the long shots are much easier to render than the dinosaurs in the close-ups. The closer the CGI creature or spaceship gets to the camera, the more difficult it is to hide the computer artifacts [distinctive patterns formed by limitations of the computer's ability to render detail], so it becomes much more difficult to fool the audience. The shots that we used the starships' stage models for were those big, lumbering, beauty shots where the starship is coming very, very close to the camera. Technology has not got to the point where it's easier to do those types of shots in the computer. It's still easier and better and more controllable to do them onstage with a model that you can physically light."

Bill George anticipates that it's just a matter of time before CGI will be used for big beauty shots as well, but he adds, "Even when we do something completely in the computer, we still usually make a prototype model of it. Because there's nothing like being able to pick something up and look at it."

In a sense, the stage model of the *Enterprise*-B is also an important part of the CGI model as well. Since the key advantage of a model over CGI is the amount of detail the model has, ILM digitized photographs of the stage model *Enterprise*-B and placed them on the computer-generated model to create a level of detailing that computer artists couldn't easily match.

The same technique was used for the CGI *Enterprise*-D, which was created for the scenes in which the ship is far away from the camera, and also for scenes where the ship goes to warp. Bill George says, "We wanted to do a real stretch effect, which we've tried in the past but with limited success. With the computer-graphic model, we literally can stretch the spaceship very much like rubber as it goes into warp."

Affectionately known as the "rubber-band shot," this stretching sequence appears in the opening credits of *The Next Generation* series. At the time that sequence was originally created, Bill George says, "The process used was called 'slit-scan,' which is very, very time consuming, and very, very exacting." With an almost conspiratorial whisper, he adds, "One of the reasons that flash occurs in the opening credits when the ship goes into warp is because we switched from the six-foot model to the two-foot model. We used the two-foot model for the stretch effect, and the six-foot model for the flyby. Well, they didn't quite match, so that's why the flash is there—to cover the fact that when we're switching from one model to the other, we kind of used it to cover the discrepancies between the two models."

But not all the model work done for *Generations* was of a scale that could fit on a stage. To film the crash-landing of the saucer, ILM ingeniously used its parking lot instead.

As Bill George describes it, "We built a saucer section that's twelve feet across, put it on a crane, and smashed it to the ground. Since the model itself was made out of fiberglass, it was pretty resilient and we were able to patch it between takes. After all, it pretty much just crashes into dirt and little, teeny trees, so it wasn't being too badly damaged and we could shoot a number of takes of the scene. We also had two or three cameras going at the same time, so we ended up with a huge library of footage for the film editors to work with."

The ILM parking lot also stood in for the saucer section itself for one sequence near the end of the film. Bill George says it was one of the "funnest" days on the show for him. In the movie, he explains, "It's about a day after the crash, there's a major evacuation taking place, and people are actually walking around on top of the saucer. In order to achieve that shot, Paramount sent us twenty costumes, and twenty people from here at ILM donned them and went out to the parking lot and walked around on a big piece of blue material. Then they filmed us in various scenarios of boarding shuttlecraft, and I got to be one of the science officers."

B'Etor and Lursa's Bird-of-Prey crew relax between takes on the Paramount lot. At least, we *think* they're relaxing.

The big piece of blue cloth Bill George and the others walked around on was used in each frame of film to optically separate the images of the people from the background, and then composite them into a shot of the miniature saucer section itself several times over, making it appear as if a hundred crew members were actually on top of it.

This blue-screen technique was also used to create a memorable moment in the film's climactic confrontation between the two captains and Soran—a moment in which physical set design was an integral part of the final movie illusion. The scene is the one that shows Picard's attempt to stop Soran's torpedo from launching, which results in the accidental "cloaking" of the launching platform, creating the onscreen impression that Picard is floating in midair above Soran's compound in the desert of Veridian III. The coordination between the two areas of the film's production necessary to create that shot fell into Herman Zimmerman's hands.

As Zimmerman recalls, "That was a particularly difficult problem to solve. There's an interface always between opticals and principal photography on the stage or on location, and we're very careful when we do those things. There's even a separate camera crew to shoot the opticals, usually.

"In this case, the problem was compounded by the fact that we were in a location that meant everything had to be, literally, manhandled up a mountain. All the camera equipment, all the scenery, all the props, all the actors themselves had to be ferried several miles from the closest bivouac point to the place where the shooting was to be done. *And* we had a large platform that had to disappear. So we reinvented an old magician's trick."

Dropping his voice as if to not get caught revealing a trade secret, Zimmerman describes the illusion. "There's a disappearing-table trick where the table is set for dinner and there's a flash and the table is empty. And you don't know what happened to the dinner. Well, what happens is that the knives, forks, and plates, goblets, flowers, food, et cetera, are glued to a table that rotates, and it hides inside the base of the table by flipping, making it all seem to have disappeared in an instant.

"So we took a page from that old parlor trick and made a torpedo launcher on a platform that rotated so it could be hidden inside the base of the launcher. It will

William Shatner has his makeup adjusted in this wonderful photo showing how complex the making of motion pictures can be. In addition to actors Shatner and Malcolm McDowell, there are 36 people in this one photo—37 if you count the photographer. The actual number of studio crew members on location here was about 150—not counting about 30 additional construction workers and drivers—all necessary for the shooting of the climactic sequence in which only three people will appear! Also note that despite being on location in the desert outside Las Vegas in the middle of summer, additional lighting from the spotlight on the platform in the background is *still* required.

not appear to do any of that in the picture, but what it allowed us to do was have a very heavy base for a rocket launcher that seems to disappear. I timed the crew. The first time they did it was eleven minutes and that's pretty good timing, I think. Thereafter, they did it in five or six. With the crew standing by at something like fifty thousand dollars an hour, you want to minimize the amount of time it takes to make that set change." Then, Zimmerman concludes, after principal photography was completed, Patrick Stewart was suspended in front of a blue screen on a Paramount stage so he could be composited into his midair position in the footage of the cloaked launcher shot on location.

The end of principal photography usually means the actors' work is over—except for being hung in midair, or rerecording dialogue, or being on call for any one of a number of last-minute fixes and enhancements. However, for the staff of ILM and the other people involved in postproduction, the end of principal photography marks the real start of their work. In fact, ILM expects to be working on sequences for *Generations* into October of 1994, despite the film's mid-November release date.

But as Bill George points out, that's not an unusual set of circumstances, especially when compared to the postproduction schedule of another ILM movie. "We were actually working on *The Empire Strikes Back* here at ILM, *after* the movie was released in the theaters. There's a scene at the very end where Luke and Leia are in the hospital ship, and Lando and Chewie are in the *Falcon*. When George Lucas was looking at the sequence, he thought that it wasn't clear where they all are in relation to each other. So there's a shot where you start off on the hospital bay, and then you pan over to the *Millennium Falcon*. That was the shot that they were working on while the film was already released in the theaters. A couple of weeks later, they replaced it with that image."

As the opening date for *Generations* comes closer, though, no one is expecting that the schedule for completion of the film will get as tight as that for *The Empire Strikes Back*. Indeed, the making of the first *Next Generation* film has been remarkably trouble-free, due in no small part to the fact that the team that's making it has been honed by years of television experience under Rick Berman's direction, and by their desire to take a project they love and move it into a new arena.

As Rick Berman looks back on the process of guiding *The Next Generation* to its next incarnation, he reflects, "When you go to the big movie screen, you're dealing with a myriad of things that you have always yearned to do: Being able to tell a story that doesn't have to begin and end in five acts and in forty-three minutes—something with a bigger sweep to it, something that stands on its own. To be able to use locations and to get your crew out on location. To be able to have far more complex optical sequences. To be able to have scenes where you have the hundred extras as opposed to the fifteen that the television budget allows you. To be able to spend the time to do the work properly.

"Every television director in his heart wants to film two script pages a day. But he's forced to do seven pages a day because that's the nature of the business. When you get to do two pages a day, which is what you do in movies, you can take the time to do them right. The cameraman and the director can work together and can choreograph shots and can work with the actors and rehearse, and make things much more sophisticated, and much smoother, and much more thought-out to look better and sound better."

But it's clear that the all-consuming passion to create an even better version of *The Next Generation* than that which has become the most successful syndicated television drama series of all time also has its downside—the ability to enjoy what the audience will take for granted as it sits in the theater on opening day.

When asked if there are any scenes or moments in the

movie that stand out to him as shining examples of what he set out to do, Berman can only sigh wistfully as he says, "I've seen the movie so many times. Sometimes, I'll see it as I work on a ten-minute act for five hours. Other times, I'll sit down and screen the film for two hours straight. And that's the way it's been going for the last month." But his enthusiasm for the film doesn't stay contained for long. "There are times when things surprise me," he continues. "There was a scene in a set called Stellar Cartography. It's a seven-page scene in one room with two people. And we were terrified that it was going to be deadly dull. But it's not. It works very, very wonderfully.

"Then there's a scene between Picard and Troi in his quarters. A very emotional scene that works beautifully."

By now, Berman's feeling of excitement about the film overtakes everything else. "Obviously, the crash of the *Enterprise* is the biggest action-adventure sequence. But to my delight, the battle and demise of the Klingon vessel is an incredible action-adventure sequence in the movie. As is the opening with Kirk in the deflector room of the *Enterprise*-B. So, there are continual surprises for us. Those are just some of the ones that have surprised me, by standing out more than I maybe thought they would have. But we've changed so much—and we've been fiddling and changing and reordering things for the last five weeks—that it's kind of hard to get specific about things that were surprising. Because they continue to surprise us on a daily basis."

If STAR TREK GENERATIONS can still bring such excitement to someone who has worked on it for almost two years, who knows every in and out, every twist, and

The Stellar Cartography Room aboard the *Enterprise*-D. This is the dramatic setting for the crucial scene in which Picard—and the audience—finally realizes what Soran is planning.

every plot nuance, then the odds are excellent that the audience is going to be thrilled.

But if anything gives a true indication of how a film will be received, it is by observing how quickly the studio decides to move ahead with a sequel. In Hollywood, a notoriously conservative town when it comes to spending money, the decision to make sequels is not usually addressed until worried executives see what the opening weekend box-office earnings are. Yet in the case of *The Next Generation, three* months before *Generations* was scheduled to open, Rick Berman and Paramount had already begun planning for the next movie.

As Rick Berman puts it, "The 'buzz' on the film has been very good, and everyone seems quite excited by it."

Almost thirty years have passed since Gene Roddenberry's creation was first presented to the world, and thanks to Paramount and Rick Berman and the producers, writers, cast, and crew of STAR TREK GENERATIONS, the future he imagined is in good hands, with no end of adventure in sight.